I0676448

Flamed Out

Valona Jones

Flamed Out

A MAGIC CANDLE SHOP MYSTERY

Valona Jones

This is a work of fiction. Names, characters, places, and incidents are a product of the author's imagination, or are used fictitiously, and any resemblance to actual persons living or dead, business establishments, events, and locales is entirely coincidental.

Flamed Out
A Magic Candle Shop Mystery
Book 5 of 5

ISBN Trade Paperback 979-8-9923571-2-7
COPYRIGHT © 2025 by Maggie Toussaint

Contact information: maggietoussaint@darientel.net
Cover art by Martha Whidden

Muddle House Publishing
1146 Tolomato Drive SE
Darien, GA 31305

Published in the United States of America

Acknowledgments

This book is dedicated to Craig.

Critique partners Marion Deland, Gayle Nastazi, and Carolyn Rowland helped sharpen this manuscript. Thanks also go to my editor, Beth "Jaden" Terrell, who helped with the final shaping. I am also delighted to have Matha Whidden as my cover artist for books three through five of this series. She's so talented and her covers are awesome! Any mistakes in this book are my own.

Chapter One

The winged lion winked at me, and I reared back in surprise. How could a rock-solid object move an eyelid? Impossible, as there was no flesh or blood in this mythical statuette. Even so, my intuition flared.

I'd been discovering my psychic abilities over the last ten months, but this oddity didn't fit with anything I'd learned. How could an inanimate object, even one representing such a powerful creature, bat an eyelid? And why now? This particular item had been in The Book and Candle Shop for nearly three weeks and never once moved on its stony perch.

Weird. Perplexing. Troubling, even.

Was this a magical message?

If it wasn't magic…was I losing it? A terrible fear swept through me.

Not now.

Not when everything was so right.

My sister, Sage Winslow, pinged me right away on our twin-link. *You okay, Tabs?*

Busy, I replied as I studied the winged lion on the shelf. Nothing different about his fierce large wings or his sturdy lion body. I squinted to make sure of what I was seeing. Nothing there. Was I losing it? Didn't want to go there.

Perhaps it was a message from beyond? I stared fixedly at the statuette. *Come on, lion, wink at me, I double dog dare you.* It stared at me steadily, no give to his stone eyelids.

I exhaled slowly, trying to figure this out like a rational person. No secret message. No decline in mental abilities. But I saw what I saw. Hmm.

As usual, Sage had no wait in her. *Both cats went tearing out of here and through the cat door to the shop. Tabby, if you don't answer me right this second, I'm coming downstairs and braining whoever is bothering you.*

My black cat Harley thundered toward me and leapt into my arms. His sister Luna twined herself around my legs. I would've snuggled them both, but Harley filled my arms. His noises of contentment soothed me. Recently I'd wondered if he was a familiar since he knew when I was in distress. This added another chip into the "yes" pile. He'd known I was having a moment and come running to help.

Even though Sage's new guy had a calming effect on her, she hadn't lost her hair trigger of emotions. I better follow up. *No need. It sounds strange, but I believed the winged lion winked at me. Totally caught me off guard. Took me a second to realize it wasn't a housecleaning issue. I'm fine but a bit puzzled.*

Harley took that moment to jump down and curl up on the cushioned wicker chairs of our book nook. His sibling joined him.

Understood, Sage said in my head. *I'll go back to sprucing up my lettuce containers for next weekend's plant sale. We'll see you at dinner tonight with a green salad and garlic bread.*

Dinner. Right. Quig and I didn't entertain, per se, but having my sister and her boyfriend over for dinner made me feel like I was doing married life right. *Sure. Sorry for spooking us both. That eye shimmer put me in serious reverse for a moment.*

No worries.

It wasn't fuzz, but it never hurt to dust. I extended my duster, bent my body at an angle to reach the statuette, and bit my tongue for good measure. Then I moved farther down the aisle to check for any other cleaning issues in the shop.

The doorbell chimed, signaling the exit of a customer my part-time shop clerk, Eve Serratt, had been checking out. I'd caught the curious looks she'd sent my way earlier. Another shopper stepped up and asked Eve about the history of the building.

Their voices faded as my fingers trailed casually across the primary color display of taper candles, hung in pipe-organ style, each hue giving off a distinct scent. I loved how the citrus and beach scents melded with the tang of forests. Then, as I strolled toward our sales counter, I rang each overhead wind chime in turn, the resonant tones tingling my spine in a good way.

"What's going on? You seem antsy today. Something worrying you?" Eve asked, coming to meet me halfway.

I glanced around and saw we had a few shoppers, so I kept my voice soft. "You're right. I can't settle today. Feels like a storm is brewing." If I mentioned I'd been spooked by a winking winged lion, she'd think I was losing it for sure. But she must've wondered what the thundering cats meant. Perhaps she thought the cats were playing and Harley needed comfort instead of me.

"I see." Eve wore flowing orange batiks today, and she'd added a coordinating turban to her ensemble, giving her a radiant earth-mother-gone-tropical vibe.

Truth be told, I envied Eve's stylistic ease and her bold colors. I tended toward neutrals in classic styles, like chinos, jean skirts, that sort of thing. Boring, I know, but it was a casually professional look that worked for me. At least I'd bowed to Eve's fashion advice on sandals. We both wore the same brand of strappy sandals with cushy soles today.

Her fashion sense wasn't all I envied. She grew up in a magical household and had years of experience wielding her craft. Thanks to her generosity and kindness, she'd shared some of her knowledge with me and Sage, teaching us how to ward The Book and Candle Shop. In addition, Eve taught us how to pinpoint focus our twin-link telepathy so no one could eavesdrop on our private conversations ever again.

"Decided I'd put all the extra energy to work. I'm on a mission," I explained. "No more dust bunnies in our shop."

Eve shrugged. "You're fighting a losing battle there. Dust happens."

I made sure the nearest customer was far enough away so she wouldn't overhear us. "Is there a ward for dust?"

"Unfortunately not. It's old school all the way." The door chimed. Eve greeted the new customer and hustled to the register.

"Ms. Tabby, do you have a minute?" another woman asked.

The voice sounded familiar but when I saw her, I didn't recognize the demure young woman dressed in shades of grey. But something about her eyes tugged on my memory. What was her name?

Good thing I had a decent shopkeeper's smile now,

and I kept talking in hope my memory would suddenly ping. "Yes, I do. How've you been?"

"Good. School is awesome, and I have a new roommate this year. But that's not why I'm here. I need your help, though I'm sorry to bother you again."

Her face twitched into a scowl as she spoke, and her name surfaced. Fawn Meldrim, the Savannah College of Art and Design art student I formerly dubbed as "Blue Hair." Only now her chin length locks looked brunette with the tips an electric blue. She'd replaced her Goth look with a soft grey tee and charcoal shorts, completed by Chuck sneakers with bright green laces.

"I'm happy to see you." My professional smile softened into a genuine one. "You're growing your hair out, Fawn. It looks nice!"

"I needed a change. One of my summer courses focused on the value of presentation, and it made sense to work on my look, so I started over with my clothes and hair. A friend helped with the colored tips."

"It's a flattering cut and still gives you an artistic edge. Now what was this about needing my help?"

She wrung her hands. "There's been a...*homicide*...in our family. Uncle Willim is gone. I need to know who killed him and why. Will you take his case?"

Hmm. An investigation. My relationship with the Savannah Police Department was fine as long as I stayed out of their business. But perhaps thinking about a murder would settle my nerves. "When did this happen?"

"A few days ago. Dr. Willim Rosemont is actually my great uncle. Or, he was. I spoke with him last week, and he was absolutely hale and hearty. I only have a few family members left, and I'm devastated by his murder. The paper reported he had an accidental fall, but that can't be. Someone ended his life on purpose."

Willim. I remembered that unusual first name from a recent *Savannah Morning News* article. A prominent psychiatrist had plunged to his death on the ubiquitous Stone Stairs of Death, the flight of steps that led people from Bay Street down to River Street. Not for the faint of heart, those thirty-three steps were steep and gave me vertigo. I always avoided them and took an alternate route down to River Street.

But this wasn't about me. It was about Fawn's uncle. "You have my sincere sympathies. I didn't know your uncle. When did he pass?"

"Today's Friday, so he died Monday evening. The newspaper hinted that his death was a suicide, that he flung himself down the stone stairs. However, there's a story going around that someone shoved him. Another rumor says black magic drove him to it."

Black magic. I barely knew anything about regular magic. Worse, I didn't know if Fawn was a member of the paranormal community, but she often visited our shop with her art school buds, so it was possible. Too bad I couldn't ask her outright.

I believed her concern about her uncle. Her aura positively shimmered with a truth vibe. So, there was a case to solve. I remembered more of the article now. Rosemont had been on Bay Street late in the evening and plunged down the infamous stone steps. Those were treacherous in broad daylight. We had a rain shower on Monday night, so the stairs were slippery and dangerous. This guy had been a psychiatrist to Old Savannah. No telling how many secrets of Savannah's movers and shakers he'd known.

Did those secrets get him killed? If not, why was he downtown so late on a work night? I itched to take the case. "Was he married?"

"Yes. But they lived apart. His estate went to his kids and also his nieces and nephews like me. He donated his house on the square to the city to become a museum. I got five thousand bucks when his lawyer read the will Wednesday afternoon."

Eve must've had the hearing of a bat because she drifted over and jumped into our conversation. "This is about Willim? I knew him. He stopped by often to shoot the breeze with MawMaw. His death is a tragedy. He will be missed by so many people. I can't believe the doc's gone."

"He's my uncle," Fawn said. "I asked Ms. Tabby to find out who killed him."

"Killed him? I heard it was either an accident or suicide," Eve said.

Fawn stomped her foot. "No. Willim never had dark thoughts like that. He was a natural-born caretaker. I'm certain my uncle was murdered."

Eve gasped and sagged against a bookshelf. "Oh, no. Willim was such an icon."

Old Savannah was the largest "small town" I knew. It amazed me how various people were related or connected to each other. "I didn't know him," I repeated to Fawn, "but I believe what you're saying."

Tears misted in Fawn's eyes. "Thank you."

"Something this big will rattle the bones of the paranormal community for years," Eve said. "Yes, definitely get Tabby involved. We need one of our own investigating. The cops don't have an *in* with people like us."

There was an answer to one of my questions. Fawn had paranormal ties. The tightness in my chest eased, and I relaxed my tense shoulders.

Thanks to my late mother's insistence on keeping us twins isolated from everyone, Sage and I grew up clueless about our modest psychic abilities and our peers. We had few connections within the paranormal community. But I had an intuition for the truth, and I believed Fawn was right. I wanted to say yes, but something Eve said made me hesitate.

"Why does his death have such import?" I asked Eve.

After a quick glance at Fawn and then back at me, Eve leaned in confidentially. "Because Willim is, I mean, was, on the Paranormal Council."

The group I'd been hiding from my entire life.

Chapter Two

"Smells great in here, like an Italian restaurant." Larry Rau placed the hefty bowl of salad on the island counter. "Thanks for inviting us to dinner."

Quig stepped close as soon as I rose, which was awkward because I was lifting the heavy pan of lasagna from the oven. Marriage to Dr. Octavian Henry Quigsly IV was everything I'd thought it would be—the fantastic evolution of our childhood friendship and deep affection for each other. But there was a downside I hadn't expected. He acted very possessive toward me when other guys were around.

It didn't bother me when we were alone, just the opposite. However, in front of others, his posturing annoyed me. He'd been this way when we were dating, and I had no problem with it then, which was why I'd delayed discussing this with him. Back then, I'd enjoyed the extra attention. Now it seemed unnecessary. Did he think I'd flirt with my sister's boyfriend? I'd married Quig and promised myself to him.

"Careful, I might drop dinner." This wasn't the time for a discussion of trust issues. But it looked like we needed to have that conversation.

"Of course," he said. "Let me take that dish for you."

I handed it over, gratefully. As the host, I should suggest a conversation topic, but my mind blanked.

Sage smirked at my hesitation, sensing my dilemma without any telepathic exchange. "How's married life, newlyweds?" she asked.

"It has its moments," I said, unable to keep a wry tone out of my voice.

"Absolutely," Quig added and drew me close for a kiss.

He kept it short, thank goodness, and I gave him The Look, the one that meant "not right now." I did not want to put on an intimate display in front of my twin and her boyfriend.

Sage roared with laughter. "Yeah, Quig, knock it off. No need to prove your mutual attraction to us. We know what y'all have been doing over here."

Oh, boy. I didn't want to talk about bedroom activities either. Quickly, I moved the salad bowl to the table, dressed the greens, and blurted out the first thing that occurred to me. "Something odd happened today. Fawn Meldrim, a SCAD student that hangs out in the shop, asked me to look into her uncle's death. Fawn believes he was murdered."

Larry's eyes widened. "Her uncle?"

So far, so good on this topic. I mustered on. "Yes. Her great uncle actually. Dr. Willim Rosemont. She said he was a psychiatrist. You know him?"

"Yeah, you could say that." Larry's tone sounded choked. "He's the Senior Magistrate on the Paranormal Council. Or he was."

My jaw dropped. Not just on the council but the head of it?

It seemed like every time I turned around lately, I heard talk of this group. For nearly thirty years, Mom's secrecy kept us wary of strangers and tethered to our Bristol Street home. I'd never heard of the council until this, my thirtieth year.

After Mom died last fall, Sage and I scrambled to make ends meet and to deal with other paranormals we encountered. All of our recently acquired experience came via the school of hard knocks. Mistakes were made. It would have been easier to start this journey with more skills and experience.

Everyone was staring at me. Oops. Not the time to get lost in my thoughts. Luckily, I didn't need to search for something to say. Words tumbled out of their own accord. "This is going from bad to worse. What did I get myself into?"

I wouldn't mind taking on a low-profile case but that never happened. This one certainly wouldn't be low profile. Further, our district police captain, Captain Kenzo Haynes, and I had a love-hate relationship. He had asked me to be a police consultant. I'd turned down the job, of course. I had no choice. Mom's number one rule was fly under the radar.

Plus, my paranormal investigations bent every rule cops followed. I often took a person's measure by viewing his or her aura. Snooping in their homes or work areas gave me access to energy residue in those spaces. Sometimes I went invisible to avoid discovery, to get into a locked area surreptitiously, or to eavesdrop. Sage could pick locks on sealed doors super-fast, so she often helped me snoop.

Bottom line, none of the evidence I collected off-the-books was admissible in court or was written in police reports. Cops were very keen on having court-worthy evidence to prosecute criminals.

"I hear you, Tabs. Seems like we can't shake a stick without tripping over that blasted council these days,"

Sage said. "I prefer autonomy over having a ruling body. Do other paras feel this way?"

"As a whole, the Paranormal Council is tolerable," Larry said, "but you hear about them these days because you are now known to the community. You're one of us."

This discussion felt bizarre. However, both Larry and Quig had paranormal talents and knew more about the magical world than Sage and I did. When our foursome battled Jeanine Acworth a few months ago, Larry spoke in my mind and went invisible. Quig showed he was a mirror talent when he reflected Jeanine's bad mojo back on herself.

Sage wrinkled her nose at Larry. "You told me your family has always had someone on the council. With your brother and parents gone, does that mean you'll be tapped for your brother's seat?"

He glanced at Quig first before turning back to Sage. "Aunt Althea sits on that board now. I grew up with her son. He wants her seat when she retires."

I digested this news, envying Larry's easy familiarity with this. He knew many paras due to growing up in the community.

"What role does she have?" Sage demanded.

"Althea Morgan was the Junior Magistrate. Now she's the acting interim Senior Magistrate until they fill Willim's vacant seat."

I'd been listening to this exchange while fingering my locket, a comfort behavior that helped center me. This topic ignited my amateur-sleuth curiosity. "Your aunt benefitted from Dr. Rosemont's death?"

"No way." Larry snorted. "The Senior Magistrate hears an unending tidal wave of complaints, endures special interest jockeying, and wrangles a nightmare of administrative red tape. Everyone insists that their issue should be the council's top priority. I wouldn't wish that job on anyone." He paused for a long moment. "Willim excelled at it, though. He kept us out of the public eye and managed our disputes in-house."

"If he was so good, why did someone kill him?" I asked.

"There's nothing to indicate he was murdered," Quig said from over my shoulder, jumping into the conversation for the first time. "He had a bad fall."

Larry ignored Quig's remarks. "Willim had a talent for reconciliation, evidenced by his long success as the psychiatrist to Savannah's movers and shakers."

He sounded like a good guy. Now I wish I'd met him. I'd never known either of my grandfathers. "His leadership role was to make everyone happy?"

"Not exactly." Larry's cheek twitched. "Few people manipulated the council because Willim convinced everyone he had things under control. He assured them that in the big picture unseen forces were at work."

"What big picture?"

"The paranormal community is a thread in the everyday fabric of Savannah, but only if we go undetected. With his education, Willim realized we were in danger of genetic drift and nearing our ecological threshold. That in turn makes us susceptible to population stressors and adverse effects."

Sage and I exchanged a worried glance. My eyes hadn't glazed over, but it was a near thing. "What's that mean?"

Larry brightened. "That old saw of safety in

numbers is true. Bottom line, we need a larger population to maintain genetic viability or..."

"Or what?" Sage demanded when Larry's voice trailed off.

"Or the community declines until we go extinct."

Extinct? "That sounds ominous."

"It is," Larry said.

Earlier this year, we'd encountered energy vamps from Chicago. "There are other communities — we're not the only ones."

"Sure, but the closest one is in New Orleans. Ten cities that I know of have councils." He gave me a pointed look. "Also, some paras choose to live in isolation."

"Why don't we hold an event every year so the young paras can meet?" I countered.

"Good idea," Larry said, "but most paranormals prefer to stay put."

"This a lot to take in, but I have a question," Sage said. "Only Mom reproduced in our family. Auntie O never had kids. Is this why we twins have been pressured to reproduce?"

Larry's face flamed bright red. "You two aren't the only ones feeling the heat. Every young adult in the community has the same pressure from their parents, including me."

A phrase he said earlier resurfaced in my thoughts. I needed clarification. "What 'adverse effects' did you mean as population stressors?"

"Disease, famine, and war." Larry paused. "Witch hunts. All of those can pressure a population."

Whoa. Definite population stressors. I shuddered. "Let's hope paranormal persecution is over."

"History proves when things go wrong, people point fingers at us. That's why keeping paras inconspicuous is the council's main job."

His answer sparked another question. "What happens when paranormals make the news?"

Larry hesitated before saying, "Depending on the threat level to the entire community, different strategies are employed."

Uh oh. I gripped the chair back before me until my knuckles turned white. I dreaded where this was headed. My aunt had worked for the council for many years. As an assassin. "Auntie O?"

"Or one of our other agents. Believe it or not, our judicial system is not harsh overall and rarely results in death. Rogue paras are reminded of the council's power and what happens if they go astray. The warning resolves most issues."

I had a light bulb moment. "That's why we twins hear so much about these people now. Because we aren't registered with the council, we are assumed to be rogues. They're watching us."

"Doesn't matter now." Quig moved closer to me, enveloping me in a veritable cloud of his delightful scent and body heat. "You're a Quigsly now. Anyone who comes after you has to go through me first."

I managed to stop a snort of laughter but couldn't hold back a smile. Quig had always looked out for me. Now he was my self-appointed bodyguard. I had enough talent to take care of myself, but I turned, patted his chest, and caught his eye. "Thanks for having my back."

"Always."

His penetrating gaze heated every part of my body.

Not only was I head-over-heels for him, but he felt the same way about me. Some days I pinched myself to see if my new life was real.

"Speaking of Willim," Larry began, "I have been wrestling with questions about his death. Quig, why does his death certificate says the manner of death is 'Undetermined?'"

"My findings are confidential," Quig said. "As are my lack of findings."

I brightened with understanding. "Suicide by plummeting down steps isn't a check box on an autopsy form. I assume you networked with the cops about their thoughts and learned nothing new. Given that Rosemont had a talent for persuasion, his mediation role likely didn't create enemies. That leaves his toxicology as a possible source of information. Any outliers there?"

"Again, I can't comment specifically on my work, but it takes weeks and sometimes months to get tox screen results. Due to budgetary concerns, we test for a standard panel of likely chemicals. Because of Rosemont's status, I requested extensive testing. That adds time to the process."

Sounded like Quig had a few suspicions. "Dr. Rosemont's death feels off to Fawn and now to me, but there's no proof his fall wasn't an accident. His mysterious death intrigues me. All I need to do is figure out who wanted him gone."

Quig removed his glasses to clean them. His stare intensified and warmed places deep inside me. "I'd prefer you avoided police matters now that we're married. Your safety is very important to me. Please don't put yourself in harm's way."

Ooh. This could turn into our first fight. I wanted to please him, but these investigations satisfied my soul. If I was very careful, I could do both because they weren't mutually exclusive. I decided to talk around the matter to sell my perspective. "The police aren't investigating."

He rubbed his eyes and then gazed at me again. "There's no evidence of foul play. However, if someone killed Rosemont, investigating his death would likely put you in danger."

"I see." Safety was encoded in my husband's DNA. However, he'd hadn't expressly forbidden my involvement. He'd stated the request as his preference.

Which suited me because the mystery of Rosemont's passing pulled at me like a rip tide.

Everyone who lived at the seashore knew how to survive a rip current. You rode it until it gave out, then you swam parallel to the shore and slowly made your way back to the beach. Those who fought the current didn't make it. If this investigation was a rip current, I felt certain I could handle it.

"I don't know about the rest of you," Sage said, breaking the prickly silence that had fallen over the room, "but my mouth is watering for Tabby's lasagna. I can't wait to bite into those comforting cheesy layers."

"I could eat," Larry said.

"Coming right up," I said.

Thanks for the save, I sent Sage on our twin-link as I moved the lasagna to the table and began dishing it out on plates.

We're investigating, right? Sage asked. *I saw that glint in your eye.*

Damn straight.

Chapter Three

After Sage and Larry left and the dishes were done, Quig and I got ready for bed. As I brushed my teeth, I wondered what confidential matter got Willim Rosemont killed. Did someone have a secret baby, a criminal record, or unethical earnings? Psychiatrists asked many questions, so I was certain he'd heard people professing all of the deadly sins.

Quig nuzzled the back of my neck as I put the electric toothbrush on its charging station. His arms slipped around me from behind, and we watched us in the mirror. My face flushed with warmth. Was this what married life looked like?

"I'm a member of your family now," I mused, as much for myself as for him, my thoughts stuck on the word secrets.

"And I'm part of your family. That's what happens when two people love each other and vow to spend their lives together. I would do anything to make you happy."

"I am happy."

"I sense a 'but' coming."

"You're right. Something has been bugging me. We made promises."

"We did. I promise to love you with all my heart. Always. I will never stop loving you. You are my very life, Tabby."

His gentle touches made it hard to think. "Me too. I mean, the same thing. Oh! You know what I mean."

"I'm glad you feel the same way, love."

Taking a firm grip on my thoughts, I returned to the topic I wanted to discuss. "About those promises. Before we were married, you said you'd disclose your talent after we were married."

He stilled. "So did you."

Quig's body language revealed more than his soft words. Was he hiding something? On the other hand, shouldn't I give the man I love the benefit of the doubt? "You know about my talent. As an energetic, I give and take energy. I can also make intuitive guesses about a person's emotional state based on their aura."

But that wasn't everything. I'd never mentioned my ability to bend light and become invisible. If he found out, would he think I was a freak of nature?

"Mmm," he murmured, his hands massaging my scalp.

I shivered with anticipation. Ever since our friendship deepened, his touch was like catnip to me. I loved being with him. And marveled that he was mine.

"It's only fair you share your secrets with me," I managed to say.

"Have you shared all of yours with me?" He rained kisses on my neck.

"Most of them." Darn. Why'd I say that?

"You hold up your end, and I'll hold up your end too."

I swatted playfully at his arm. "Get serious."

"I'm very serious. About you. Can we discuss this later? I am devoted to this being the best night of our lives."

Though I wanted answers, I also needed him, right now. Turning in his arms, I did some gratifying exploring myself.

"Thought you'd see things my way," he murmured.

~*~

I usually fell asleep wrapped in his arms, his heartbeat a soothing lullaby in my ear. In the natural order of things, my relaxed body usually subsided into sleep too.

But I lay awake, remembering every time I mentioned his family secret, Quig distracted me, not that I was complaining about his diversions. I enjoyed everything about him, about us, but doggone it. Why wouldn't he confide in me?

For that matter, why couldn't I accept that everything else was perfect? Why did I push in this one area? I was married to a man who delighted in showing me affection. Would my need-to-know mindset wreck a very good thing?

We loved each other.

Unbidden, another thought popped into my mind. Sage and her former boyfriend Brindle loved each other, but it wasn't enough. At least they found out before their lives became legally entwined with shared property, marriage, or kids.

Many couples broke up and managed the aftermath fine. I didn't want anyone but Quig. He was everything I needed. After my mother passed, I'd naturally turned to my best friend for consolation and when all the comforting was said and done, he kissed me, oh so tenderly. I kissed him back.

That thrill never faded. Every day with him felt like that magical first kiss.

Why couldn't I let this go? He had no issues with my talents, known or unknown. And yet, my curiosity insistently flared like a candle on a windy night. Funny, I hadn't used that expression in a while. Mom and Auntie O always said it with a laugh because we were candle-makers. Grandma used the phrase too, long before there ever was a song with a similar title.

I rolled over, and Quig came with me. His warmth comforted me, until blessed sleep eased my concerns. I may have unanswered questions, but this man, this life, were exactly what I wanted.

Chapter Four

The morning of Dr Willim Rosemont's memorial service arrived. Though Sage and I shared our family's treasure trove of black dresses, those alluring gowns weren't appropriate for this solemn occasion.

Trouble was I'd eaten a steady diet of desserts since getting hitched two months ago, and nothing fit the same. My choices in mourning attire were dismal, until I'd remembered that A-line navy-blue tank top dress in the back of my closet that used to be too big, and I never got around to returning it.

Oddly, the more I fussed about today's attire, the more Quig beamed. Once I donned the blue dress, and it worked, I came to my senses. Good grief. I'd nearly started an argument with my husband because he said how wonderful I looked.

Our drive to the service passed quickly, and I aimed my air conditioning vents directly on my face. August in Savannah could be a scorcher, and this year was no exception. Quig dropped me off in the drive-through breezeway. I stepped in the lobby to wait for him and discovered it was hotter than a July sand dune inside.

The air wasn't cool in the funeral home's auditorium either. Possibly because the mourners were packed tighter than sardines. Quig sat on my right, my twin on the left. Beyond Sage came her boyfriend, Larry. On the other side of Quig was his buddy Herbert R. Ellis, who also was our attorney.

During the service, a chaplain led prayers and

hymns and gave a short talk on a life well lived. Eulogies came next. In particular, three members of Savannah's City Council and Captain Kenzo Haynes praised the doctor as compassionate and characterized him as a valued leader in our community. A lady behind the family echoed the praise of Rosemont's contribution to the community. No one from the family row offered any words of remembrance. They looked solemn and shocked.

I knew that feeling.

Mom's death last fall happened quickly. It turned out she'd shared her lifeforce energy too many times with her cancer-ridden friend. Mom's body drained to the point where it couldn't recharge, and she passed in her sleep. I'd been in shock for her funeral because I would've helped her if I'd known she was pushing her limits so severely.

I stirred from my musings as local singing phenomenon Peaches McVeigh stepped up to the microphone, backed by a full ensemble, and sang "The Old Rugged Cross," "My Soul is Anchored in the Lord," and "You Raise Me Up." Her powerful, bluesy voice filled the hall, and my eyes weren't the only ones there that teared up at the raw emotion of her set. She ended her performance by blowing a kiss heavenward and saying "Love ya, Doc."

The chaplain announced that the committal would be later and private. Meanwhile, the family would meet and greet mourners in the reception room.

I glanced at my watch. The entire service lasted forty-five minutes, but in the heat, it felt like it'd been hours. I longed for cooler air, and I would've stepped outside for fresh air except it was even hotter out there.

What I wouldn't give for a cold pack around my bare neck and another slap dab on top of my head. As we made our way to the reception, I listened to what people were saying all around me. After all, I'd come here to snoop, but partially to honor the man who gave so much of himself to Savannah.

It was impossible to hear a single voice with so many people talking. Not quite the snoop-fest I'd hoped for. All I knew was Willim Rosemont had been well respected and that I needed to attend a Peaches McVeigh show. I'd been mesmerized by her singing.

Beside me, Quig asked Herbert in a low voice, "What will the council do now?"

Recently, I'd learned Herbert was on the Paranormal Council, so it was a reasonable question for Quig to ask his best friend. However, I was surprised he'd ask something so hush-hush in a throng of people. But then, who would know Quig meant the Paranormal Council and not the Savannah City Council? Or who could hear them speaking with everyone else yammering? With surreptitious glances right and left, I realized no one was paying any attention to their conversation.

"Usual procedure is to appoint an interim, and they've named Althea Morgan as the Interim Senior Magistrate," Herbert replied softly. "That's temporary as she can't manage her Junior Magistrate role plus the Senior one for long. No one could."

I'd never met Althea Morgan. I didn't have any idea if she was my age or older. I silently hoped the council stayed bogged down administratively for a long time so they wouldn't focus on me or my twin sister.

"Is she here?" I asked Herbert, meaning Althea.

"Yes," Herbert said with a glance Larry's way. "She was in the second row, right behind his family. She's the godmother of Rosemont's son. The two families have always been close."

There'd been one female on that row. "The blonde woman wearing a fascinator?"

"That's her trademark style for formal occasions. She loves those fancy wisps of hats."

I remembered her. She'd been stoic up until Peaches sang the last tune. Then she'd cried her eyes out. I'd sensed the loss was more than of a work buddy.

"Don't be spilling your guts, Ellis," Larry Rau said. "Your esteemed colleagues would have your head if they knew you were indiscreet."

"Stuff it, Rau," Herbert said. "Nobody is interested in your opinion."

"You have no authority over me. In fact, I could make your life a living hell."

"You wish."

Their argument surprised me. I had no idea these two men didn't get along. Worse, it made me wonder about their history — and if I could fix it. Meanwhile, I showered them with good energy.

Finally, it was our turn in the receiving line. I murmured, "I'm sorry for your loss," to Rosemont's widow and the others in the receiving line as I shook their hands. Everyone in our group followed suit, and we cleared that bottleneck.

Unfortunately, a scowling Savannah City Council member, Jasper George, stepped in front of us. "A word, Dr. Quigsly."

Despite his elected status as the County Medical Examiner and Coroner, Quig reported to the City

Council. He gave the man a quick nod and leaned close to whisper in my ear, "I won't be long."

I'd heard those words before in meet-and-greet settings like this. A quick glance around the room showed the seats were taken, so I could stand or prop myself against a wall. Maybe someplace quiet would work.

Larry and Sage headed to the refreshment table. Herbert glanced at me, and I nodded toward an empty corner of the room. We threaded our way through clumps of people, and it was a relief to have this semi-private space to ourselves.

"Quig won't be long," I said to start a conversation.

Herbert snorted. "Councilman Jasper George will bend his ear to the breaking point. That man is so set on career achievement that he pressures everyone."

The man in question always struck me as an odd duck. For one thing, his torso seemed overly long perched atop short spindly legs. Was it mix and match day at the body parts farm when he was born? "Oh? Does that help him get ahead?"

"Only if he does it to people who curry favor. Quig is neutral in the world of Savannah politics."

Herbert's answer confused me. Quig's job was straightforward. "What favors could he grant in the morgue?"

"You'd be surprised," Herbert said softly.

My eyes widened in alarm. "What does that mean?"

Herbert shook his head and focused on the crowded room.

That was weird. Maybe the heat bothered Herbert too. I tried another topic. "I didn't know you and Larry Rau were at odds."

Herbert startled out of his musings. "Larry is an acquired taste. His brother Johnny even more so. What's more, the Raus are users."

Johnny was no longer on this side of the dirt. My one and only contact with him was finding his body in Larry's home. At the time, everyone thought Larry was dead because the two brothers strongly favored each other in appearance.

"You have my complete attention. Larry's dating my sister. Explain what you mean." I would do anything to protect my twin, and vice versa. "How do the Raus use people?"

Herbert turned to face me. "He homed in on Sage the moment her previous relationship ended. Larry isn't a wide-eyed innocent. He has many failings. Some might say more than most."

Contrary to Herbert's distrust of the man, I'd always felt Larry was a better fit for my sister than her previous beau. Maybe something else flickered under Herbert's veneer of cool. He'd made no bones about wanting to date me, though I was already smitten with Quig when Herbert met me. Perhaps he'd wanted a shot at dating Sage?

"Trouble dead ahead," Herbert muttered softly.

I saw the female entertainer closing in on our corner. Unlike Herbert, I relished having the chance to speak with her. For investigational purposes, of course.

Peaches McVeigh sauntered up to Herbert and mugged him. Technically, it was a hug, but she was really into it. Herbert endured the contact with a pained expression on his face, sparking my curiosity. For a man who didn't show much emotion, he'd sure acted different today. Did these two share a history?

"I need a ride home, Sugah. Care to help a gal out?" Peaches asked, her hand cupping his cheek.

"Hello yourself," Herbert said. "I'm flattered you asked. Was looking for a reason to leave anyway."

"Purrfect," Peaches drawled.

"Hello, Ms. McVeigh, I'm Tabby Quigsly. Your singing during the service was beautiful," I said to make my presence known. "How are you holding up?"

"Hey, darlin.' You don't mind if I steal the hottest lawyer in town, do you?"

"You have my blessing." I glanced at Herbert. "Is your cat okay?"

"Lately Violet has been indulging her inner vixen and staying gone days at a time."

Interesting response. Still, Herbert's laxity made him an irresponsible pet owner. "What if something happens to her out there in the world? Is it right to give her so much autonomy?"

"Violet can take care of herself."

Peaches and Herbert left as Larry and Sage returned. "The punch is bland, the cookies are soft. Worse, there's nobody here I care to chat up," Sage said. "You ready to go?"

"Almost. Waiting for Quig to finish speaking with council member George."

"Done any snooping yet?"

"Between the heat and the loud conversations, I have a killer headache. I want to go home too."

"Stay right here, Sis," Sage said. "I'll wrangle your husband for you, but it's gonna cost you a trip to the beach. Can we go this afternoon?

No way. All I could think about now was air conditioning. "First thing tomorrow."

Chapter Five

Early the next morning at Tybee Island beach, Sage and I walked down the shore a ways until the people thinned out, and we found privacy. My sister plunked down at the crest of the high-water mark, and I joined her. We sat quietly absorbing the wave energy and the refreshing onshore breeze. In minutes, my shoulders relaxed.

If I could live on the beach, I would. It centered me like nothing else. Same for my sister.

"More than ever, I want to investigate Dr. Willim Rosemont's death," I began, digging my bare toes in the warm sand. Sage glanced over at me, questions in her eyes, so I continued. "After hearing how respected he was in Savannah, I need to find answers for his niece, Fawn."

Sage turned her face to the sun and sighed. "Larry says Rosemont was a man of power. He'd be a hard man to murder. Since he had ties in the normal and paranormal worlds, where would you look for his killer?"

"Murder isn't a foregone conclusion. He could've accidentally fallen down those steps. In my experience, clues go cold fast. I heard there's a political push to officially call it an accident and close the case. That rumor spurs my curiosity."

"Larry also told me Rosemont lived alone. His wife and kids moved out long ago because he never had time for them."

I scowled. "Since he was active in both worlds, he likely didn't have time for much else. Even so, he recently had a night out with friends. Hmm. That disconnect feels relevant. Maybe he was all about his power and his personal needs. If so, he wasn't the kind and compassionate man touted at the memorial service. Did he have a dark side to his personality?"

"Don't know. But enough about him." Sage gave me a long considering look. Then she smirked. "Did you tell Quig yet?"

Her wry but gleeful tone irked me. I didn't appreciate the change of topic. I wanted to brainstorm case questions for her to ask Larry. "I have no idea what you're talking about."

"Right." She gave a soft chuckle. "He'll probably create a new list of rules regarding what you can and cannot do. He is keenly focused on being your husband."

"His protectiveness doesn't bother me." I felt compelled to defend him. "It means he cares for me."

Sage scowled. "Guys with control issues can get physically rough. I'm worried for your safety. Especially, you know, with the other…"

This was like pulling teeth. Why couldn't she come out and say whatever it was? "Quig isn't like that. Ever. He's very considerate."

"If you say so."

Her poking around in my life made me snappish. "And what's this other thing you referenced?" Sage looked so smug that my irritation twisted into concern. I reached for her arm, feeling the rightness of our physical connection as our energies joined. "What do you know?"

"Can't fool me, Sis. You're preggers. When were you going to tell me?"

"What?" I repeated, dumbstruck, my hand falling away.

"Pregnant. Knocked up. Expecting. Bun in the oven. With child."

"No way…we are waiting to have kids. Why do you think I'm pregnant?"

"Let me count the ways. My sun-worshipping sister, who is never bothered by heat, is too hot multiple times every day and even now shading her eyes. Your appetite is wonky. Plus, you've got a cute little pooch to your belly."

"Wait a minute." I reared back in surprise. "Sure, I've put on weight. Quig wants ice cream every night, and he fixes me a bowl, too. The 'pooch' is marriage weight, same as going off to college adds weight. I'm not fat, merely rounding a bit. No cause for alarm."

"You know how babies are made, right?" Sage arched an eyebrow. "One would think a sensitive with your skillset would've realized your new status before I did."

Her smugness cut through my defenses. My irritation partially deflated. Was her suggestion even possible? Nah. "Is this why you wanted a beach day? To get the lowdown on an alleged pregnancy?"

She beamed bright energy my way. "Nothing alleged about it, Tabs."

Fresh panic struck me at warp speed. My brain would not compute. This would not do. I hurried to explain my version of the facts. "I stopped taking birth control before the wedding because it takes a while for that to get out of your system. We've been using protection. Except for once on our wedding night." Heat suffused my face. "We ran out."

"Atta boy!" She hooted with laughter. "Tabby, it only takes one time, as Mom always said."

I shivered despite the warm day. If I was *pregnant*, it would be a done deal. But how could I have missed such an important detail about my body? "Why are you so sure?"

Sage stared at the cresting waves before she spoke. "Your inner aura is thicker in your baby area and over your boobs. The outer aura glows silver and orange. Plus, I believe your sacral chakra is more balanced."

I knew she read people's auras, same as me, so her characterization of mine was likely correct. But sacral chakra? My visual field narrowed to her face. "Since when do you know what a chakra is?"

"Larry and I meditate together. He's helped me balance my chakras that were out of sync. From what I can tell about yours, you seem *more* below your belly button, if you know what I mean."

I vaguely knew what chakras were, but for Sage to comment on mine felt intrusive, even if she was my twin. I covered my belly with my hands. "You've surprised me. Can you see other people's chakras?"

"No. That's advanced stuff. I can sense yours because it is like mine. Your belly is...*more* in an intriguing way. And you smell sweet, like cake."

"I do not." I glared at her. "I showered this morning."

"Tabby. Get a grip. I see and sense your significant body changes: a radiant face, glowing skin, and rollercoaster emotions. You've started napping. Your condition is obvious to anyone who knows you like I do. We'll stop for a pregnancy test kit on the way home. I'm certain it's true, and I'm delighted for you. After all, if you reproduce, the pressure is off me."

I couldn't grasp the p-word, much less buying a test kit, so I ignored the suggestion. "Quig's Mom keeps bugging me for 'news.' She claims I'll have a baby before next summer. Her attitude and certainty on the topic are super annoying." I sobered. Was my isolated childhood and sheltered life causing me to be naïve?

The gears in my head whirled. Darn it. If Sage was right, then Milly Quigsly was spot on.

Now that I thought about it, my body felt different. Not only in the way clothes fit. In the way they felt on my skin. And I'd noticed my work sandals felt wrong on my feet. Speaking of feet, I had a new habit of rushing home to put my feet up in the evenings. And I enjoyed resting a hand over my belly.

Huh.

Maybe it wasn't the ice cream.

"I can see you're on the fence. Let's do the math," Sage continued. "If you got pregnant on your wedding night, you'd be two months along, and the baby will be full term by the end of March, if I calculated right. Is your gynecologist one who takes maternity patients?"

Another chill slid down my spine. I couldn't wrap my head around the word pregnant. "I have no idea."

"What does your belly feel like?"

My hand curled protectively around the rounded area. "It doesn't feel different, except for being a little extra." A stray thought hit me between the eyes. "Is something wrong with me or a possible kid since I can't feel anything?"

"You're blooming with good health. The kiddo should be fine. Don't freak out. I've tried to see her aura, but it's murky." Sage raised a hand to forestall a protest. "Baby Girl is likely too young for her aura to be fully formed. We need information. I don't feel comfortable winging it. Not on something important like this."

My ears closed after she described my aura. "Murky isn't good."

"It isn't necessarily bad either. Too bad Dr. Rosemont is dead. He would've known who to recommend."

Rosemont. My unsolved case. Couldn't dwell on that now. "Quig is a doctor, but I can't mention pregnancy to him until I'm certain. It would be awful to raise his hopes if I've only got an ice cream belly."

"Right. That's why we need to find out if you are preggers. We need to buy a kit."

"Okay. You've worn me down. I'll do a test." Motherhood meant entering a different phase of life. I took a deep breath, needing to think about any other subject. "Enough about me. Tell me about Larry. Y'all doing okay?"

"Better than that. We are super chill." Sage's smile stretched from ear to ear. "We love the same things, and he makes me happy. The *romance* part is smokin' hot. Who knew, right? I have never felt better."

I didn't need to hear the steamy parts. "From the outside looking in, y'all are a good fit. You're content in a way I've never seen before—as if you found the means to be you and be less upset with the world."

"Yeah. Weird, huh? I finally got the right guy. Took me long enough."

Remembering Herbert's negativity about Larry, I asked, "And you feel like you are each contributing and benefitting from the relationship?"

"Of course. Why do you ask?"

"Something Herbert said. He doesn't care for Larry."

She shrugged and dragged her fingers through the sand. "It's mutual. Larry doesn't like Herbert either. Wonder what caused their friction?"

Southerners excelled at holding grudges, and our city was a small town in many ways. "The discord could be recent or generations old. You never know in Savannah."

~*~

Sage and I huddled together in my bathroom after I took the pregnancy test. My emotions skittered around like grease in a hot pan. Did I want it to be positive or negative? What would Quig prefer?

My aunt and his parents would be thrilled if I had conceived. But Quig and I were newlyweds, though we'd been living together since the first of the year. We'd barely scratched the surface of learning to be life partners and sharing bank accounts. What would it be like with an infant added to the mix?

Another question squirreled around in my head. Would my cat Harley accept a kid in his domain? He'd better or he'd have to live with Sage. I didn't want to banish Harley, of course, but a kid would take priority.

No need to go too far down the what-if road. I reread the directions of the kit to slow my thoughts. The test kit showed a control line in the viewing window. If the test area showed even the faintest hint of a colored line besides the control line, that meant I was a mom-to-be.

As if I'd conjured the color, before my eyes a second line formed and darkened to match the control line.

"See?" Sage asked, hugging me and jumping up and down. "You're gonna be a mom. Yay!"

Her joy overtook me and became mine too. I jumped with her, until I stopped. "Maybe I shouldn't do that."

Sage shoved my phone at me. "Call him!"

I shook my head. "This news is too big. I will tell him in person. Tonight."

Chapter Six

"Your buddy's here," Gerard said.

Coming into The Book and Candle Shop and acting like this was any other day was tough after learning I was pregnant. I glanced up to find my weekday shop clerk standing in the threshold between my stillroom and the shop. "Not my buddy. Which cop is it?"

"The grumpy one."

Oh joy. I hadn't had the pleasure of Detective Nowry's company in two months. I didn't want to see him particularly, but when the man wanted my help, he circled relentlessly, like a shark on the scent. I'd helped him solve other homicides, saved his hide when he'd been spelled by a witch. Maybe he was here to offer a belated thank you.

Fat chance.

I nodded at Gerard and headed his way without taking off my work apron. I liked having that additional covering over my womb — more protection for the baby. My shop clerk stepped out of my path and edged toward the alley door. "I'm going across the street for coffee. Want a cup?"

"Iced coffee would be great. Oh, and a BLT sandwich, if you please. Charge everything to my account."

"Will do."

Gerard disliked the detective. He'd been caught before in Nowry's suspect net and interviewed aggressively. The harrowing experience changed him, made him distrust cops, especially this one. He loped out the alley door.

I turned my attention to the sixty-something man walking my way. It was unusual for Detective Nowry to drop by alone. Usually his partner, Sharmila Belfor, accompanied him. Even though Belfor was all business, somehow, she smoothed Nowry's rough edges. Until I knew what Nowry wanted, I would be cautious. Not only did I keep a counter between us, but I also pushed out a psychic barrier to make sure no bad vibes came my way.

Or to the baby.

My left hand curved over my womb.

The shop door chimed as Nowry entered. He wore a dark suit, even though the outdoor temperature registered in the nineties. The two customers in the shop didn't even glance up from the books they were perusing in the back corner.

I loved it when people got so absorbed in the good vibes of the shop. This place was a visual, auditory, and olfactory treat. Many tourists said they felt like they'd come home as soon as they walked through the door. You couldn't fake that kind of reaction.

All too soon, Nowry stood before me, easing his bulk down on the bar stool by the counter. "Ms. Quigsly."

"Detective. To what do I owe this honor?"

"Due diligence," he rumbled softly in his deep voice. "City Council is pressuring the department to close the Rosemont investigation. Captain Haynes hates anyone telling him what to do, but that's between us, and I'll deny it if you repeat it." He cleared his throat. "Anyway, we want you to consult on this case."

Consult. His boss had tried to hire me full-time in June. I said no, of course. So, he forbade me from doing my brand of snooping. That hadn't deterred me one bit.

Plus, I had already decided to investigate the Rosemont case, though I hadn't snooped in his house yet. Quig wished I wouldn't put myself in harm's way, but I could investigate in a safe way. That way we both got what we wanted.

And I was the mother of his child-to-be.

Yikes.

Sage's predictions of Quig laying down rules about what I couldn't do while pregnant rang out with Cassandra-like surety in my head. Quig would put his foot down on anything that might impact our baby's safety. In any event, I had to be super careful if I snooped. And do it safely. I couldn't endanger the baby.

"Are you all right, Tabby?" Nowry asked. "You look...pale."

I shook off my musings. "Sorry. Lost in my thoughts. I attended Rosemont's memorial service yesterday, along with half of Savannah. The tributes paid to the man made him seem a saint."

"No man's a saint, but Doc helped many people. You'd be hard-pressed to find someone who disliked him."

"Besides his wife and kids?"

"No love lost there, and that couple didn't reside at the same address. There were no police records of fights or allegations of abuse. From what we can gather, they were incompatible and led separate lives."

"Why not divorce and start over? Why be stalled

dead-in-the-water like that? Their choice doesn't make sense to me."

Nowry shrugged. "Some couples view their wedding vows as etched in stone."

I nodded but immediately had second thoughts. If I partnered with a spouse I couldn't live with, I would move on. No way that would happen with my guy. A warm glow filled me as I thought of how much in love Quig and I were with each other.

"Hope this doesn't sound rude, but isn't it standard procedure to start questioning the people who knew the victim?" I asked. "Have you questioned his wife to rule her out? Did she inherit a boatload of money when he died?"

He gave a terse nod. "We interviewed her. She is shaken by his death. Anxious too, but I don't know if that's her normal demeanor."

"And the life insurance?"

"Goes to his two kids. His wife, Sherrie, inherits the modest home where she's living. However, she will lose the current stipend he provided and must find a job. Financially, it was in her best interest if he stayed alive."

Hmm. "Were the kids staying with him the night of his death?"

"They were not. We have security camera footage from two Savannah locations showing Rosemont with nightclub singer Peaches McVeigh, your lawyer with my partner Belfor, and the group's drummer paired with, of all people, Lilah Acworth."

He spat out Lilah's name as if he'd tasted rotten fish. I understood the aversion. Lilah was a difficult person and a narcissist. "Sounds like a good starting point for a suspect list, if this is a homicide."

"That's why I'm here. We need to do another round of interviews. Peaches is in South Carolina with her band, including the drummer. Lilah's in the wind. Althea Morgan, who is the family's point of contact, is booked solid with appointments. Attorney Herbert R. Ellis won't return my calls. I hoped, as his friend, you would encourage him to come forward."

Herbert wasn't a fan of the detective, though he put up with the cop because they both had relationships with Sharmila Belfor, Nowry's partner. Herbert was Quig's childhood friend, and I had become better acquainted with him over these last few months. Herbert was no one's fool. He didn't volunteer anything to cops. His philosophy was his business was his business and no one else's.

I considered the matter before I spoke, tapping my short fingernails on the glass countertop. "Herbert is the only possible suspect you can interview again, and you're stuck because you can't reach him. Sorry, I won't help with that. Having been through a police interrogation myself, I understand why he'd dodge your calls."

Nowry swore under his breath. "Sharmila won't twist his arm either. She's supposed to be on my side, not on her boyfriend's side."

"Why isn't she here with you?"

"Since the hit-and-run accident and her hospitalization this summer, she's been assigned to the Cold Case unit. The higher ups put her on desk duty, so I'm flying solo. Belfor is different now. Being unconscious for days and then doing physical therapy to regain her mobility took the wind out of her sails.

My gut says she's gonna request that posting become her regular assignment."

Empathy welled in me for his associate. "I hadn't realized, but I understand how harsh life can be. I'm sorry you may lose her as a partner. You two had synergy."

He gazed away for a long moment before pinning me with his glare. "She's a good detective, but no cop wants a partner who's been spooked. I'm wondering if this old dog can handle breaking in another eager detective. They come in thinking they know everything, when they don't even know what they don't know. It's enough to make me walk away from the job."

"You're retirement age?"

"Blew right past it, but there's nothing for me at home. My wife died years ago, and I never developed hobbies. Got no kids. Retirement will be a prison sentence for me."

Okay, that was more information than I wanted. How could I wrap up this conversation?

I gave him my best customer smile because I'd rather snoop on my own than get tangled up with the Savannah PD. "You'll figure it out when you retire. As for consulting on the Rosemont case, don't count on me. I will discuss it with my husband, but Quig views our evenings as our exclusive time."

"Newlyweds." He sighed. "I know you want to do it. Work your charms on him. Women always manage to get what they want."

I didn't care for his snide comment or his knowing what I wanted. Indignation simmered in my response. "I have a fulltime job and a husband. My primary focus has shifted to hearth and home." As I spoke the words, I realized how true they were. I wanted to spend time with Quig. I hoped he always was this happy to come home to me.

"I'm disappointed to hear that. The captain won't be pleased."

Tough. Pleasing the captain wasn't on my to-do list, but I shouldn't antagonize the detective. "I enjoy solving puzzles, and that's how I became interested in police cases. While I still enjoy puzzles, I love being married more."

Nowry got a distant look in his eyes. "I felt that way about my wife. I see so much darkness while I am at work. I didn't want her tarnished by that. She was the best part of me."

We exchanged smiles. How strange. We were having a moment. That our mutual priority had been, or in my case still was, to make our spouses happy.

Nowry lumbered off and drove away, freeing my clerk to emerge from the stillroom where he'd been hiding.

"Thought he'd never go," Gerard said. "Your lunch is in the back, and I even remembered to request extra bacon on your sandwich."

"Thanks. I am ravenous." I ate with him at the register, feeding Harley my extra bacon so he'd quit twining around my legs.

A customer checked out and afterward Gerard switched into interrogation mode. "What did the detective want?"

"Me. I mean, he wanted my help on the Rosemont case."

Gerard's lips twisted to the side. "Hmm. Quig know

about that?"

"Not yet, seeing as Nowry just left. I'll tell Quig tonight." Maybe I should mention the investigation request first thing when we met for dinner, so he wasn't thinking of additional ways to protect the baby in my womb.

If my husband was adamantly opposed to me sleuthing while I was pregnant, would I do it anyway?

That was no way for our marriage to begin, but try as I might, I couldn't think of a compromise that would work. Unless my husband wanted to sleuth with me.

Chapter Seven

After work, I made macaroni and cheese, meatloaf, cornbread, green beans, and sliced watermelon for dinner. Quig might notice that wealth of his favorites and wonder if I was buttering him up, but at this point, I was using every resource to ensure he was in a good mood. I had no idea how to successfully present my desire to investigate Dr. Rosemont's death, but I hoped something would occur to me.

Once everything was prepared, I rested on the sofa with Harley, my feet propped on the coffee table, my hands atop my belly. *My womb.* With our baby.

On a whim, I focused my telepathy internally. *Are you in there little one? I love you so much.*

I didn't get a verbal reply, Instead, I had the sense of happiness well up inside me. Cool.

Good thing Sage waylaid me this morning with that beach trip and broke the news to me. That allowed me to wrangle the idea in my favorite place without worrying about my reaction to the news. The test kit silenced my doubts, and then I had all day to reflect on my new reality.

My lips quirked into another smile. I was going to be a mom. Incredible. Wonderful. And a whole lot of scary. I'd have the responsibility of caring for a tiny baby. That meant I'd have plenty to figure out between now and the end of March.

I didn't want Quig to think I had any doubts about being pregnant. So far, I'd carried a child without feeling any different and that suggested this pregnancy would be easy.

Quig would be thrilled about being a father.

That fact made me less anxious about telling him. Because it was good news. We wanted kids. Auntie O wanted us to have kids. His parents wanted a grandkid. Everyone wanted this.

My cat heard Quig coming up the steps before I did. Harley stopped purring to lift and cock his head toward the sound. Then he glanced at me before jumping down and padding to the door. I got the hint, and we both welcomed Quig.

To his credit, Quig acknowledged the cat with a pat on his furry head and me with a tap-and-go kiss. He dropped his briefcase by the door and sniffed the air. "Dinner smells amazing. I'm hungry enough to eat it all."

"Nothing left for me and Harley?" I teased.

"You better eat fast."

I placed the food on the table while he filled our water glasses. Quig surveyed the spread with a happy grin. "What a feast! It will be a challenge to eat so much, but I'll do my best."

"No need to overindulge. I've got watermelon for dessert. Tell me about your day."

His water glass paused in midair. "Oh. I was going to wait until after dinner to broach the subject, but my news won't wait. The Paranormal Council visited the morgue this afternoon."

I dropped my fork. The clatter was so loud that we both laughed. "Sorry," I said. "Never in a million years would I have expected those words from your mouth."

"Me neither. But Herbert walked in with Althea

Morgan, Kelsey Flowers, and Reverend Clark Gaudy. I knew of them through Herbert, but we'd never met. They knew me, of course, through my work. And they know about you, love."

Oh dear. I saw black spots in front of me until I breathed. I'd rather the Paranormal Council give me a permanent pass. I knew Herbert, of course, and I'd heard Althea speak at Rosemont's memorial service. The other two I wouldn't know if I passed them on the street. "A visit by the council would be my worst nightmare."

"They usually don't go around as a group, but Herbert convinced them to come by today to present their 'ask' in person." Quig savored a large bite of macaroni and cheese before continuing. "As per routine, Captain Haynes requested Dr. Willim Rosemont's body be held in the morgue pending results of blood and toxicology tests. I will have those back soon. The Paranormal Council is aware the body will be released soon, and they requested a full autopsy. They're certain that their former leader did not fall down those steps. They also requested that you examine the corpse to see if you notice anything unusual."

"Unusual? How would I know that in a person I've never met?" My head was saying no-no-no, but my heart wanted to do it. I'd seen a dead body or two in my lifetime. It shouldn't be difficult. And yet, why did they select me for this task? Was it an honor or scut duty? My thoughts whirled into another gear. If I said yes, my pending request to investigate this death would be a done deal. Hmm.

"They've heard of your intuition and also know you

find information the police cannot," Quig said. "What will it hurt to look? Perhaps there's residual energy on the clothes he wore or his pocket items. Nowry dropped them off at the morgue today on temporary loan from the Property Clerk."

"I'm flattered, but there's a problem. I've only read energy in living things or in places the person has frequented and laid down energy pools through time. I've never sensed energy in clothing or inanimate objects. That's a different paranormal talent. Sure, I've noticed the effects of drugs in a few people's auras, and sometimes I've sensed residual energy in places where strong emotions occur repeatedly. However, Dr. Rosemont is dead. His body no longer has an aura. It would be unusual for energy to be attached to his corpse."

He arched an eyebrow. "Isn't unusual your wheelhouse?"

"Well, yes, but I investigate my way. I don't do well with outside pressure or deadlines. Besides, Nowry requested my help with the official police investigation earlier today, and I turned him down." Guilt welled in my throat. I wanted to investigate the man's death on my own, and here Quig was dropping the opportunity in my lap.

Better clarify that with him. "However, I am interested in conducting an unofficial investigation. Fawn Meldrim asked me to look into her uncle's death. I say a cautious yes to the Paranormal Council's ask. However, I'd prefer to limit my sleuthing to Rosemont's home and office. Corpse-reading never crossed my mind. Besides, I thought you'd already done his autopsy."

"Let's circle back to the investigation request in a minute. Rosemont's wife requested no autopsy for religious reasons, though she didn't specify a religion. Since his cause of death is officially undetermined, I conducted a physical observation, ran blood and urine analyses, and conducted noninvasive testing."

"What's that last one include?"

"X-rays for the most part."

"Why didn't you just say X-rays?"

"Depending on the X-rays we sometimes add soft tissue scans."

"I get it. But if the family says no autopsy, and the samples you collected are normal, how can you justify an autopsy?"

"That's why Captain Haynes requested your help on the corpse. If you find anything odd, or get a vibe on a particular body part, I can do a deeper forensic examination, honoring the family's wishes and yet hopefully yielding the exact cause of death. Don't worry. I won't use your name in any paperwork or justification. I will say his former associates requested an autopsy, and upon review of my notes and what the cops have since learned about Rosemont, I reexamined my initial findings."

"I see. You won't get in trouble with the City Council again?"

"Nope. After they tried to replace me with an inept Medical Examiner last spring, I am their favorite person."

Sounded like Quig had his end all thought out. But what about me? The cops wanted me to be an energetic hound dog. While the idea was appalling, it would shoehorn me into a position to investigate the man's death. I could get a broader view of his life on my own terms.

A dark thought arrowed into my head. "I'm being asked to find something, and if I find nothing, will I get blamed later for wasting taxpayers' time and money?"

"Nothing like that. I promise. Will you examine his body and items on him at the time of death?"

"Yes, but don't get your expectations up. Like I said, the type of paranormal read the cops want isn't within my abilities."

"It will work out. I'm sure of it. Let's go immediately after dinner, so that there's no one around and no pressure on you. Afterward, I'll text Nowry to return Rosemont's property to storage. Then we're both off the hook with the official investigation."

"Okay, I guess." I didn't want to do an investigation at the morgue, and I couldn't dredge up any enthusiasm about going there tonight. All I knew was, now wasn't the time to share the news of my pregnancy.

~*~

Three steps into the morgue and a wave of nausea stopped me cold. Quig was busy turning on lights and pulling open Rosemont's storage drawer, so he didn't notice me sag against the wall. I'd never had trouble with the atmosphere here, but something pungent battled the usual chemical scent. "What's that horrible odor?"

"The custodian mopped in here right after I vacated. He's on a kick of adding essential oils to his all-natural floor cleaners. I usually don't mind it, but this version is pungent. As if he dumped a whole bottle in the mop water."

"Whew! I'll say. It certainly is strong." Nothing in my collection of essential oils smelled like burnt pine cleaner infused with rotten strawberries. With good reason. It was an awful combination. "You may tell the custodian your wife is not a fan of this foul brew."

"Will do. Meanwhile, I'll clear the air with my fume hood's exhaust fan. Have a seat or step out in the hall. It'll smell better in minutes. This unit's air flow is phenomenal."

I opted to step into the hall. Oddly, the hallway had no trace of the gross scent prevalent in the morgue. Perhaps the custodian couldn't tolerate the normal morgue odors and was only scenting floors in there. I held my locket for comfort, filled my lungs with clean air until the nausea subsided.

Quig joined me with a large tube of gel in his hands. "I have menthol if you need it."

Unsure what effect that strong scent would have on me tonight, I passed. "No thanks. I'm sure the fan did the trick. I will try menthol if the stench persists."

When I entered the morgue this time, the air quality had improved. I turned my attention to the drawer and body Quig had withdrawn from the freezer wall. First, I noticed the tag on the pale toe. Then I saw the white towel draped over Rosemont's private parts.

His body had little meat on its bones. I'd say Rosemont hovered between skeletally thin and lanky. Perhaps he'd been a lifelong runner to be so thin. Mom used to say it was hard to keep weight off after she turned fifty. This man was easily sixty, but he still had a full head of white hair. His skin tone reminded me of a white stone. His finely chiseled face drew my eye.

Even in death, the man looked handsome, so I

assumed he'd been popular with ladies.

"See anything?" Quig asked over my shoulder.

"Not yet. I'm mentally cataloging his face. With those movie star features, he must've had every woman in Savannah chasing him."

"One would think that, but he didn't date. If he attended a formal event he always went stag after he and his wife Sherrie separated."

Quig's tone turned wry when he mentioned the wife, prompting another question from me. "Did he date men?"

"No data on that, though I've heard that he and his live-in gardener were good friends."

"But he was with Peaches McVeigh the night he died. She's a woman."

Quig smiled. "The jury's still out on that."

"On her gender or their friendship?"

"Both."

I shook my head. "That is a complication I didn't expect."

"What about his energy?"

"Ginning up my nerve. Luckily, I don't need to touch him for that."

"Be careful about touching him, if you decide to do it. His neck is broken, thanks to the fall, as is one arm and an ankle. If the worst happened, and he fell off the table, any post-mortem injuries could be difficult to explain."

"Yes, we do not need to make things worse." With that I held my breath and switched to my other vision. As predicted, no aura surrounded his body. I scanned him from nose to toes without sensing any energy vibrations at all. The only thing I sensed was the unrelenting finality of death. Whatever plans this man had for his future, he'd run out of tomorrows.

I stepped back and glanced at Quig. "As I thought, he lacks an energy field. There's a knot on the back side of his head. Nothing else caught my eye."

"The knot is likely from the fall, though the fall and a head bump were so close in the timeline proximity I didn't determine the order of their occurrence. Thanks for trying. I'll slide him back in the freezer. His personal property is laid out on the adjacent exam table."

I didn't move because Rosemont's head injury nagged at me. "The head knot feels significant. Since the cause of his fall is in doubt, it's possible he was struck before he fell."

Quig sealed the drawer. "Anything is possible. Except if he had been physically struck from behind, the five people with him would've seen it happen. And, he would have fallen forward, not backward. However, you mentioned it twice, so I'll make a note of it."

"Sounds like a 'Murder on the Orient Express' situation."

"Could be. That's what I'd like to find out. Meanwhile, see what you sense about his personal items."

In both visions, I studied the linen pants and shirt, briefs, belt, and sneakers, all in shades of white. Nothing stood out as unusual. The other items on the table were his billfold, phone, and keys, and they had no extra feel to them. Then I saw the pocketknife. It glowed like a beacon in my other vision.

"That's some pocketknife," I said.

"Whitlin' jack," Quig said.

"He whittled?"

"Big time. Very much into making duck decoys. I hear there are hundreds of them in his home."

"I've never known anyone who whittled." I glanced over at the freezer wall. "Did he have extra calluses or cuts on his hands?"

"Good question. I'll doublecheck his hands when I reexamine the head gash. Let me pack this stuff up, and we can go home."

The hall light flashed. The door opened.

At the squeak of hinges, my intuition urged me to hide. I ducked under the exam table and went invisible. Guilt hit me fast—was this harmful to the baby? Probably not. I was merely moving light differently around my body. Quig was too far away for me to make him invisible. Besides, he had every right to be in his morgue.

A Night Security guard stepped around the corner. "Working late, Doc?"

"Reviewing a case, Oscar. I've been asked to wrap this up quickly, and I have a few uncertainties. I couldn't suss out what bothered me until I got home. Came in to make notes and decided to review the man's personal property."

"It's all good. Have a nice evening, sir."

"Thanks. You, too."

The man's visit took less than two minutes. Footsteps retreated. Then the door opened and closed. A brooding silence filled the air. Dang. How was I going to explain this? I'd have to tell Quig my last secret.

"Tabby?"

Argh. I couldn't hide indefinitely and with the bright overhead light in here, I couldn't stay invisible for much longer without suffering the consequences. I sighed and became visible under the exam table.

"There you are!" Quig leaned down to help me up. "How'd you do that?"

I stepped away from him as soon as I stood, unsure if he would be appalled by this talent, and gave an honest answer. "I think about hiding, and it happens."

He seemed to be considering that…and me. "You couldn't trust me with that information?"

Not the reaction I'd expected. I hated seeing that hurt look from his eyes. "Only a few other people in the whole world know I can do this. My own mother didn't know. It's always been a secret, and I've been afraid what people would think of me if they found out. It's freaky."

"It's scientifically impossible, but that only means no one has studied the phenomena. I am curious about it on several levels."

I thrust out my hand, palm up. "No one, and I mean, no one, is studying me. I am not a living, breathing, pathology sample to be examined under a microscope."

He laughed. "Don't worry. I'd kill anyone who tried to do that."

His aura throbbed with menace. "I believe you."

"Okay if I touch you now?"

Suddenly, I wanted that more than anything in the world. "Yes."

He held me tight, caressing my head, neck, and shoulders. Then he nuzzled my neck as he settled us both into his desk chair. "When you disappeared, I nearly lost it. There are no hiding places here except for the cold units, and I knew you weren't inside one of them. My heart stopped a few times. I worried that you'd vanished permanently."

I hugged him fiercely, relieved that he didn't recoil from my touch. "Nope. I'm still here."

"You're okay? It doesn't harm you to become, er, transparent?"

I swallowed around the lump in my throat. His mind was quick, and he needed to understand my secret talent. I trusted him as much as my twin and my shop clerk Eve, but still. Maybe I should be sharing these thoughts with him. "I'm fine. I get into trouble if I bend the light too long. But I wasn't invisible for five minutes, so I'm good."

"Whoa." He lifted my chin to stare into my eyes. *"Bend the light?* I assumed you didn't know how it happened. That perhaps the trigger was a fear reflex, and it was an instinctual, chameleon-like response."

Yikes! I'd made him suspicious. I tried to push away from him to gather my thoughts, but there was no give in the man. "I meant what I said. I bend the light. It's like a gear you shift a car into. I don't know the stepwise process, but I think about going invisible, and then no one sees me."

"What about objects you hold?"

"Those go invisible too, though the more I'm holding, the faster the energy burn. If you'd been close enough, I would have taken you with me, but you were out of reach."

"I see." He paused a moment. "What happens after five minutes?"

"Though it isn't quite as exact as five minutes, I get

into serious trouble, energy-wise, if I am invisible for that long or beyond." I hoped and prayed he'd leave it at that.

"Explain."

His face filled my entire field of vision. Not in a menacing way but etched with care and concern. "It's the dark side of my talent. Unless I'm at home where I recharge naturally when I have energy deficits, I may be forced to take energy from others so that I can get home." Afraid of how he might interpret my needing energy influxes, I hastened to explain. "I hate doing it, and I never take more than a tiny amount from any one person. It is embarrassing to be in public and make a mistake that requires me to gather energy from strangers."

His pinched expression eased. "Take what you need from me right now. I insist."

"No. I don't need it now, and I don't do that. You are off limits."

"Tabby. You're my wife. I will help you in every way. You have my permission to take what you need from me anytime, anywhere."

"No. That goes against my moral code. I don't steal energy from family or friends. I can't. I hate being vulnerable as much as I hate having to gather energy when I'm spent."

"Are you overtired now?"

"I'm tired. Not overtired. There's a big difference."

A frown filled his face. "I can't quantitate the difference between tired and overtired."

Scientists.

Okay, quantitate meant he needed a number. Perhaps a percentage would work? "Let's assume a person barely feels tired between ninety and a hundred percent of their energy level. An athlete can go much lower percentagewise but still have high performance abilities because of physical fitness, but I'm no athlete. For me, tired is slightly below seventy percent. If I'm overtired, I'm well below fifty percent."

"Good to know. But as long as you recharge, you're fine?"

Air sucked in between my teeth. "Sorta."

His jaw dropped. "You can't leave it there."

"If I am overtired for an extended period, I can't recharge. That's what happened to my mom. She gave and gave energy to her friend with cancer until her recharger failed." My voice broke and so did my heart. I tried to gather myself and dash the tears away. "The irony is her friend passed within a few days of Mom. Her self-sacrifice was for nothing."

Quig blinked a few times behind his thick glasses. "I don't want you to go invisible anymore. Don't give away or burn your energy that fast, please. I need you. You're my everything. I won't survive without you."

Who knew he had a flair for the dramatic? "Don't worry. I don't routinely burn that much energy at a time." Except for helping Sage, and now that she had Larry, she didn't need me as much. Her recharger worked fine now. "I know not to go invisible too long."

His expression froze for a moment. "Is that what happened in Bonaventure Cemetery when the serial killer took you?"

"Yes. I burned too much energy to stay alive without a huge infusion of extra energy. However. I wouldn't have survived without using all my talents that day."

"Darn it. I don't want you involved with criminals or investigations, and yet I asked you to look into Dr. Rosemont's death. If someone murdered him and you search for answers, the killer might target you. Please forget I asked you. Don't investigate. For my peace of mind and wellbeing, as well as yours."

How could I deflect his request without hurting him? I had to try. "I understand your concerns. I have them too."

"I feel a 'but' coming on."

"You must be psychic. *But*, I investigate under the radar. I do it safely, and I always have a buddy."

"You mean Sage? If you're ignoring my wishes to do it anyway, take me instead of your twin sister. I can protect you."

"No offense, love, but Sage and I are an excellent investigative team. Both of us examine the person's home for stray energy pools as well as normally observe the entire collection of that person's possessions. Then we discuss our perceptions. These observations aren't things that can be quantified."

He studied me so intently, I could've sworn he was decoding my DNA. Finally, he spoke. "We'll circle back to that. Since you're determined to investigate Rosemont's death, there's another stop we must make before we head home."

Chapter Eight

The shadows on the Stone Stairs of Death, known locally as the SSOD, always spooked me. Worse, I felt the invisible pull of the dark, steep passageway. Quickly, I retreated before vertigo struck. The stark metal railings and the sleek stone ran in two long flights of stairs tied by a cobblestone landing halfway down. Every surface looked hard and unforgiving.

Quig and I stood in an alley off Bay Street looking down to River Street via this narrow stairway where Willim Rosemont allegedly plunged to his death. Historic Savannah's stones hailed from around the world, cast-offs from ships of old that needed ballast for their empty hulls. Colonists used the relics for building. After all, stones were a precious commodity in an area with no natural rock.

Centuries old, these historic stairs were a "use at your own risk" landmark for Savannah. From the top, they offered a narrow view of the waterway, and gazing straight ahead I could see lighted boats on the river below.

In a time when we take a standard size of rise and tread on staircases for granted, these individual steps were narrow and steeper than usual. They were not for the faint of heart and certainly not for the elderly, infirm, or inebriated. Many a person had broken an ankle or worse on these doozies.

The SSOD were difficult to navigate when wet or during wind gusts. We hadn't had rain since Monday, but I didn't remember if it had been windy the night Rosemont died. We experienced high winds often during the summer. But it was early yet in hurricane season, and we hadn't experienced a major storm yet. Besides, if it had been windy that night, others in his group might have been injured.

Even so, this unique riverfront access had plenty of foot traffic during the day and night. When I attempted to sort out nearby residual energy with my extra senses, I became inundated with a shadowy emotion that writhed in the air. I reared back in fear.

"What's wrong?" Quig asked.

His tight grip on my hand ensured I didn't fall. I dismissed my other vision, so once again the stairs were shaded with ordinary shadows. Though my pulse soon steadied, the edgy sensation remained. Frankly, I didn't care for dark energy or what it might imply. After all, Savannah was one of the most haunted cities in the U.S., so the charged atmosphere might come from ghosts.

I bumped out my protective barrier to fend off any threats. My shield pushed the invisible rip tide out of our immediate area, and I felt a wave of relief. I couldn't remember the last time I'd walked down the Stone Stairs of Death. Usually, I strolled down one of the cobblestone ramps to River Street instead of these calf-burning stairs.

Why didn't the party of six take a ramp? The footing was much better and less treacherous on a ramp. Had someone in the group insisted on using the SSOD?

"Tabby?"

I gave his hand a reassuring squeeze. "I'm okay. But I got lightheaded looking down the stone passageway.

61

Vertigo, though it's possible a ghost lurks around here. I felt unsettling currents too."

"Are you in danger? Should we leave?"

His concern warmed me. "Not yet. I dealt with the dark energy issue, and I'm better now that I'm not standing at the edge of the steep drop. The newspaper reported his six-person group had been out and about and planned to hit the late-night bar scene on River Street. They walked though this alley. Then what?"

"Rosemont pitched down the Stone Stairs of Death and fell to the midway landing. He had no pulse when medics arrived. He was pronounced dead on the scene. From there, he was transported to my morgue."

"How odd that he was with friends, and no one saw him fall or saw if he was pushed or shoved. He was standing still one moment and the next, tumbling down the steps. His head wound is significant. That injury could've happened during his fall, but did anyone search up here for an object that could've been used to smack his head?"

Quig frowned. "I don't know if anyone searched the flower beds up here or bordering the stairs. We can try looking with the flashlight on my phone, but I'd rather pass that suggestion on to Nowry and let the cops handle that."

"Works for me. And I am ready to go home."

"You don't want to go to the first landing and do your thing there?"

Sweat beaded down my back, and it was difficult to breathe the hot humid air. But that was normal for August. My free hand covered my belly protectively. "We can revisit that another time, if you like. I didn't pick up Herbert or Lilah's energy signatures, and I would know it if I did because I've spent time with them. This place has layers upon layers of currents, some of it very dangerous, but nothing I can pinpoint or recognize. I'd rather go home and think about what that means. Further, I'd rather not attempt the stairs at night. If there's a malevolent force here, we could become victims instead of amateur sleuths."

He glanced around. "Good point. Let's go."

It didn't take long for him to escort me to his nearby Hummer and drive the short distance to our above-a-shop home on Bristol Street. The air conditioning took away the edge of my physical discomfort, but it didn't soothe my inner turmoil. It occurred to me that someone who could go invisible like me could very well be Rosemont's killer. Sage, Quig, Larry, and Eve knew of my ability. I hoped no one else knew about my hidden talent and intended to frame me for this murder.

~*~

At home, I took a shower while Quig made several calls. He showered too, and I was still awake when he came to bed.

"What did Nowry say?" I asked.

"Got his voicemail."

"And?"

"Then I called Althea Morgan, of the Paranormal Council. She offered to do us a favor and take us into Rosemont's home tonight."

I sat up in bed. "I'm not going anywhere else tonight. That has to wait."

"Easy, babe. I feel the same way. I told her we'd reschedule."

"I'm not keen on going there with her, anyway. She

benefitted by Rosemont's death. Auntie O said Althea was a white witch. Being there with her at night, when paranormal activity is highest, strikes me as a foolhardy thing to do."

"I hadn't thought it through, but I take your point. She is a woman of power and a suspect. I looked up the abilities of white witches online. She could be anything from a good and benevolent witch to someone who turns others to stone. Had to believe she'd be that vindictive, since she was a mother."

For so long, Mom had told us twins that we weren't witches, that we were energetics. However, it gradually dawned on us that the way we give and take energy, and even the ways I imbued my candles with good vibes and Sage vitalized her plants, that Sage and I met the general criteria of witches.

Neither of us embraced that label.

Quig must've somehow sensed my sudden alertness over the word witch.

He opened his arms to me, and I cuddled with him, listening as his breathing evened. After the eventful evening, I was sure I wouldn't sleep a wink. Then Quig began rubbing my back, and my breaths slowed. Tomorrow was my day off from the shop. I'd deal with everything after getting a good night's rest.

My last thought as I drowsed down into sleep was that Larry Rau, my sister's live-in boyfriend, shared my talent. Larry could also bend light to go invisible.

Chapter Nine

The next day, Quig didn't wake me when he left for work. After rising before ten, I puttered around the apartment, catching up on laundry and other chores. When I viewed my clothing choices and remembered how tight everything felt, I suddenly had a new purpose for the day. My wardrobe needed an update.

I scrolled through a local, big name department store's online catalog. Much to my surprise, there were no khaki pants. Everything was skinny legs this and stretchy fabrics that. Lots of pretty dresses caught my eye. They'd be cooler to wear in these dog days of summer. I checked prices and realized I could go broke buying a new wardrobe. Next, I went to a popular review site and learned that several local stores that sold gently used kid's clothes also carried maternity clothes. That's what I needed.

Despite the heat outside, I felt excited to go on an adventure. Each shop had items I needed, so I bopped from one secondhand shop to another. Finding a top here, a dress there, a nightgown elsewhere, until I had a collection of professional wear and casual clothes that would last all week, and I was still under three hundred dollars. Upon the last shop clerk's recommendation, I braved the pricey department store for new undies and shoes a half-size up.

Finally, I made it upstairs to our place with all my loot. I flipped laundry from washer to dryer, started another load. Then I propped up my feet and browsed with my laptop to find a new novel.

Whatcha doing? Sage asked on our telepathic twin-link. *I can feel your brain humming with joy.*

Realized this morning that I hated tight clothing, so I went shopping.

Without me?

I knew she'd react this way and sought to soothe her ruffled feathers. *I wanted to take my time, and I knew you had the candle shop today. It's been a fun morning, but I'm home with my feet up for a bit. In the interim, I've learned a lot about maternity clothing and found several cool thrift stores.*

Did you tell Quig about the baby?

I winced. *I meant to, but last night he asked me to screen Willim Rosemont's body and personal effects as well as visit the place he died. None of that inspired sharing our good news.*

And this morning? You chicken out again?

I overslept. All that going and doing wore me out. I needed that extra rest.

Won't Quig notice the new clothes or the credit card charges?

I pay for my credit card. I'm not sure if he notices my clothes or my spending. Seems like he focuses on my curves.

Ack! I don't want to hear stuff like that. Tell him about the baby. Today.

Uh oh. My twin was in a bossy mood, and she disliked being left out of my activities. *I meant to do it already, but then he asked me to investigate a case, the one I wanted to investigate.*

Tabby, you'll feel better if the baby isn't a secret. You don't want him to hear it elsewhere.

You'd tell him?

No. I'm on your side. I'm your family.

Oops. I'd hit another landmine topic for my sister. *He's family too. Both of us must remember that. We're not alone anymore. You've got Larry. Doesn't he have opinions on what you should and shouldn't do?*

If he has, he knows better than to say anything around me. I wouldn't tolerate that behavior for a red-hot minute. Sage paused. *Did you make an appointment at your gynecologist?*

Not yet. One step at a time, Sis. This baby isn't coming out for seven more months. Quig will want to go with me for that first appointment, so I need to coordinate the date with him.

Well, then, do it.

I didn't reply, and she must've gotten busy in the shop. Which suited me fine. I didn't need anyone telling me what I should do, not even my twin.

After looking at baby stuff in the shops, I realized we'd have to make room in the apartment for a nursery and the paraphernalia that went with raising a kid. It was overwhelming to contemplate so I closed my laptop. My eyes drifted shut, and I didn't fight the urge to rest. Just for a few minutes.

My phone rang, and I jolted awake. Took me a minute to realize where I was. Wow, I'd been deeply asleep. In the middle of the day. That was highly unusual. I answered the call. "Hello?"

"Ms. Quigsly, you have any idea where Herbert R. Ellis is?" Detective Nowry rumbled in my ear.

I still thought of Ms. Quigsly as Quig's mother. "Tabby, please. And I don't know where Herbert is. Have you asked Sharmila?"

"Detective Belfor said her boyfriend was busy last night, and they didn't spend time together. She was no help at all. He doesn't answer his phone. I don't know if it is intentional or if something happened to him."

I cast about for an idea until something occurred to me. "Did you try his mother? Perhaps his parents needed his help today."

"Good idea. I should've considered that, but I am concerned his unavailability means he has something to hide."

Herbert was also my attorney, so I knew his character well. "He's a good person. He wouldn't kill anyone."

"Everyone will kill given the right motivation."

"Must be awful dark in your head with those gloomy thoughts. Innocent until proven guilty, remember?"

"These days, cops assume a suspect is guilty until proven innocent."

Having sat in his interview room multiple times now, the truth of his statement resonated in my ears. "How sad for the world."

"Heard you went investigating last night."

"I did, by invitation."

"What did you learn?"

"I thought Quig left you a message."

"He did, but I want to hear it from you."

Crossing my fingers, I gave him a sanitized version. "I viewed Rosemont and his personal property. Didn't notice much but the lump on his head. Quig said that could've come from his fall. My intuition tells me someone hit him, forcing the fall down the SSOD."

"He mentioned that in his message. Even though Rosemont couldn't have been struck without anyone noticing, patrol officers are scouring the area for a rock or another dense object that might have struck him.

You didn't find any answers at the top of those stairs?"

"Nothing useful."

He swore under his breath. "I'm catching heat on this case. Haynes wants it closed, but it doesn't feel ready. Why did that group choose to go down those stairs?"

"I had a similar thought. The ramps are easier to descend. If you can find out who suggested using the Stone Stairs of Death, perhaps that's your killer."

"If only I'd thought of that," Nowry growled.

His sarcasm wasn't lost on me. Time for a little pushback. "Tell the captain I don't sniff out killers. My process and my intuition work differently than standard police procedures."

"Your process better develop leads, or you can expect a visit from the captain. He thinks you are the best investigator in town."

Darn it. I didn't need that pressure. "Perhaps he said that to spur you to find new leads."

"He doesn't care where the leads come from. He demands results."

"That man needs to take a chill pill."

Nowry hung up without replying. Had I pushed the limits of our acquaintance by criticizing his boss? Nowry and I had several close connections in recent months when he'd opened up to me, and I had rescued him from a powerful witch's spell. It wasn't fair for him to waffle and leave me guessing.

The real question was why there was pressure to close this case so quickly? After several minutes of serious contemplation, an answer came to me. The killer felt vulnerable, exposed by his actions. He or she wanted the focus off the case and on something else.

Was it someone on the force? Or perhaps a civilian who had put pressure on the Captain? Regardless, I wouldn't stand down. I wanted justice for Rosemont.

~*~

A knock sounded on my door, snapping me awake again. Darn it. Why couldn't people leave me alone? This was my day off.

However, I rose from the couch and padded to the door, my cat scampering ahead of me. That raised my hopes. Harley must know the person outside. I peeped through the security hole and beamed my delight. My caller was very familiar to me.

Quickly, I unlocked and opened the door. "Auntie O! Did you have a nice trip? Please come in. It's great to see you!"

"Tabby!" Auntie O stepped in, placed a grocery sack on the nearby console table and hugged me. The hug continued until I felt tingly all over. Was she sharing energy? Weird.

When she finally released me, she grinned like a Cheshire cat. It was infectious. I grinned back. "Can I interest you in something to drink or eat?"

"I brought you a treat," Auntie O said, bustling off to the kitchen.

Her sunshine yellow outfit suited her happy mood. I trailed her to the kitchen and sat on a bar stool. "Looks like you went shopping in Florida."

Ice clinked in glasses. "I did. It's hard to find bright yellow clothes elsewhere, but I fell in love with this outfit as soon as I saw it."

"The color suits you."

"And you, my dear, look like I woke you from a nap. Your man keeping you up all hours of the night?"

"Guilty of napping on my day off, and my man needs his sleep too."

"He's earned that rest, though I have to say I was somewhat concerned by the delay."

I heard her words, but I didn't understand what she meant. I drew a shallow breath and asked, "What are you talking about?"

"Your news!"

My news, I silently repeated. She knew about the baby? "Did Sage tell you?"

"Sage didn't say a thing. I just know." She set a glass of ginger ale and a plate of ginger snap cookies in front of me. "How do you feel?"

I sipped the chilled drink, suddenly remembering I'd forgotten to eat lunch. Since she knew, I blurted the words out loud. "I'm going to be a mom."

She patted my hand. "It's written all over your face. You're glowing with motherhood."

Something wasn't adding up. "You felt it all the way down in Florida?"

Auntie O pursed her lips before she spoke. "I'm highly attuned to you and Sage. When I'm away from home, I think of my nieces every day. Even from a distance your energy felt different. I wasn't certain what that meant, but I hoped and believed you'd done the family proud."

"How can you check on us remotely?"

"It's all good, dear. Energy is energy as I'm sure you'll come to realize. Don't you worry about a thing. You're coming along fine. How's Quig feel about becoming a dad?"

I glanced down at the untouched cookies, tracing the condensate on the side of my glass. "He doesn't know. I only found out yesterday because Sage told me I was pregnant. I didn't believe her, until she nagged me into taking a pregnancy test. She was right."

"Of course she was, and this is joyful news."

"Why can you two see what is happening inside me, but I am the last to know?"

"Not the last," she reminded me.

Ugh. I didn't care for her stink-eye. "Well, the last Winslow. I mean the last one in our family."

"We are attuned to each other's currents. Yours are different now. Much stronger. Brighter too. Like a beacon."

My hands protectively covered my womb. "Is that bad for the baby?"

"The baby is fine. Oh, it's so wonderful to say that! You girls put me through the wringer with your waiting around to start a family. Frankie will be thrilled when he hears the news. He's going to be a great uncle to your daughter."

Frankie was Auntie O's partner. He'd had family troubles and health issues of late, but it wouldn't be right if he heard my news before my husband. "Wait. You can't tell him until I tell Quig. Promise me. I don't want Quig to hear it through the rumor mill."

Auntie O squared up her posture and crossed her arms in a tough-person stance. "That's on you. Call him right now."

"No. I have to tell him face to face."

"Tell him tonight at dinner because I can't hold in my excitement."

Dinner. My stomach lurched. "About that. Is it normal that I have no appetite?"

"Marjoram felt that way for the first trimester. Don't

you worry, though. I am making a celebratory pot of chicken and dumplings for you two lovebirds tonight. Have a ginger snap, dear."

Cautiously I sniffed, and the scent of the cookies appealed to me. Most foods didn't smell good lately. I ate a cookie and then another. "These are good. I need to stock them in our pantry."

"I brought two packages. That should give you a good start."

"I might eat a whole bag right now."

"Moderation, dear. It takes practice when you're eating for two. And we'll need to make sure you're eating a balanced diet of foods that are good for our baby."

"Food would be fine if it didn't come with such strong aromas. By the time the meal comes along, I am nauseous from smelling it cooking."

"How about if I cook all your meals at my place?"

Aack. I couldn't allow her to do that. I wasn't helpless. "I'll figure it out, Auntie O. You focus on Frankie. He needs your good cooking to gain weight after his heart issues."

"No reason I can't do both until you get used to the changes in your body. Nice outfit. I see you've been shopping too."

"Yeah. My clothes didn't fit right anymore, and I found it aggravating to squeeze into them. Did you know I couldn't find any khaki maternity pants?"

"Shocking. Though I must say that sundress looks splendid on you. Maybe it was time to update your style. It's something we women do multiple times as we age."

"My classic style suits me, but I was unwilling to be

stuffed like sausage meat into clothes that squeeze the baby…or me. The baby and I needed more room."

"Mmm." Auntie O refilled my ginger ale.

"You heard about Dr. Rosemont?"

"I did. Willim was a wise leader. You knew him?"

"Never met the man when he was alive. Since then, I've had a close encounter with his corpse, a few of his personal possessions, and more."

"Oh?"

The hopeful note in her voice confused me again. "Two independent parties asked me to investigate his death."

Her eyebrows rose. "What did you find?"

"My senses tell me his death wasn't an accident, but I found nothing useful to police using my extra senses."

She studied me for a long minute. "You must be careful about your investigations now that you've got a baby on board."

I sighed heavily. "Even though Quig asked me to investigate Rosemont's death, he will say the same thing."

Chapter Ten

"I'm pregnant."

In the microseconds that followed my announcement, my husband's expression froze, his eyes rounded. His cheek twitched. Why didn't he say something? The suspense was killing me. Shadows clouded my heart. I couldn't breathe. I couldn't think.

Time stretched like saltwater taffy.

Finally, finally, Quig's face wreathed in smiles, and he whooped with joy. He gathered me in his arms and bounded all over the living room, spinning us in tight circles. "You're pregnant!"

The ceiling swirled and so did my gut. Nausea threatened. I pushed against his chest. "Whoa! Stop, please. I'm happy to celebrate, but your euphoria makes me dizzy."

Quig halted immediately, a grin filling his entire face, his aura pulsing with radiant vibes. He tossed his glasses on the counter, then caressed my face. "This is so awesome. Right? It is wonderful news, even though we had talked about waiting?"

I gave a slight nod and wished I hadn't as the room revolved again. "Yes."

He knelt and tenderly kissed my womb, then glanced up at my face. "You're okay? No illness or anything?"

"I'm good. Some appetite and equilibrium changes. Twirling, for instance, is not okay."

Quig rose and kissed my lips, my forehead, my

cheeks. "Got it. I'm thrilled we're pregnant."

My heart sang with delight. "You'll be a great dad."

"And you'll be the best mom ever."

He hugged me again and we stood there, wrapped in each other's arms, slow dancing. I sank into him, my curves nestling perfectly into his muscular frame. I beamed into his chest, relieved he didn't call our baby a mistake.

Why had I put off sharing the news? My off-kilter emotions must've drowned out clear thinking. Oh well. We'd figure that out too. We were in this together.

His stomach growled, and I raised my head to meet his expressive gaze. "I have more good news. Auntie O is back, and she prepared our dinner, which is warming in the oven."

"It smells as wonderful as you do, but dinner can wait. I need to share the news with my parents. They'll be over the moon."

And they'd ask a million questions of both of us and want to come over. I wasn't ready for their third degree. "Can we do that tomorrow? I'd like tonight to be about us."

"You bet. Anything you want, Mom-to-be."

"A back rub would be great."

His gaze heated. He scooped me in his arms and strode toward our bedroom. "Coming right up."

~*~

The next day in the shop began like any other day, that is, until Lilah Acworth stormed in like a 200-mph hurricane. Her aura snapped with dark currents.

I instantly formed an invisible barrier around me and the baby. Harley flashed his tail up and looked as if he would pounce on Lilah. I didn't know how to reassure him without speaking aloud to him and his littermate Luna, who was Sage's cat. I sent them images of their dinner bowls upstairs, and they skittered out of the shop as if the hounds of hell were on their tails. I didn't blame them for their speedy exit. I'd avoid Lilah if I could.

Lilah stopped in front of me, way too close for comfort, and shook her bony finger in my face. "You sicced the cops on me."

For once, I had a clue about what Lilah was talking about. Willim Rosemont's death. I made a show of stepping around the counter to add distance between us. "I was consulted about the case. Nothing I said indicated you were guilty. If the cops questioned you, it was because you were with him that night. That made you a person of interest in this murder. Not me."

Her voice turned shrill. "That isn't fair. I had nothing to do with his death."

"Keep your voice down. This is a place of business."

Lilah huffed her displeasure. "The council is suspicious of me, and now the cops are elbows deep in my life. They think because my daughter killed someone that I'm felon material too. This is your fault, Tabby. If you hadn't blasted onto the paranormal scene, Savannah psychics would still be under wraps and out of the spotlight. You've upset the energy balance, and my family is taking one hit after another. This must stop."

She had it all wrong. Sage and I didn't seek publicity. It found us. Out of the corner of my eye, I saw Gerard Smith crab-walk toward the stillroom. He didn't want to turn his back to Lilah. Smart. I hid my lips from Lilah and mouthed "coward" to him. He grinned.

"Well, Missy?" Lilah demanded, hands fisted on her hips. "What do you have to say for yourself?"

Asking her to leave wouldn't solve anything. It appeared she needed to talk this out with someone. It made no sense that she'd chosen me as her confidante. Or had she turned to me? Could be that she'd turned on me and come here to gloat.

What a mess. Dare I risk being supportive? Would she accept basic human kindness from someone she considered trouble?

I didn't want her as an enemy. It made sense to placate her, to treat her more as I would anyone who came here with a problem. "I understand how being detained at the police station upset you." Even the thought of sitting in that interview room gave me the willies. "It has happened to me more than I'd like. Here's some free advice. Put it behind you and move on with your life."

Her fierce eyes glittered with anger. "What life? My daughter is dead. I have no family. I have nothing."

Of all the guilt trips she could've laid on me. I'd lost family recently. I understood better than she knew. Keeping my voice pitched low, I said, "I hear you, and I understand how grief can knock you down. Keep putting one foot in front of the other, and you'll find your way."

"Losing a parent isn't the same as losing a child. I brought her into this world. I was responsible for her." Her lower lip trembled. "I failed her."

Dear Gussie. I towed her into the stillroom for more privacy, and Gerard scurried out. "Jeanine was thirty years old. She made choices that put herself in danger. She killed Johnny Rau and planned to kill more people before taking on the entire city. Her actions aren't on you."

She stared at me as if reading a message on my retinas. Her aura had calmed down a bit, so she only needed to accept the fact that she wasn't mad at me. I beamed happiness and light at her.

Lilah shuddered. "Cops don't think that way."

"Law enforcement must rule out everyone in the deceased's circle. While it felt personal to you, it was an exercise in pressuring you to volunteer something that supported their theory of the crime."

"I didn't kill Rosemont, but I should've paid more attention to what my daughter was up to. She'd still be here if I had known her intentions."

"Lilah, pardon me for speaking plainly. Jeanine brought troubles on herself. You should be relieved she didn't drag you down the drain with her."

"Is that so?" She looked down her sharp nose at me. "You expect me to just get over this awful guilt I feel for failing her?"

"I expect you to process the blame."

"Hmph." She clenched and unclenched her fisted hands. "You're a lot like Marjoram. She didn't tolerate whiney friends either."

I felt a smile touch the corners of my lips and killed it. Even though the compliment was backhanded, it didn't feel sincere. More like a platitude. I'd said enough. What would she do now?

"Something's different about you," Lilah said, sniffing the air.

A different topic. Interesting. "New clothes."

"I see."

Truly, I hoped she didn't.

"Your life is playing out the way your mother and aunt wanted. You and your sister came fully into your powers off the grid, and through time the council forgot about you. Tell me this, are you the next assassin or is Sage? Everyone knows that power runs through your family line."

And there it was. The dig at me. No way could I turn the other cheek to that barb. Conscious of three customers browsing in the nearby shop, I said under my breath, "We're not having that discussion here or anywhere."

Lilah edged closer and whispered loudly to me. "I'm shunned because of my daughter. Jeanine should take the heat for her actions. Not me. More importantly, she should be in line for a Paranormal Council seat. She deserved it."

Ah. There was the truth. She'd expected to become a proud parent of a council member and now due to the paranormal power that Sage and I wielded, Lilah resented us for being alive when her daughter was dead.

I glanced though the doorway into the shop to check on the three customers again. One was looking at a book and the other two were sitting in the wicker chairs near the bookshelves chatting. Even so, I kept my voice soft. "Neither Sage nor I aspire to the council, if that's your concern. We want to be left alone."

"That genie is out of the bottle. Mark my words, you'll become their creature. They won't let power like this alone. They will get you, one way or the other." Lilah paused a moment, sniffing the air and eyeing me with suspicion. "You know the difference between a white witch and a dark witch?"

What was with the sniffing? Did different witches smell different? "Are you talking about 'The Wizard of Oz' version of witches?"

"Bah. Who needs labels? Those of us in the paranormal realm wield magic. We're all witches of some kind. 'Normals' have inherent magic too, but they can't access it. And my sweet Jeanine was an angel."

I barred my arms. "A matter of opinion."

"Lucky you. You're a survivor, Tabby. My daughter became a Dark Witch."

That was one way to rationalize Jeanine's killer tendency. Her goal had been to take over Savannah and punish the entire city for their alleged hatred of the paranormal. I kept my musings to myself and tried a summation to get rid of Lilah. "Look, I don't know who killed Willim Rosemont. I didn't finger you to the cops. I don't have a vendetta against you or your kin. All I want to do is to make candles. The council is not in my future."

"So you say." Lilah flounced out.

~*~

While setting the table for supper that night, I kept thinking about the package that came today for Quig. Who would be sending my husband a box through the mail? Since it wasn't addressed to me, I couldn't open it.

Therein lay the rub.

"You got something in the mail today," I said when he didn't open it immediately.

"Who's it from?" he countered as he finished laying

out the plates.

"I didn't recognize the cryptic name. N. Y. Biz."

"Oh." He paused, turned his head to the side, and chuckled. "Oddly enough, I know exactly who that is. 'Not your business' was a catch phrase a friend and I said to each other as kids. Wonder why he resorted to a code name?"

Darn my emotions. It wasn't like me to be bothered by unexpected mail. Even so, I was relieved to know the sender of the package was a male friend. I quipped, "Not my business."

That brought another laugh.

"Let's eat," I suggested.

Quig sat, forked up a mouthful, ate, and swallowed. "Whatever is in that package, it'll keep until we finish this lovely feast your aunt prepared, Mom-to be."

I smiled at his new pet name for me, but it didn't divert my curiosity. "Aren't you curious about the box? I've been dying to open it."

"Why didn't you?"

"It wasn't addressed to me."

"Doesn't matter. You have my permission to open anything that comes to our mailbox."

I let out a long breath. "Thanks. The same for you opening anything of mine."

"Glad that's settled. Let's eat. I'm famished."

I enjoyed the pork chops, scalloped potatoes, asparagus, cornbread, and chocolate pudding. Unsure of what foods would work well with my touchy nose and queasy stomach, I started with potatoes. Stayed down, no problem. Same for the meat. All of it turned out to be fabulous and digestible.

"You're enjoying the meal. Good," Quig said. "I

mean, you're eating for two now."

"Got news for you, buddy, it isn't wise to mention how much a woman eats."

"I am merely commenting on the mother of my unborn child eating a normal-sized meal for a change. I'm delighted this food suits your finicky palate."

"I was hungry for it, that's for sure."

"Feel free to grab seconds. I'm getting more."

The memory of this morning's queasiness stayed my hand. "I'm full. No sense pushing things to the max. Little Thyme needs some room to grow."

"Our *son* will be named in the tradition of my family, or there'll be hell to pay with my parents. He'll be called Octavian Henry Quigsly, V."

He seemed to have forgotten that women in my family only had daughters. But I didn't want to argue and risk upsetting my stomach at the table. Let him have the satisfaction of thinking it might be a boy, for now. "Isn't there a rule that when you repeat a family name so many times you have to start over with a new name?"

"No way. The fun will be deciding what to call him. I was thinking Tavvy, since that's what my grandfather was called, but it would be confusing because it sounds too much like your name. My dad is called Henry. Maybe Hank?"

"You wouldn't capitalize on him being the fifth and call him Quint?"

"Hmm. Never thought of that. I suppose Quint Quigsly isn't any more of a mouthful than Quig Quigsly."

"Sounds like a tongue twister to me. How about Quinn?"

Behind his dark framed glasses, his eyes narrowed. "Isn't that a girl's name?"

"Nope. A guy I knew in college was named Quinn."

"I'll take it under advisement."

I broke out in laughter and pushed my empty plate away. "You sound like a lawyer."

Instead of laughing, his face went still. "Speaking of lawyers, I should open that package."

He hurried to the hutch where we put the incoming mail and brought the small box to the table. Soon we both stared at the phone inside. One number was listed in the contacts.

"What's this about, Quig?" I asked, all manner of conspiracy theories dancing in my head. Was he a secret agent, or worse, a sleeper agent?

My tone alerted him to my concern. He gave me a fleeting smile. "I'm sure this is from Herbert. I'll call the number provided."

Herbert. He was talking about our attorney, Herbert R. Ellis, also known to me as Quig's best friend. Relief shivered through me. I leaned forward and then thought the better of that. Bad form to squish the baby. A good wife would clear the table, so he had a modicum of privacy, but I wanted to hear at least one side of this conversation. So I stayed put.

"Hey, buddy. What's up?" Quig asked. "And before you answer, you're on speaker phone, and Tabby is here with me.

"It's fine to include her. As for the other, nothing good. I had to leave town abruptly."

"What's with the code name?"

"I'm being set up to take the fall for Rosemont's death. I can't let that happen. You know my family's expectations. I haven't done my duty to the family yet, so I can't go to prison. Not for a crime I didn't commit."

Though his explanation prompted more questions, I practiced patience and studied Quig. His brows were bunched as if in deep thought.

"Running isn't the answer, pal," Quig said. "It makes cops suspicious."

"I'm not worried about them. I've got bigger problems. The balance of power on the Paranormal Council shifted with Rosemont's death," Herbert said. "They're pressuring you about clearing the case, right?"

"Yes, and his head wound is antemortem. That means he was murdered before he went down those stone stairs," Quig said. "The council wants Rosemont's death to officially be an accidental fall. My hesitation and initial labeling the means of death as undetermined didn't sit well with them. They contacted me again and asked for Tabby to look into the case."

Herbert swore aloud and then apologized. "Sorry, Tabby."

I grinned. "It's okay."

"No, it isn't. You're good at what you do. Once they couldn't get the accidental death rammed through Quig's office, they must have decided I would be the sacrificial goat to make the case go away. I'm sure you'll prove he was murdered. If so, I predict both of you will find legitimate evidence pointing to me. I'm doomed."

I was stunned. Herbert sounded upset and genuinely concerned someone would trick me with false evidence.

While I pondered the realm of fake clues, Quig asked, "Why?"

"Who is the better question. I suspect the Rau family. They're trying to get me off the council. My disgrace would force that. Then they will select an ally to take my seat. Rosemont kept the factions from each other's throats."

"I get the politics of it, but I don't understand why you're the patsy," I said.

Herbert sighed heavily. "It's centered around my talent. How I make things come out in my clients' favor. That's why they're tarring me with this crime. They want me gone."

I gathered my breath to ask a follow-up question, but Quig held up a hand and spoke instead. "We understand the pressure you're feeling about the investigation. What can we do to help?"

"I'm worried about my cat. Violet wasn't home when I left. Will you check on her? Make sure she has food and water. I'd ask if y'all would take her in, but that's too big of an ask. And this is embarrassing, would you get rid of the leftovers in the fridge? I didn't think to do that before I dashed out of there."

Despite the dire situation, cleaning out his old food and caring for the cat were small asks. Of course, we'd tend to his requests. After all, his telepathic cat was the reincarnation of his Aunt Violet. I was about to say so when Quig beat me to it.

"We'll drive out there right now and tend to things. Should we call you back afterward?"

"No. Keep the phone, but I'll send a new number and check in soon. Thanks." Herbert ended the call.

"That was weird," I said. "And he sounded

paranoid as well as certain he has to hide."

"His fears sound well-founded. Let's store our leftovers and drive to his house, unless you're too tired to come."

"Not tired at all, and I wouldn't miss this for the world."

Quig's work phone rang then. Another death in the city. They needed him immediately. "Duty calls. Our trip to Herbert's place is on hold for now. Violet will be okay until morning."

That poor kitty, all alone out there. "I can check on her tonight."

"I'd rather you didn't go out there by yourself at night. If the council or the cops are watching his place, it could put you in the wrong light."

His words made sense, but, oh, how I wanted to help. "I get it."

"Something else you should know about the council member's death. When I examined scrapings from Rosemont's head wound microscopically today, there were gold paint flecks. You are onto something about that bump on his head."

Though his findings validated my intuition, the murder weapon wasn't found. "Last I checked, there's nothing gold on the Stone Stairs of Death."

"Right. But I'm ninety-nine percent certain a gold object caused blunt force trauma and precipitated the man's deadly fall."

Where did the weapon go? No one saw or found a gold item that night or after, for that matter. I mused out loud, "The killer could've taken it, or perhaps the killer was invisible." The last idea gave me shivers. If invisibility was in play, I was vulnerable. I gulped at the realization. This case wouldn't settle out the way the powers-that-be wanted. Further, solving it also put a target on my back.

Quig spoke so softly, I didn't hear him. "What'd you say?" I asked.

His face flushed, something that rarely happened. Quig took a moment then shrugged before stating clearly, "Or, Herbert diddled with their thoughts so no one remembers what really happened."

Oh. This was about Herbert's concern that he was too successful as a lawyer. I wanted to know more about his paranormal talent, but we needed to stay on point. My experience in sharing energy was that it only worked for one person at a time. Hmm. "While I don't understand how that is possible, I still have a lot to learn about magical abilities. However, to manipulate so many people at once would've taken a very powerful individual."

Quig winced at the word manipulate before he headed to the door. "The paras on the council are that strong."

No wonder Mom kept us twins under the radar as we grew up. The paranormal leaders made their own rules and enforced them. I sighed as Quig gathered his wallet and keys and said, "Either way, things look bad for Herbert."

Chapter Eleven

I was asleep when Quig returned from his call-out, so I was unable to ask him the questions I'd formed during his absence. Knowing Herbert had a persuasion talent had piqued my curiosity. Had he gotten his legal clients off through trickery? Since I was his client, I had the right to know. Consequently, I rose before Quig's alarm sounded to start making coffee and pancakes.

One thing I'd learned right away about married life is that the adage of "the way to a man's heart is through his stomach" had the ring of truth. I hoped sweetening the pot gave me an edge today. If Quig was in a very good mood after breakfast, he might be more inclined to answer my questions instead of skirting them.

His eyes lit up when he joined me in the kitchen. "What's all this?"

I kissed him good morning. "Breakfast. I got an early start today and wanted to do something special since you worked late. I missed you last night."

"The late night goes with the job, but thanks for the extra effort. It's appreciated."

We noshed on breakfast. I waited until he was sated and yet still had a few minutes before leaving for work.

Finally, he pushed back from his plate. "That was excellent, love. Thanks."

"You're welcome. Although to be transparent, I have a few questions. I want to know more about Herbert's talent. I'm concerned that if his ability became widely known, his clients, and me specifically, will be in jeopardy."

Quig's smile didn't quite reach his eyes. "First off, I won't let anything happen to you and that's a promise. Second, it wouldn't be good for either council if paranormal abilities headlined the newspaper or TV stations. No one benefits from that. In principle, everyone in this city is on a level playing field, but the world doesn't work that way. People tend to clump in groups. If there weren't the division of paras and humans, our community would be separated by class distinctions, economics, or something else. Our planet's human ecosystem, if you will, is dynamic and ever-evolving."

A good answer, of course, but it didn't shed light on my worries. Time to cast out my fishing line again. "Thanks for that reassurance. However, I still have concerns. At one time, you mentioned that you and Herbert became friends as kids because of your similar abilities. I assume that's related to your family secret, but I need to know. Can you also do that? Manipulate people's thinking so things come out your way?"

Quig flinched. He stared at me, sadness rolling off of his aura in erratic waves. "I should've known you'd put that together. We needed to have this conversation at some point, but I wasn't ready to tell you. I've been apprehensive about your reaction when my core talent was revealed."

His woeful expression twanged my heartstrings, but I had to have it spelled out plainly. "So, it's true. You manipulate people's thinking?"

His steely gaze held mine. "I can to a limited extent, but I don't use the ability unless I'm threatened, in harm's way, or unless it's an outcome I desire very much. People with my talent operate under a strict moral code ninety-five percent of the time."

The atmosphere became prickly, his skin paled. "I see." And I was beginning to understand something else. He'd wanted me very much…was I the other five percent? My breath hitched at the possibility. I had to know. "Did you manipulate me?"

His answer was a long time coming and very soft. "Yes, though I didn't want to do it. I'm not sure I can explain it to you. I'm not supposed to tell you, but I don't want anything to come between us."

Omigod. It *was* true. I had to remember to breathe. "Why?"

"Because you're my mate. I knew the first time I saw you. People in my family recognize their other half on sight."

I almost said "I see" again, but I couldn't stop trembling. With his confession, he'd ripped the bedrock of our life together apart. Worse, he'd tricked me.

Were my feelings for him even real?

Somehow, I managed another breath. "What are you?"

Would he tell me? I needed answers. For me and the baby.

He took his time replying. "As you discovered months ago, I have an accentuation ability, so I can be a force multiplier for someone with your talent. When you wield energy near me, I make you stronger."

"I appreciate that, more than you know, but that wasn't how you influenced my thinking. I repeat, what *are* you?"

"I'm your husband, the man you're in love with, the man who loves you with every molecule in his body. You're my everything."

"And?"

He gazed at his empty plate. "This is extremely hard for me. I don't want to lose your respect. You've previously said people are unkind about the label for your talent, but they are bitterly cruel about mine. We're Enervators. In scientific terms, we transmit airborne pheromones and transdermal dopamine, chemicals that compel people in close proximity to please us. It's how males of our species secure their mates."

That made sense though I needed time to consider all the aspects. Why was he so tense? "People call my family psychic vampires or leeches instead of Energetics. What do they call you?"

He didn't speak. Didn't look my way.

Panic ebbed, surged, and swirled through my body. The quieter he became, the more anxiety pounded my body. My fingernails bit into my palms. "Quig, I need to know."

The void of waiting for his response was worse than hearing whatever labels the Paranormal Community called his talent. He'd mentioned chemical attractants and securing a mate. That sounded like a natural process in the animal kingdom. Far as I knew, scientists didn't believe humans used pheromones to attract a mate. So what Quig was talking about was either an adaptive feature or a throwback situation, if I remembered correctly what I'd learned in biology class about evolution.

Quig drew into himself and sighed. "Parasitic

manipulators. The process of acquiring a female is addictive to us and our mates, though we are in no way parasitic. The more we're with our chosen female, the more she wants to be with us and vice versa." He paused for a moment before going on. "The effects are cumulative and synergetic."

His admission stung. My legs pumped, scooting my chair back too fast and nearly tipping me onto the floor. Was our baby safe? "You're…drugging…me with air particles?"

"Not exactly, though I understand how you arrived at that." He interlaced his fingers on the table, his expression pensive. "You love me, Tabby. You've loved me from day one. I didn't create your feelings for me. They were always there, only latent. Courting you opened a pathway to those emotions."

Dread throbbed like a splinter in a finger. The cloying scent of maple syrup made me nauseous. I couldn't process what he'd done, especially with all of his quibbling over semantics, but it felt like he was still hiding something from me. "What. Else."

"The timing of our engagement shower was no coincidence." His raspy voice sounded like a leaky tire. "Mom planned it on a full moon at Dad's request." He glanced at his lap before looking up. "You became pregnant on our wedding night. It always happens that way for my family."

My mouth gaped open. "No way. We used protection. Mostly."

He shrugged. "Doesn't matter. When it's time, my swimmers penetrate any barrier. The full moon and my earlier, ah, ministrations, assured you were very fertile."

His matter-of-fact statements about our intimacy had the effect of pouring burning oil on my skin. He knew what would happen that night, but I didn't. That wasn't right. Anger snapped in the air around me. I glared at him. "You impregnated me against my will?"

He met my gaze, though he held his breath. "I did my duty to the family. Our son will arrive in March."

My blood heated. "*Duty to the family?* Those are the exact words Herbert used about Sharmila."

"Easy, babe. It's a lot to take in all at once, but we love each other. We planned to have children. We talked about that several times. You love the life we created together. So do I."

I wanted to throw up. Instead, my spine stiffened. "In light of what you've revealed, I beg to differ. You *groomed* me and impregnated me. I had no choice in this."

He reached for me, and I jerked away from him. No way would I allow him to keep dousing me in chemical attractants.

A single tear rolled down his cheek. "Tabby, I'm the man you've always known and trusted. Your friend through thick and thin. I love you."

My skin felt too tight as thoughts careened through my head. I was appalled by what he'd done. Was any of our marriage real? I didn't feel like a zombie wife, but maybe his "charms" made it so that I couldn't sense my true emotions. No, that couldn't be right. I loved living on Bristol Street. I enjoyed making candles. I was still myself, but he'd admitted altering my biochemistry to *acquire* me.

This sucked.

My whole world crumbled around me.

I blinked back tears, unwilling to destroy us, but I couldn't blindly accept that he'd enslaved me. And yet our relationship hadn't had any speedbumps to date.

I knew of another relationship that was rocky, though. "Is Herbert grooming Sharmila too?"

At his terse confirmation, I continued. "No wonder he was so upset a few months ago when she went home from the hospital with her parents. She eluded his grasp, and therefore he lost his proximity to his future Baby Mama."

Another realization surfaced. "Except for us going to our jobs, you've barely let me out of your sight since we became friends-with-benefits last fall. I must've been an easy mark to fall into your snare so easily."

He took his glasses off, rubbed his eyes. "I always enjoy your company. The pheromones hastened our relationship along but be honest. We have real feelings for each other. Both of us."

I thrust my hand out like a traffic cop. "Don't speak for me. I didn't feel romantic toward you until movie nights started. I hadn't felt romantic toward anyone in a long time. Did you do that to me? You secreted attraction goo all over me so other men didn't interest me? That's how you got me to sleep with you, isn't it? You rewired my mind and body."

"None of my pheromones activated until a few years after puberty. My parents worried I was defective. But our biorhythms have always aligned. If you take a deep breath and think about this, you'll realize you always felt comfortable around me. I patiently waited until you were ready to settle down before I made a serious push for you. We shared our growing feelings the night of our first kiss. I will never forget that moment."

He looked at me, hope flickering in his gaze, but his aura remained flat, those currents no longer lushly resilient and full of allure.

"I'm horrified by how you deliberately took advantage of me," I said.

"You know my deepest, darkest secret. You're all I've ever wanted. You are why I get up in the morning, the one person in the entire world I want to spend my life with, and the person I sleep beside every night. You are and have always been the heart of me. That's why we're so close. Our bond is my way of thanking you for loving me. You are my life."

It felt like steam shot out of my ears. My voice grew shrill as emotions spiraled into chaos. "I gave you *everything*. All. Of. Me. You hijacked my biochemistry and forced my addiction to you. I absolutely hate what you did. You stole my life. You took my freedom and shackled my future. I-I-I can't stay here."

Tears in my eyes, I grabbed my purse and fled out the door.

Chapter Twelve

Somehow I made it to my car. I didn't know where to go, I only knew that I needed to get the hell away from here, to get away from him. My hands shook so bad, I couldn't start the car. I'd trusted him. And he'd betrayed me. Hijacked my biochemistry.

My heart shattered into a million pieces.

Where are you? Sage asked me. *What's wrong?*

I couldn't handle telepathy at the moment. Words wouldn't come. I sent her an image of my steering wheel.

Don't move. I'll be right there.

She must've flown down the steps because seconds later, she opened the car door and drew me into her arms. I couldn't hold the sobs inside. Oh, how I ached. Everywhere.

"What. Did. He. Do?" Sage gritted through her teeth when I ran out of tears.

I couldn't speak. I tried but only a moan came out.

"I'll kill him," Sage said. "He doesn't deserve to breathe ever again. I'll rip his fingernails off and make him eat them. Force him to choke to death on his own body parts."

I held her harder, afraid she'd do it. "Don't." My voice sounded raw and thready.

Sage held me at arm's length. "Tell me."

"Hurts. Need to go."

"Where?"

"Away. From here."

"Done." Sage guided me around the car, belted me in the passenger seat before she landed in the driver's seat. She pointed the vehicle toward Tybee and drove as fast as she could. "You got any money?"

I blinked. I'd grabbed my purse on the way out the door. "Debit card," I managed to say.

"Good. I ran out of the house in shortie pajamas, no shoes, and no wallet."

Sage whipped around Savannah's historic squares on two wheels and sped through yellow lights.

"Slow down," I managed.

"I want to know what happened, but we need caffeine first. Your phone's ringing."

I glanced at the screen.

Quig. Again.

I silenced the call. No way was I talking to him. He'd made his bed. He'd lie in it. Alone.

He sent a text message next. It read, *I understand you want nothing to do with me right now, but I pray you change your mind. If you check on Violet, spend as long as you like at Herbert's place. He won't mind, and I need for you to be safe. I need you, always...*

I didn't answer. I couldn't.

A short time later, armed with supersized sodas and a dozen donuts, I stopped trembling. I felt numb. And bewildered. And empty where the love should be. As if someone had sucked all happiness from my body.

Sage pulled into a shopping center and parked away from the stores. "We're miles away now. Talk to me."

I told her everything, but the telling reopened the wound. I felt too hot, too sweaty, too dizzy. Uh oh. I opened the door and threw up. Everything came out. The heaves went on forever. Finally, they eased and I hung there, vomit-flavored drool trailing from my lips.

Sage handed me some napkins from the glove box.

I wiped my face and sat back in my seat. "Sorry."

"Don't apologize. Hold on a sec while I move us to a fresh location."

When we stopped again, I said, "I need ginger ale."

"First, we're reclining your seat, and I'll rub your wrists with an ice cube."

It felt good.

Really good.

"You didn't know he was influencing you?" Sage asked.

"No. I love touching him, love being with him. Love him touching me."

"Because when he touched you, you wanted more?"

I nodded solemnly, then winced at the movement. "Always. My sun rises and sets on him. He's been a constant in my life."

"Damn him to the moon and back. He does not deserve you. You are the best of us. The nicest, kindest, hardest working person in the world. He stole your free will, kidnapped your future, and planted a baby in you without your permission."

I clenched my teeth together to keep my chin from quivering. I felt the need to defend him, and there's no way those words were coming out of my mouth.

"Thank you." A single tear slid down my face. "And I'm not the best of us. You are. You're brilliant and loyal and the only person on this planet I trust implicitly."

Sage's thumb dashed away the tear. "Always. And I will kill him for hurting you this bad."

My stomach rolled, and I cradled my belly to hold it

still. "Don't."

"You still love him?"

"I do. But is it real? I need to stay away from him long enough to be me again. Then I'm banking on my intuition guiding me. Until then, he's my estranged husband, and I'm keeping the baby."

"Of course you are. And you're moving in with me. I won't let him near you. We'll send Auntie O to get your clothes."

"Forget it. I can buy new things. I don't want any of us in there right now."

Sage tapped her face with her finger. "I always thought there was something off about how musky his apartment was. Now I know those were his pheromones and part of his covert seduction."

"He can't change what he is any more than we can."

"You're defending him? After he betrayed your trust? Stole your innocence?"

"Just stating facts. No wonder he concealed his family secrets before we married. I would've run across the country to get away from him."

My sister's eyes brightened. "We can still do that if you want. Road trip to anywhere."

The idea warmed the ice in my blood. Then reality loomed. We had a business to run. More to the point, we had to sleep on Bristol Street to recharge. "We can't. The shop."

"Piddle on the shop and everything else that ties us down. Auntie O will step in and help Gerard and Eve. After all, this could be construed as partially her fault. She's been pressuring us since we were eighteen to get pregnant."

"Not her fault. I made the choice to be with him."

"Because you are under his influence. He drugged you, Tabs. Like a dope fiend."

"I know." My words came out whisper soft. Anger still simmered deep inside me, but my emotions were all over the map. My fingers sought the locket he gave me. My comfort talisman. I felt better as soon as I touched it. Then I wondered if he'd dosed it with something addictive that went through my skin and that's why I loved it. This was so mixed up. I needed his arms around me, needed to feel him rubbing my back.

But was it me or drugged-me thinking that?

"To the devil with all men," Sage declared. "Let's go to the beach. At least I'm dressed for that."

Quig's suggestion popped into my head. No. Shouldn't do that. But I wanted to check on the cat. "Oddly, I want to go to Herbert's place."

"You're running into his friend's arms? What fresh hell is this?"

"Herbert isn't there. He's off the grid because he believes he's being framed for murder. His cat was on walk-about when he scratched off, so he asked me to check on Violet. I have permission to be there."

Sage shifted the car into gear. "Makes sense. The energy out there is good. Maybe it will boost your energy."

We rode out to Herbert's riverside home. I called the cat's name over and over once we got to his driveway. She didn't come, though I felt her presence in my head.

Be kind to your mate, Violet shouted in my head. *He can't help what he is.*

What are you talking about? Where are you? I replied.

Staying in the woods.

Why?

Bad things are happening. It is darn inconvenient to skulk around in the bushes.

Sage and I have come to top off your food and water. You are always welcome at our place in town.

Might take you up on that offer. Stay as long as you like. Neither Herbert nor I mind. Especially if you practice forgiveness when it matters.

Why are you being so cryptic?

I'm a cat. I'm allowed.

I turned to my twin sister. "You hear any of that? Violet is out there in the woods, talking a bunch of gibberish."

"Didn't hear a thing. But I expected she wouldn't be here. She's a survivor, Sis. Like us."

The house was locked, so I looked around until I found a fake rock sitting in a flowerpot of withered leaves under a tree. No natural rocks here. Must be a key keeper. It was. We let ourselves in.

It barely took a minute in the kitchen to refill the automated food station and refresh her water bowl. With relief, I noted the cat-sized doorway in the kitchen door. Violet could gain access to the house whenever she wanted.

Sage had wandered off inside the house and called to me. I followed her voice into the primary bathroom. It was nearly as large as the bedroom. The shower drew my eye. It was at one end of the room, through an arched doorway. The tiles were in shades of very light grey with a decorative black tile border above the edge of the white floor tiles. Overhead a giant shower device looked like it would deliver a waterfall of water.

My clothes felt grubby. I felt tired. I glanced longingly at the shower again. "We shouldn't."

"We should." Sage grinned and turned on the water. Let's shower with our clothes on. Then we'll wring them out and put them in the dryer. Herbert won't mind at all."

I wasn't sure about that, but what the heck? This was the strangest day of my life.

The shower felt magnificent. The energy of the spray drew me under it again and again. Sage hunted up towels and a bathmat while I indulged in the simple pleasure of being washed clean, then she joined me, and we shared the shower.

Our fingers were wrinkled when we dried off. Herbert's thick grey towels were amazingly soft.

"Herbert must be loaded to have so many personal luxuries," Sage said. "Maybe I should dump Larry and let Herbert ooze his mojo on me."

"His mojo must not be that potent. Either that or Sharmila is immune. They started dating before Quig and I did."

"His house isn't musky like your place. Maybe Herbert isn't doing it right."

"Maybe he wants her to choose him. I wish I'd had that choice."

"I don't want to think about men any more today. While you showered, I asked Eve to cover for me at the candle shop. I'm not letting you out of my sight today."

"You think I'll go back to him?"

"You'll do what you want regardless of my feelings about that dirty, lowdown, rotten, scallywag. I'm here for damage control and to make sure you don't drive in your condition. I checked, and Herbert has ginger ale and bread so I can make toast for you. We'll share a light snack while our clothes are drying."

Her voice trailed off, and I wondered why. Better ask. "What are you thinking?"

"I'm thinking Sharmila may keep clothes and shoes here. We're about the same size. I might borrow an outfit from her. That would be a big help for me. I didn't come dressed to go shopping."

Air whistled in through my teeth. "Not a good idea. We've imposed on Herbert enough."

Sage grinned. "At this point, what's one more transgression?"

An hour later, we'd emptied his refrigerator of leftovers, as requested, and cleaned up all evidence of our presence. Sage had borrowed Sharmila's halter dress, and I'd reluctantly donned a pair of Herbert's comfy gym shorts and a faded polo shirt. Sage had folded both of our escape outfits and stashed them in the trunk before we left.

Back in town, we hit several maternity and kids' clothing stores. I bought three more dresses, a shorts outfit, and a nightgown. Sage and I also stopped by our favorite shoe store and bought sandals.

I yawned. "What a morning. I'm glad you're with me, Sis. I would still be seething and crying if not for you."

"I'm flattered but believe in yourself. You're a strong woman. You would have made peace with what happened and figured out a way forward by yourself, but this way is better. Speaking of which, you're staying with me now, right?"

"I am. Until I know how I feel about everything that happened."

Tabby raised a finger. "Hold that thought. Larry's calling."

They chitchatted for a few minutes then I heard Sage say, "She's here."

He said something else, and Sage asked me, "You up for a snooping trip through Rosemont's house?"

My tiredness vanished in a heartbeat. Focusing on the case would put my feelings for Quig on the back burner. I was all for that. "Yes."

"We'll meet you there in fifteen minutes."

~*~

My phone buzzed in my purse. Sage smiled at me. "Quig?"

"Again. He's not giving up."

"You have something he needs very badly. I'm sure his parents have been pressuring him to reproduce too."

"He can kiss my grits right now because I have nothing to say to him."

"Good for you."

We neared the historic square where Rosemont had lived. "Does Larry ever talk to you about the council?"

"No. It hasn't come up."

"Herbert told me Rosemont's death shifted the balance of power. That Larry's family will soon have a majority on the council."

"Argh. I hate politics. None of that matters to me, Tabs. I want a man who gets me, who wants me for who I am, and who can deal with the scary stuff. I can talk to Larry about anything and everything. I've never felt so free in a relationship."

Her happiness echoed forlornly in my heart. I was delighted for her, but my sadness felt weighty as a ship's anchor.

Sage found a parking spot a few doors down from

Rosemont's antebellum mansion on the square. Her eyes brimmed with excitement. "This is the first house we've ever searched in broad daylight. The first house we've ever walked in by invitation instead of sneaking in. I feel legit and empowered."

I managed a fleeting smile. Then Larry greeted us and walked us inside. I hadn't gone more than a few steps into the inlaid marble foyer before I stopped cold.

"What is it?" Sage asked.

"Energy pools and not the good kind. They are hot and dangerous."

Sage went into her other vision. "I see them now. You're right. They appear to be writhing. Are they Rosemont's?"

I studied the pools in the entryway again. "I believe so. Let me walk around for a few minutes. There is an energy current flowing through here."

"I'm not sensing anything but the pools," Sage said. "Your paranormal talents must be more sensitive than mine."

Aware of Larry hovering at Sage's elbow, I muttered, "Sometimes." I closed my eyes until I had a better sense of the overall vibe here. In general, I wasn't an expert at sensing human energy without humans attached to it, but in an old place like this that had been lived in for generations, there were tracks where energy had been laid down.

In my other vision, these rambled along, as if drunken cats made the paths. Some were much darker than others. Though I'd never met the man among the living, energy-wise it appeared Rosemont had a troubled soul.

Staying in my other vision, I followed the acid-strong energy trail to an office. Instead of the path circling and leading out the doorway, it dead-ended at a side wall. Worse, I knew with a growing certainty I'd found something that needed finding.

"Something is behind this wall," I said.

"Does it matter?" Sage asked.

My intuition screamed the answer inside my head. "Yes."

Larry studied the wall. "I don't sense anything."

"There's something here that needs to be found," I insisted.

Larry tapped on the wall. "That's odd."

"How so?" Sage asked, her aura throbbing. "And before you say another word, my sister isn't odd. I trust her intuition over anything we see with our eyes."

"Easy, love. I didn't mean anything personal. Oddness is as subjective as normality," Larry said. "Normal is what we're individually used to. I also trust Tabby's intuition. What prompted my use of the term is the wall material. The other walls in this room and in most of the house are plaster. This one is drywall, and it's painted a slightly different shade of white."

"So? What's that got to do with the price of tea in Savannah?"

Her use of one of Mom's sayings brought a fleeting smile to my face. "Haven't heard that one in years."

"Seemed the right time for it," Sage said. "And I don't understand the relevance. Why is the type of wall important?"

"Plastering a wall is learned art. Most carpenters today with an iota of work experience can decently hang drywall. Plaster experts are much harder to find."

I connected the dots in my head. "This wall is more

recent than the others?"

"Absolutely. Why did you key in on it?"

"A dark current led me here."

"You've gone to the Dark Side?" Larry quipped.

I winced inwardly. "Not funny."

Sage poked Larry in the chest repeatedly with her finger. "Tabby is the epitome of sparkling light. She would never embrace anything dark."

God bless sibling loyalty. I beamed at my twin.

"Sure," Larry said. "How can we examine this alleged find? The council gave us permission to search this place. They didn't say we could tear down walls."

Sage grinned. "They didn't say we couldn't."

Larry blinked as if astonished. "You're right. Not sure it's the best idea, but I agree that this is important. This room has a different vibe than the others." Then he turned, looked around the room, and opened the closet. "Aha!" He waggled a long golf club at us. "Got something. Stand back."

Sage and I retreated to the doorway. Larry whapped the club many times in the exact spot I indicated and then a little lower. The air clouded with dust. I covered my mouth and nose with the bottom of my shirt. The drywall cracked and fell.

Then a skeleton fell out of the wall.

I screamed.

Chapter Thirteen

Sage and I clung to each other in silent horror as we stared at the bones on the floor. The skull drew my eye as it wobbled closer to me. The macabre teeth looked fierce in their death grin. There were two holes in the top part, a discrete round hole in the front and a larger hole in the back.

From my extensive viewing of forensic TV shows, I believed the two holes were likely the entrance and exit wounds of a bullet.

How did a dead person get inside the wall? I sent to Sage via our twin-link.

I'm stunned, she replied.

"I'll notify the council and the cops of our finding," Larry said, touching Sage's shoulder. "Y'all good?"

If being shocked out of your gord by bones falling out of the wall was "good," then we were fine. "Sure," I managed when Sage kept silent.

Larry stepped out into the corridor and began making calls.

"Oh, Tabby," my sister said in a wobbly voice. "You are an incredible finder. I don't know who this is or how he or she got dead, but you found them. Because of you, a family will have closure."

"Perhaps. There's a chance the opposite may be true. I might have killed their family's hope that their loved one was alive." The longer I stood there, the more the room wavered. My knees felt weak, my stomach roiled with nausea. "I don't feel good. Think I might throw up."

"Come with me." Sage wrapped her arm around my waist and steered me away from the remains. We ended up in the kitchen where I sank into a chair. Sage wet a cloth a dabbed my forehead and wrists.

"Thanks. Any chance there's some ginger ale?"

"Tip your head back and keep this wet cloth on your head while I make myself at home in Rosemont's pantry."

Soon, I had a glass of ginger ale and a plate of crackers to settle my tummy. I sipped and nibbled until I felt better.

My thoughts turned to the dark pools and trails of energy that occurred throughout the house. Rosemont had to have made them. He'd laid down energy in singular paths throughout this house, time and time again.

I glanced around the kitchen in my other vision, but no stray currents flowed through here, only a few dark pools. Did that mean only one body was hidden here? How long had Willim Rosemont owned this house? Knowing that might give us a timeframe to identify the remains.

As time passed, my stomach settled, and my head cleared. I felt better, but I didn't move from my seat. I longed to go home, but we'd been directed to stay put. Sage played games on her phone. Larry went into executive mode and directed the authorities to the skeleton we discovered, only he claimed that the wall already had been cracked and he helped it along.

A familiar voice boomed through the house. "Where's my wife?"

Quig! The mere sound of his voice soothed my

troubled soul. He would handle things, for sure. I was still supremely upset with him, but perversely I wanted the security of his embrace. Talk about being conflicted.

"Tabby?" he called.

Sage looked at me and shook her head.

"I have to," I said softly. "It will be all right."

Over my shoulder I spoke loudly, "Back here."

Quig hurried in, his face a near-rictus of pain. He plucked me out of the chair and hugged me. Damned if I didn't hug him back. "I've been going out of my mind with worry all morning. I came as soon as I heard. You okay?"

I inhaled his familiar fragrance like a junkie getting a fix. "Mostly."

He held my gaze and clung to me. "Mostly? Do you need to lie down? Is the baby okay?"

"The baby is fine. I'm fine too. Finding a body in Rosemont's wall made me queasy. I needed a break, so we came in here."

Quig glanced over at Sage, ignoring her militant scowl. "Thanks for helping Tabby. I felt her distress as if it were my own."

"Of course I helped my sister," Sage said. "Let her go. She's upset with you. And you're being you, flooding her with your addictive pheromones or whatever."

Quig's jaw dropped as he studied my face. "You told her my family secret?"

"She won't tell anyone else. She's my twin. I couldn't explain to her why I was upset without telling that part. Thank you for the hug. I feel better now."

I tried to push out of his arms, but he wasn't having

that.

"I'm taking you home. Right now."

"What about your job?" Sage asked. "Don't you have to declare the bones dead? And then examine them closely?"

He nodded. "Did it on the fly. Georgie Mac from the rescue squad did the paperwork and will take everything to the morgue. My mission is to drive Tabby home."

"She wants to stay with me," Sage said.

"She doesn't know what she wants. But she's not herself right now, and as her husband, I say she needs to rest in our bed at home."

"That might be true, but I need to hear it from Tabby."

I handed Sage my car keys. "I want to go with him for now, but I will see you later today."

Quig arched an eyebrow, but he kept his thoughts to himself. "Let's go home, love."

He made as if to scoop me up, and I protested, holding up a hand. "I can walk."

"Okay." He led me out of the house, into the bright sunshine, and then into his Hummer.

Once we were seated and belted in, he turned to me and said, "You scared me. I didn't know where you were, only that you weren't okay. You didn't return my calls."

"I couldn't talk to you because I was certain this would happen," I said wearily. "I need to process what happened. I am very upset with you, as I stated earlier, because of how your talent works. I'm not a minion, bimbo, or merely your baby mama. I am a living, breathing person dealing with a double dose of my own hormones now."

"I can't help what I am or who I am," Quig stated simply. "But it is not in my DNA to harm you. Not ever. I would step in front of a speeding car for you, take a bullet for you, whatever it takes to protect you."

"Stay away from speeding cars and bullets," I said. "I don't want anything to happen to you either, but I'm angry with you. I won't put my child in harm's way."

"Our child," he corrected.

"Our child," I echoed.

He drove us to our place, parked his Hummer in the alley instead of the garage.

When he tried to carry me up the steps, I planted my feet. "I'm pregnant, not injured. I can walk."

"Please. Allow me to help you. I see how tired you are."

I glanced at the steps, and they stretched impossibly long. What the hell? "Okay," I said, guiltily eating up the pleasure of his touch. When we were inside, he placed me lengthwise on the sofa. I silently congratulated him on the choice, as the bed would've been a bit much at this juncture.

"Forgive me?" he asked, sitting at my feet. "I did what I did because I love you."

"Sounds like a line from a song," I said. "And the answer is no. A few hours is not enough time for me to process how you manipulated me into being your wife and the mother of your child. I value freedom. Our country's government is based on freedom and inalienable rights. You trampled mine."

His eyes glistened. "Please. Hear me out. I can't function when we're at odds like this. I took today off. Luckily, there was only the one emergency call-out and since it was Rosemont's house, I went there. I was on my way to the scene when Larry Rau phoned. I had to see you with my own eyes."

"Why wouldn't I be okay?"

He gazed away again. "Some women who marry into our family have difficulty during pregnancy, childbirth, or labor."

I eyed him suspiciously. "You're mentioning this possibility now? After the fact? Shouldn't this have come up during one of those will-we-have-children conversations?"

"Don't be like this, Tabby. My life is bound to yours. I'd hang the moon and stars for you."

"And what other freedoms will you take away if I agree to stay with you?"

"That's it. I promise."

"Your promise isn't worth much today. Look at this from my perspective. I trusted you absolutely. When you groomed and impregnated me, you broke that trust. On the plus side, we've been friends for a long time, and I've always enjoyed your company, even before the grooming occurred. On the negative side, I detest what you did. It makes me question our entire history. I can't tell if my feelings for you are real, or if you created them."

"You love me. We are real."

"I can't trust my own thoughts, feelings, or actions, thanks to your manipulations to make me your perfect wife."

"I did a lousy job of it because you left me," he groused.

"I never said my leaving was permanent. I need a few days to think, and I can't do it when you're influencing every breath I take. If you truly love me, you'll give me the physical space I need."

"But...what if...you don't love me? Our bond is complete."

Bond? That was the second time he'd said that word. What the heck? "For you maybe, but not for me."

Quig muttered under his breath, his shoulders bowing as if the weight of the Atlantic Ocean rested on them. "Please, don't leave me. I'll give you as much space as you want, but I need to know if you want to be with me."

"Why bother to ask my feelings when you've made sure of them with grooming? Isn't it obvious I need a break?"

"Please. Don't go. I need you."

"And I need to sort this out."

"So, you don't want to be with me?"

"Why do you keep asking me that? Isn't it obvious?"

"Words matter."

A migraine stuck. The lights pulsed. I lashed out. "No. I don't want to be with you. Are you happy?"

He didn't talk for the longest time. "I will move into our spare bedroom. Don't go."

"You think I don't understand simple biology? Pheromones are airborne. Keeping apart in our home won't bring the mental clarity I seek. I will stay with Sage for a few nights. I am completely safe there. I will detox from whatever you've done to me and know my own thoughts. Then I'll let you know where I stand."

"I'm truly sorry your feelings are hurt. My biology governs how I function. Every couple in our family goes through the same process. I am unable to be with you any other way."

Of course my feelings were hurt. What did he expect? "What does your mom think of being groomed?"

His eyes rounded. "She doesn't know. Dad never told her."

"That's unacceptable. Would you have told me if Herbert hadn't spilled the beans, so to speak?"

He didn't answer. I wanted to yell at him and at the same time, to lay down and cry my eyes out. I needed to pack some items and get out of here. That was what I needed to do. I shouldn't be this close to him. But I made no effort to rise.

Quig pulled his glasses off and studied them as if they held all the answers, then tossed them on the coffee table. "The rule in our family is men don't tell their wives. You figured it out with Herbert's help. He didn't do me any favors. I don't like that Larry Rau is staying with Sage now. He might try something with you."

"He's been nothing but nice to me, and Sage is happy with him."

"Of course. He's on his best behavior until he burrows into your good graces."

"That sounds gruesome but so does being programmed to be your wife. I feel like I joined a cult."

"It's why we don't reveal that secret. You can't tell Mom. Ever. It would kill my dad."

"I'll bet." I pushed off the sofa. "I'm packing a bag for a few nights. I won't be far away, but don't contact me unless there's an emergency."

"The emergency is happening right now." He stared directly into my soul. "You love me. I know it's true. I feel the connection deep in my heart. It's why I went the extra step with you. We have a true bond. Because I was so sure of you. Of us."

"Your truth and mine are at odds right now. Give me a few days to think my own thoughts, unless you would rather cut bait and start fresh with someone else."

Quig started to reach for me, then sat on his hand. "I don't want anyone else. It's always been you. I love everything about you, except for you walking out on me this morning. I didn't love that. I hated it. I wish I could grant you all the time in the world to figure this out, but please know, every minute away from you will be torture for me."

"I know how that feels, as if part of me is missing. For there to continue being an us, I need to check in with all of me, not just the parts that crave you all the time."

He hung his head. "I want and need you to stay. But I love you enough to risk everything."

I packed my bag super-quick. Tossed in three of everything, toiletries, clothing, shoes. Grabbed my tablet and phone charger. And then I returned to the living room. "See you later."

He didn't reply in words. Sadness and grief radiated from his body. His eyes looked utterly devastated. Tears streaked down his cheeks.

My immediate impulse was to console him.

Was that my impulse or his? His, most likely. I ruthlessly pushed myself out the door, down our alley stairs and then climbed up Sage's alley stairs.

Sage was watching out the door for me. She grabbed the suitcase from my hand. "Took you long enough."

My lip quivered. "I think I broke him."

"Don't feel sorry for that man. He brought this on himself."

That was my twin. Blunt and to the point. I blinked back tears. "We had a good talk. He understands my perspective. I tried to listen to his. He said he didn't have any choice. It's encoded in his genes. DNA made him do it. Weird, right?"

"It's downright wrong. You're your own person, not his love slave."

"That's not how I feel. He's hurting and so am I."

"You're tough. You'll survive."

"It doesn't feel that way. I ache everywhere. For him."

"That means you're detoxing."

I shook my head. "Soul-searching shouldn't feel this awful."

"You'll be better soon. Meanwhile, Auntie O is bringing dinner. Frankie is still in Chicago."

~*~

Auntie O arrived with a chicken and grapes pasta dish, a broccoli with walnuts salad, sliced watermelon, homemade rolls, and a sheet pan of brownies.

She gave me her sternest look. "Tabby, I worked too hard to get you married for you to leave your husband. At least you had the good sense to become pregnant before you left him."

"We had a disagreement. I didn't leave permanently. Just needed space to clear my head. When I'm with him, I'm part of a couple. I need to be an individual for a few days."

"How's that going for you?" Auntie O continued.

"Terrible. I feel awful. I'm a hot mess right now."

"Time will tell," Auntie O said. "The answer will become clear very soon, I predict."

"You'll go back," Larry said. "The Paranormal Council knows little about couples in Quig's family line, except they never divorce."

"Hush, Larry," Sage said. "Tabby needs our support. If you can't do that, you're not the man I thought you were."

Larry grinned at her. "Never doubt I'm your guy. Took you a while to figure it out."

"Quig said we had a true bond." I stabbed my fingers through my loose hair in frustration. "Whatever that means."

"Ah, I am beginning to see. He needs you at home, but you need a short break. This break is for you to sort out which of your emotions are real." Auntie O dished up a plateful of food and set it in front of me. "Eat. My great niece needs good nutrition and a drama-free household."

"I'm not hungry. It feels wrong to eat as if everything is okay." I clutched my tummy and realized I felt nauseous again. "Excuse me." I hurried to the bathroom, threw up, washed my face, and dampened a washrag. I took it with me to bed.

I cussed silently under my breath, hating how weak, betrayed, and bereft I felt. Tears fell until I had none left. It took forever for my breathing to even. The anguish in my heart remained, as did the ache in my empty arms. Though it was all shades of wrong to miss him when I was angry with him, I did.

What was I going to do?

What could I do?

I carried our child, a living being who depended on

me to protect her.

Adulting was hard. I wanted to hide here in my old room until the world went away, until I knew who I was again, who I was meant to be.

But the world didn't wait upon my convenience. I had responsibilities.

Like working in the shop tomorrow.

I set an alarm on my phone and automatically checked my messages. Nothing there.

How deflating.

I'd asked him to give me space, which is what I needed.

Only now that I had it, I'd rather have him.

Chapter Fourteen

The next morning, Auntie O brought me ginger ale and plain crackers in bed. "Do as I say and things will come around with your morning sickness. Don't move other than to eat a few crackers and sip sparingly on the ginger ale."

I sniffed and the crackers smelled just right. I stuffed a whole cracker in my mouth. "Thanks."

Auntie O perched lightly on the bed. "Go easy with those. Nibble like a mouse until your stomach agrees with morning again."

Caffeine was my morning go-to. "What about coffee?"

"Ah. Coffee is highly aromatic. The scent may trigger morning sickness all by itself."

"Ugh." I stared wistfully at the juice glass of ginger ale. "I have a lot to learn, don't I?"

"All new mothers-to-be do, and yet babies grow and thrive despite what you do or don't know."

I tried a tiny sip of the ginger ale. It was hard not to gulp the whole amount, but I did as Auntie O specified. She was right. My stomach felt fine with five salted crackers and four ounces of ginger ale. "How'd you know about the crackers and ginger ale routine?"

"It worked wonders for your mom."

Her aura fluttered. I realized I'd switched to my other vision as soon as I felt better. I didn't usually spy on family members' auras so this felt weird. Then her aura settled down to what I considered a normal healthy aura. Did she catch me looking and somehow wrangle her aura to look perfect? If so, that was a nifty skill. But the flutter couldn't have been good. Was something going on with her?

I sat up more and gazed at my aunt with my peripheral vision. Her hair was less tidy than usual, lines etched her face, and her shoulders and back were hunched. Was my situation stressing her? If so, I had to fix this.

"Whatever it is," I said aloud, "it will be all right, especially if you're concerned about me. I'm strong, and I can handle what life throws at me. Last night, I was more emotional than usual, but it had been an unusual day."

Auntie O shook her head as if to clear it. "I let you down, dear. If I'd known Quig could hurt you this bad, I would've protested the match and kept you two apart.

"Quig has been the bedrock in my life for as long as I can remember. He said he had no choice in how he wooed me, and apparently, neither did I."

My aunt studied her hands before she replied. "Heritage and talents are undeniable. Like you, I expected to be a simple candle maker. I had no aspirations to anything else. And then my intuition sharpened to a razor's edge, and I discovered my knack for the unthinkable. I knew how to take a life with my mind. Willim Rosemont on the Paranormal Council realized what was happening before I did, and he taught me the code of conduct and trained me to use my powers for the good of our community."

"Neither Sage nor I had any idea about that aspect of your life until recently. You have always been a stable, guiding presence in our lives, and we're thankful for that. That code of conduct you received must have been a magic sauce. The circle of people who knew about your talent must have been very small. Your secret is safe with me now and for always."

"Thanks," Auntie O said, "Quig's talent, whatever it is, is yours to keep as well. Your love for him is etched on your face and heart. I'd never do anything to hurt either of you."

I reached for my locket, the one that always brought me comfort when I held it. Then I stopped. Quig gave me the necklace. "You sound surer of my affection for him than I am. I miss Quig so much it hurts to breathe. Is he okay? Does he hurt as much as I do?"

"If you want those answers, you know who has those answers. Your husband. I urge you not to take long to decide. This separation is difficult for him. I sense his distress." Auntie O patted my leg and sighed. "It's a shame Rosemont is gone. He would have been the perfect counselor for you, but you can't take this discussion to a normal counselor."

I nodded. "First, I'm not going for counseling. I'll sort it through myself. My true feelings will make themselves known. No matter what I decide, he will remain in my life because of the child we've conceived."

"That sounds reasonable."

A stray thought demanded to be voiced. "Do you regret not having kids?"

"Of course I do." She stopped for a minute. "I've never shared this with you, but when I was married to Edgar Colvin, I conceived three times and miscarried three times. Edgar wanted children so he divorced me when my obstetrician said no more pregnancies. That made me sad, but luckily, I was able to coparent with your mom, so I helped shepherd and mentor you girls."

My hands wrapped protectively around my womb. "I hope I carry this baby to term."

"Sage and I will help your kid along with gentle pulses of energy if needed."

"Since we're sharing personal information, I've always wondered this. What happened to my dad? I have no memories of him after a certain point."

"Ah. This question has been a long time coming, and yet, I don't have an answer for you. Marjoram and I searched for Adam Winslow to no avail. I don't know what happened or where he went. One day he just wasn't around."

"He vanished without a trace? You can tell me the truth. I won't be heartbroken if he ran away from his responsibilities. Sad maybe, but at least it would beat not knowing."

Auntie O shook her head, her gaze resolute. "Got nothing for you."

"What about telling me why your parents Dwayne and Rosemary Waltz are buried in the Wayfare plot at Bonaventure Cemetery?"

"You're an adult now, and that's a reasonable question. Dwayne was the bastard son of the Wayfare heir. Mr. Wayfare had no sons with his wife, so we are Wayfares by blood, not marriage."

"We're the illegitimate side of the family."

I quickly relayed the information to my twin. She shot me back her response. *Cool.*

"Any other questions?" Auntie O asked.

"Not that I can think of."

~*~

Fawn Meldrim knocked on Sage's alley door after I'd dressed for work the next morning. I still felt wobbly inside, but I was determined to keep putting one foot in front of the other. Since I was the only one home, well, me and two cats, I answered the door.

"Do you have a few minutes, Tabby?" Fawn asked.

"Sure. Come inside." I closed the door behind me. "How'd you find me?"

"No answer at your place, so I tried here. I need to talk to you."

"I have to be in the shop by ten."

Fawn nodded. "This won't take long."

"How can I help you?" I asked, sensing her edgy vibe and the odd currents in her aura.

Her hands clenched and unclenched at her sides. "Is it true? Did you find a body in the wall at Uncle Willim's place?"

Only the right answer would do. "Yes."

Her face blanched, then she paced the room. "I don't know...I mean, it can't be possible...But what if it is...What does that mean?"

While she stared at me through anguished eyes, her aura flashed bright as heat lightning. I injected a vibe of calm in my voice to soothe her. "The remains I found weren't in any way recent. The person had been dead for years. Only bones remained."

Fawn stopped and gnawed on her lower lip. Just when I was about to prompt her, she blurted out, "I might know who it is. But I hope I don't. I mean...she's supposed to be living a fine life elsewhere. Or at least, that's what I always told myself."

Her jolting thoughts didn't quite connect for me. "If you knew the person in the wall, I'm all ears."

"You see, I always thought the world of Uncle Willim. But there was this incident ten years ago. My cousin, who was my best friend, disappeared. Kimmy was last seen in his company. Mom and I suspected he caused her disappearance, but we couldn't prove it. I know this contradicts how I feel about Uncle Willim, but I'm a conflicted person. I wish I'd known you then. I would've hired you on the spot."

I gave her a wry smile. "It wouldn't have done you any good. I was working hard at denying my talents until these last few months. It is only in the last year I've used my talents to solve crimes. What was your cousin's last name?"

Fawn grimaced. "Her name was Kimmy. Her mom is not your favorite person. Lilah Acworth. That's why Lilah got so spun up when Jeanine disappeared and then died. All of her kids are now gone. That made a deficit of paranormal population growth in her skill area. Lilah is no longer in good standing in the para community."

Lilah Acworth. I'd rather it be anyone else in the world than someone related to her. "How come I never knew Lilah had two kids?"

Fawn shrugged. "Dunno. Kimmy was three years older than me, but we got along great despite our age differences. She wasn't a social butterfly. Kept to herself most of the time. Rumor had it that Kimmy had a different dad than her sister. Some said Uncle Willim was her father."

"Whoa. That's a bombshell. Dr. Rosemont and Lilah had a baby?"

"That's the rumor. Maybe your husband should check the skeleton's DNA against that of Willim Rosemont."

Not going to happen because I wasn't willing to share my separation from Quig with anyone outside the family. Plus, this news about the skeleton's possible identity suggested Fawn had a motive to kill Rosemont. Lilah too. "I'll see. Meanwhile, I need to finish getting ready for work, unless there's something else?"

"You see why it's upsetting if the body is Kimmy Acworth. I want her to be alive and well elsewhere. I don't want to know about her getting killed and stuck in a wall for ten years."

"I understand. It's possible the bones can't be identified. Keep this to yourself for now. We don't know that Rosemont killed the person who used to be those bones. It's possible the victim died elsewhere, and Rosemont solved the problem of his/her death by concealing the evidence. He knew he could keep that secret as long as he lived. On TV shows they call that controlling the scene."

"Either way, I hate the outcome if it's Kimmy."

"I recently learned the hard way that I can't control everything in my life. This is definitely out of your control, and it would be best if you went about your normal schedule for now. If you make a fuss, you could become a target, and neither of us wants that."

"Thank you," Fawn said. "For talking me down from that mental ledge. I want you to keep working on Uncle Willim's case. Either way, I need to know what happened to him and to those bones."

Her orange aura color grew larger then shrank back

to its former size. That confused me. Was she lying? Or worse, was she realizing the cases might be connected and that she was putting me in danger by asking me to investigate?

Now that I had a baby on board, I didn't want my life cut short for any reason.

Fawn stopped at the door and glanced back over her shoulder before leaving. "Thank you for hearing me out. I didn't know who else to tell. I appreciate what you do for our community."

I slumped down on the sofa. With no easy solution for either case, I hesitated to seek them. My efforts might destroy Rosemont's reputation and put myself in harm's way.

Barely five minutes later, a crisp knock sounded at the door. "Tabby! Open this door right this instant."

Chapter Fifteen

Argh. This was turning into the longest morning ever. How I wished I was ensconced in our apartment two doors down. People thought twice about knocking on Quig's door. Especially my relatives.

I gathered myself mentally and physically then opened the door for my aunt. "You have a key," I stated plainly as I slunk back to the couch. "Why didn't you let yourself in?"

Auntie O shut the door and followed me to the living room. "I sensed that girl over here. The kid that used to be all Goth-y. What did she want?"

"Fawn Meldrim wanted to know about the old bones I found. She is worried they belong to her missing cousin. I didn't know she had a missing cousin." I glared at my aunt, cross with all the mornings interruptions, cross with myself, and wanting nothing more than to go back to bed and sleep away the day, but it was my day for the shop. "You and Mom did us no favors by hiding us away all these years. We can't keep the paranormal community out of our lives now and are hindered by our lack of history within the group."

Auntie O grimaced, an odd sight in her usually cheerful face. "You didn't miss much. People jockeyed for power, slept around without remorse, and did whatever they wanted, just like the rest of Savannah. Who is this missing cousin? I don't remember her."

Her aura flared with dark colors. I drew in a quick

breath and held it. Why was my aunt lying to me? Should I be on guard? Why did I suddenly feel nauseous? I rubbed my temples. "I can't deal with this right now. My stomach aches, and all this tension is making everything worse. I don't even know if I can take anything for it in my condition, so lying on my bed in the dark with an ice pack on my head is what I want to do. But I have the shop today."

"Nuh-uh. You aren't getting off the hook that easily." Auntie O let the silence roil. "Tell me the name."

"Why did you lie to me?" I countered.

She stilled.

This time the silence felt prickly. Was she trying to get in my head and get the answer for herself? "Why is it important to you? What else are you withholding from me?"

Auntie O walked into the kitchen, got herself a glass of water from the sink. I waited, letting my questions hang in the air between us. Whatever she was hiding, it was a doozy. I knew it in my very marrow.

"All right," my aunt said, facing me from behind the island counter. "You're right. There was a girl in our community who went missing about ten years ago, a teen named Kimberly."

"Fawn said her name was Kimmy. Must be the same person."

My aunt tapped her nails on the counter. "Then you also know Lilah Acworth was her mother."

I did know that, not that it helped. "What would Kimmy be doing in Rosemont's wall?"

"First, we don't know it is the Acworth girl. Second, I have no idea. It doesn't necessarily mean Willim was involved in any foul play. He fixed problems." At my quizzical look she continued. "A person who made problems for the community go away."

"And Kimmy was a problem?"

"She was a wild child. Always pushing the limits with everything and everyone. She put the entire community at risk with her drinking, drugging, and overt sexuality. And with her assassin training, she became a risk to everyone in Savannah. Control is everything to an assassin, but Kimmy rebelled against being controlled."

My back teeth ground together. "Her assassin training? If she was unstable to start with, why give her that training? This makes no sense."

"It was her talent, dear. Better to train her and teach her the code than allow her to kill anyone who crossed her."

Still seemed wrong to me. Poor girl. "Why did Kimmy act out?"

"She hated Doug Acworth, Lilah, this town, and herself. She was hell-bent on self-destruction from day one."

Auntie O was telling the truth now, and yet my intuition prickled. This wasn't the whole of it. Whatever she hadn't mentioned was huge. I was certain. Like Fawn, I craved information and feared it. Fear never got anyone anywhere. "What else?" The fingernails in my fisted hands dug into my palms.

Her eyebrows rose. "What do you mean?"

"You omitted something important."

"How do you know?"

"I just do."

Auntie O's eyebrow raised. "Interesting."

"Tell me."

"You are turning out to be full of surprises, Sunshine. The next Senior Magistrate will not know what to do with a woman of your many talents."

"Don't."

"What?"

"Don't distract me with the innate fear of the council I have, thanks to you and Mom."

"It could be much worse," Auntie O said in a dull voice. "If they knew your potential way back in the day, they would've shaped you into a totally different person. You would've been lost to us. We couldn't allow it. They would've ripped you twins apart without a qualm. Sage wouldn't have survived the separation. We knew Sage couldn't recharge fully, and we were delighted that you always helped her that way."

My blood chilled. What she described sounded horrible. So awful that I had a few dry heaves until I pulled myself together. "No one is splitting us up, and if you haven't noticed, Larry fills in Sage's empty places. She's a different energetic now."

"That she is." Auntie O's vision narrowed. "I advise you to be wary of confiding in her for the near future. Larry comes with good and bad attached to his family name. You remember Jeanine and her 'training' in the swamp? You would've been subjected to something similar, with several mentors available, one of them being Larry's brother. The council has always wanted a super talent to call upon. A person with the skill to kill without remorse, a living lie detector, and a ghost who can seemingly walk through walls."

I couldn't move. Breath hitched in my throat. A

roaring sound got louder and louder in my head. "No. No. No," I whispered.

"Breathe, dear. A woman of your exceptional ability can handle anything. Thanks to the way Marjoram and I protected you, you still have the autonomy to do whatever you want. It's a luxury I never had."

Her wry tone wasn't lost on me. Auntie O hadn't wanted to become an assassin. Worse, a remark replayed in my head. Recently, Lilah had mentioned that one of us twins had likely inherited Auntie O's skills. I'd always considered that the person who could kill easily was Sage. The thought of taking a life was abhorrent to me.

But I would kill in a heartbeat if anyone threatened me or my family. Even Auntie O.

My eyes widened at the realization. Jeanine had shared that her training involved pushing her beyond her limits, isolation from her family, and total male domination. I would've cracked completely.

Holy cow. I would've been the council's next pet assassin.

"You're figuring this out," Auntie O said. "Not a pretty picture, is it?"

I didn't want that brutal style of training for anyone. Much less for my sweet aunt. Or myself. Definitely not for my kid. "You were trained that way?"

At first, I didn't think she'd answer, but when she began to talk, her voice sounded choked. "The trainer indoctrinated me into the guild of assassins. But first he broke me physically, mentally, and more. He pushed until my only choice was to bend to his will. He was relentless and merciless. I've never told anyone, but I believe his violent intimacy, if you could call it that, damaged my ability to hold onto my babies."

My mouth gaped, and no sound came out for several moments. Finally, I gathered myself to say, "I-I-I didn't know. I'm sorry that happened to you. I can't image how you survived that, how anyone survives such brainwashing and torture."

"Yes, the tactics were similar." Auntie O's gaze grew teary. "Now you know why we kept you two hidden from the community. We didn't want that experience for you, and we vowed to protect Sage at all costs."

All my life I'd felt the isolation of our family unit, but looking at things in perspective, that was a hell of a lot easier to take than what happened to my aunt and mother. I owed them a large debt for their defiance of the council. "Yes. Yes, of course." Both cats came out of my bedroom and pounced on me. Harley leapt into my arms, and once I sat down Luna curled in my lap. I shuddered and shivered at what I might have become. At the life I would've led, alone, without Sage. I would've become a ruthless killer.

The next words came from the bottom of my heart. "I am humbled by the torture you endured, the life you saved me from."

"There's more."

"More?" I echoed dully, reeling from the morning's revelations.

"Contrary to the rumors that circulated, Kimberly's father wasn't Acworth or Rosemont. She was your half-sister. Your father had a brief affair with Lilah before he was engaged to Marjoram. Your mother was furious at his betrayal. Adam Winslow left when his secret baby became common knowledge, and that was the last we heard from him."

"Did you or Mom…" I couldn't voice my suspicion of what they might've done to my father, but if Quig ever broke my heart that way, he'd pay mightily. I wouldn't share what was mine.

"I didn't do anything. I don't know about Marjoram. She became guarded after Adam left. Tougher and utterly determined to protect her children."

My ears burned with heat. "I know the feeling. Being pregnant has stirred up fierce protectiveness in me. Anyone comes after any of us, and they will pay the price."

"Easy, Tabby. Take some deep breaths. If you go rogue like Kimberly did, the council will take you out too."

Oh. That was bad news. "That's what happened? I thought they would stop her by paranormal means, not by shooting her."

"Whatever got the job done. She was strong and powerful. Worse, she hated what the trainer had done to her and raged against the community that forced him on her."

"The Paranormal Council took her out?"

"I was not consulted or involved, but, given the bones in Rosemont's wall, that is the most likely scenario."

"I am trying to understand, but my reactions to these situations are visceral. The training, the reprisal, the cover-up. Kimmy being my half-sister. I never even knew she existed. I feel awful about blaming you and Mom for sheltering us from the community. I am and was so naive. Now, I am beyond grateful for that level of protection. I literally had no idea of what could've happened."

Another thought occurred to me, chilling me to the marrow. "Will they demand I go through the training now?"

"Not a chance in hell. You're past the age of indoctrination. You would kill the trainer in a heartbeat. Then they'd come after you. For a time, I wondered if Larry's interest in Sage was a cover for him in his role as an informant who'd been assigned to get close to you two."

Ugh. That damn council was determined to ruin our lives. Sage was finally happy. And getting better at recharging herself every day. Then my thoughts cleared, and I remembered how Larry looked at Sage. How good they were together, like two peas in a pod. His emotion wasn't fake.

"Larry's interest in Sage is genuine," I said. "What is the age of indoctrination?"

"Thirteen."

Appalled, I silently mouthed the number, terrified for any child who had to go through such brutality at a young age. No wonder Jeanine had hated us. She endured that degradation at puberty, and we got a pass. "That is so wrong. That means of 'training' has to stop."

"Good luck. I tried to change the process when I was your age and got nowhere, fast. It's tradition. As you are learning, the paranormal community is bound by its rules and traditions."

"Those can be changed."

"And you're the one to do it. But not right now. You are too vulnerable in your current state and must consider the future for your family. Of what's at stake."

"No one is training my daughter in that way. Ever."

"That's the spirit."

Another knock sounded at Sage's door. I groaned aloud. "You've got to be kidding me. I hate being popular. Worse, I can't sleep in because I have to go to work."

Chapter Sixteen

"Don't worry about work today. You're taking the day off," Auntie O said, patting my arm. "My Frankie flew in last night, and he wants to help. I already sent him down to the candle shop. He and Gerard get along so well. I predict they will have an excellent sales day."

If I ignored the knocking at the door, maybe the person would leave. "That's nice. Thank you."

"You need to go see your husband. That's what will fix your headache. I sense that he is not doing well."

The cats fidgeted. "I'm not doing well either. I want the world to stop until I have time to think this through and then I'll jump back into the world again, but that's not going to happen."

"No, it won't. I'm on your side, always, but your place now is with him."

"I disagree."

The insistent knock sounded again, this time accompanied by a very loud female voice. "I know you're in there, Tabby *Quigsly*. Open this door at once!"

Oh. Rats!

I cringed at that shrill voice. Both cats raced out of the living room to hide.

Quig's mother, Milly Quigsly, meant well, but her single-mindedness exhausted me. Once she locked in on a goal, she became a heat-seeking missile. That intensity got old real fast. She'd probably figured out I was here since I'd quarreled with Quig yesterday. She expected me to go home to Quig.

Bottom line, she wasn't going away. I nodded to Auntie O. "Let her in. I'll hear her out, then she must leave."

My aunt crossed to the door and opened it. "Welcome, Milly. We were about to have tea. Will you join us?"

Milly marched in like she was late for a parade. "What I need is for my daughter-in-law to return to her husband. Right this instant."

I didn't rise from the sofa, not out of disrespect but from weariness. Dealing with Hurricane Milly challenged me when I felt a hundred percent. Today I was barely at sixty percent, and her fiery emotions overwhelmed me. I struggled to keep an even tone. "Quig and I had a disagreement, and I need time to clear my head. I haven't left him. This is a time-out."

Milly towered over me, her face glowing red, her jaw clenched, her arms crossed, her right foot tapping. "You did the unthinkable. You *left* my son. He's miserable. Don't you realize what you are doing?"

High drama, Milly-style. I expected nothing less. She was bulldozing me and deaf to anything I said. A small part of me wondered if she was right, but then I immediately remembered that I needed this separation. Why should Quig's needs supersede mine?

Milly had no idea she'd been groomed by her husband. And I'd promised Quig I wouldn't tell her. That made this confrontation more complicated. "Look, I understand you're fully in Quig's corner. He is your son. You mean well, and no disrespect intended, but we will handle this ourselves. For the record, he's not the only one who's distraught. This separation hurts me too."

Fury glittered in her eyes. "Not the same at all. You are sitting up, taking nourishment, and conversing. He is not. You wounded his heart. Fix it now."

Again, that small trickle of unease caught me, but then my fingers coiled into fists in my lap. I would not let her cow me. "He betrayed my trust, took advantage of me."

Milly swatted my reply away like an errant fly. "Before friends and family, you vowed to love Quig for better or worse. Go home and be his wife."

Boy-oh-boy would I like to throw her out right now, but I needed to be an adult and clear the air. Perhaps on a subconscious level Milly knew what Quig's dad had done to her. Best to stay firm and tread as lightly as possible. "No. Taking this time out is best for me. He deceived me. I don't trust him."

"Get over it! This dust-up is inconsequential in the scheme of life."

My turn to make a gesture with my hand. "If he's ill, ask Henry to examine him. Your husband has medical training."

"Don't you think I've asked? Henry won't come. Says it will work out or not. Told me not to interfere. But he's wrong. Nothing is more important." Milly dropped to her knees, pleaded with her teary eyes. "I'm begging you. Return to him."

"No." With her kneeling and me sitting on the couch, I had the high ground. But I didn't want to be elevated in any way. What I craved was peace and quiet.

However, as a mother-to-be, I understood. I gentled my words. "I love Quig. That didn't change. But I must consider the future."

"Bull. Quig adores you. Always has. Always will. He would *never* hurt you. Quit being selfish. He needs you."

"You're wrong." Despite my fatigue, my feet itched to be moving. I rose, paced the room, and put distance between us. Auntie O, hovering in the kitchen, caught my eye, but I shook my head. This was my problem. I would solve it.

Milly sputtered at my dismissal, and I hurried to say my piece. "My sister loved a man who was toxic to their relationship. He loved her as well. But loving each other wasn't enough, so they separated. And she found the right guy later. I need to know if I made the same mistake. Until that happened to Sage, I didn't know it was possible that love wouldn't be enough."

"Someday you'll know what it's like to have a child who is the center of your universe. It doesn't matter how old Quig gets. I'll always be his mother. Except I can't help him with this. He. Needs. You."

The tears in her eyes spurred mine. Why couldn't she see I was in no shape to make life-altering decisions? I respected her devotion. But I couldn't do what she wanted. Not until I knew my love for him was real.

I dashed away the moisture with one hand and mustered more courage. "I've heard you out, and now I'm asking you to leave. Please go."

Auntie O stepped forward and offered Milly a hand. "Let me help you up, dear."

"Don't touch me. I want nothing to do with you savages." Milly stumbled to her feet. "Murderers."

She whirled and fled, leaving the door wide open.

Auntie O closed and locked the door. "I'll never understand what Henry sees in her."

The room spun. I flashed hot then cold. My stomach lurched. I ran to the bathroom and tossed my breakfast. Then I sank to the cool tile floor. Tears rolled down my cheeks, out my nose. I grabbed wads of toilet tissue for damage control, not that they put a dent in the deluge. I couldn't stop crying. I loved Quig with every ounce of my being, but I had to know the truth.

Did he force my emotions?

My weak stomach couldn't take all the stress. What I couldn't admit out loud was the other thought rolling around in my head. Was I bound to him through a junkie-like addiction?

~*~

An hour later I still couldn't settle, even though I was alone. Milly's visit left me empty, angry, and drained of energy. I wasn't buying her theatrics for one second, because that meant Quig was in worse shape than I was. No way he was as bad off as she'd stated.

Impossible.

I was the victim.

He'd wronged me by "grooming" away my free choice, indoctrinating me into his cult of one. Even now, I craved his warmth, his arms, especially his scent.

His scent. The bright freshness of Quig's natural bergamot notes elevated his woodsy aroma into an intoxicating breezy blend. It magnetized my attention. In his absence, I felt hopelessly adrift, a skiff with no anchor line, no oars.

In short, the man smelled and felt like home to me.

With no relief in sight, I decided to start the day over

and went to bed with the cats.

Much later when I wakened, I had no answers, but I was no longer bone-tired. Only a "regular" tired and oddly numb. I wasn't myself. How much of that change was from my pregnancy? Or, was I hurting the baby with this love sickness?

I was a walking conundrum.

How I longed for the shelter of Quig's arms.

And how keenly I needed the truth of my affections to be revealed.

Though Sage and Larry tried to cheer me up at dinner, I couldn't eat. I managed to drink a glass of water before returning to my childhood bedroom with Harley. My cat had been lying on me all day. At first, I'd welcomed his constant presence and purring. Then those same attentions made me feel hot and sticky and out of sorts.

I was a third wheel here.

I needed to go home to Quig.

But I didn't have answers yet. About us. About me. Going home wouldn't yield the answers I craved.

If only I could stop obsessing about my situation.

Why couldn't I focus on something else?

That question echoed in my thoughts.

Something else.

I managed a shaky breath.

I did have something else to focus on. Dr. Willim Rosemont's death. Was it an accident or murder?

If I hadn't been derailed by personal issues, I would've already visited more than Willim's home. Without new data, I could only review the information I had.

I stared at the bedroom ceiling, willing this

diversion to work.

Willim was pronounced dead on the Stone Steps of Death. He had been knocked in the head with a gold-plated object. Since there were no such items nearby, someone struck him and carried the weapon away. But Willim was with friends. How had Peaches, Herbert, Sharmila, the drummer, and Lilah missed seeing a physical attack?

Was his aggressor invisible?

Larry Rau could go invisible. Was Sage's boyfriend involved in this? Could other paranormals become invisible? It wasn't something I could ask. Was there a membership roster listing people's talents? That would be helpful.

The female skeleton in Willim's home office wall was still unidentified. Was she Fawn's alleged missing cousin? Could she be my stepsister as Auntie O said? Would her DNA match mine?

Wait. I was asking the wrong questions. Those questions would tell me more about Kimmy Acworth. Knowing the skeleton's identity wouldn't solve Rosemont's case. It might help though.

Even so, I needed to return to my original question. Who had motive to kill William Rosemont? Maybe the Paranormal Council. Possibly Fawn, since she was close to her cousin. If it was her cousin.

Herbert hid after Willim's death. He had too many secrets to protect, or did he?

Sharmila was on sick leave with stomach flu. Or, she'd gone into hiding with Herbert, and the rumors were false.

Lilah Acworth had been intimate with Rosemont. He never married her, so she might feel resentment toward him. Especially if she knew about the skeleton.

Peaches was on tour with her band, so neither she nor Grey Roads, her drummer, were in town now, though they had been when Rosemont was murdered. They must have given statements that same night.

Or was Rosemont the victim of a paranormal conspiracy? Was this a hostile takeover of the leadership group? Given what I'd learned about training teen paranormals, his death could signal a revolt by the younger generation or their parents.

Further, Rosemont had been a trainer. Hmm. Larry's brother had been on the ruling body and a trainer.

Two trainers, both on the council, both dead.

Were all trainers council members? Worse, were all council members trainers?

Food for thought.

Althea Morgan, as Junior Magistrate had the most to gain on the council by the doctor's death—she'd been promoted to Interim Senior Magistrate. According to Larry, this was a thankless job, fielding infinite problems and complaints. Though Rosemont had the personality to handle the job, Larry insisted no one else wanted that job. And she was a mom. I couldn't take her off my suspect list, but she trended toward the bottom of the pile.

I recognized council members Kelsey Flowers and Reverend Clark Gaudry by appearance. Kelsey was slightly older than me and was a healer and an empath. Her skills didn't fit your typical killer profile.

The minister Clark Gaudry made a name for himself as a faith healer before joining the council. My shop clerk Eve said Clark heard voices and was considered clairaudient. Had something he'd heard spurred him to kill Rosemont?

And there was still the matter of the victim's clients as possible suspects. Perhaps one of them had a motive. Had they admitted incriminating information during a counseling session? If so, how would I identify them?

Having an open book of suspects bothered me. When I investigated, I started with the victim and worked outward. But was I deluding myself that I was fit enough right now to investigate a homicide? What if morning sickness made me throw up on evidence? What if my brain fog never cleared?

Morning sickness sucked.

Harley snuggled close to my torso, purring loudly. I stroked his soft fur until we both relaxed. I welcomed his healing energy and the comfort and peace of sleep. Perhaps I'd dream the answers I needed.

In any event, something had to give.

I couldn't live like this.

Chapter Seventeen

The next day I pulled it together and went to the candle shop to work. I would treat this like any shift at my job and not dwell on my personal issues. With that thought in mind, I set out my candle-making supplies on the counter.

Except…my heart wasn't in it. I didn't want to waste materials and making candles when my intentions weren't pure was a waste. Instead, I did inventory, dusted, and helped with sales in the shop. I stood in front of the winged lion again. Waiting for him to blink at me again. No such luck.

While watching traffic out the front shop window mid-morning, I saw Herbert slip into Southern Tea, the restaurant across the street.

I turned to Gerard. "I need to step out for a few minutes. You okay in here?"

"Yeah. I'm good," he said.

I hurried over to the restaurant, searching the eclectic space for my lawyer. Herbert must've seen my mad dash across the street because he rose partway and waved me to his table.

"Join me?" Herbert asked.

"Yes. Thanks. I'm glad I saw you." I slid into the other chair. "Detective Nowry asked me to convince you to come in for an interview."

Herbert sank into his seat. "Nowry can suck worms for all I care. I won't help him do his job."

"Why are you here then? The detective has a few

questions, that's all."

"Forget about Rosemont right now. I need to talk with you about our mutual friend."

My throat tightened. "Why didn't you come directly to the candle shop?"

"Needed neutral territory."

Herbert risked his freedom to speak to me about my husband? Irritation roiled in my gut. "I know what he is, what you are, and I don't approve of your ways."

"Too late for that." He scowled at me, then began again. "Quig needs you. Consider how many times he's come to your aid. Don't you have it in your heart to help him now? His life is in danger."

In danger?

Herbert's aura showed he was telling the truth. But his claim sounded unbelievable. Like what Milly had said yesterday. Like something bizarre from myth or legend. Was Quig's best friend asking me to put him first?

My spine stiffened with resolve. "Get real. Dying from a broken heart?"

"From being away from you. His very life is linked to your presence."

"Impossible."

He arched an eyebrow.

I gulped air. His claim couldn't be true.

Could it?

Had this quest to find my truth hurt Quig? I leaned in close to whisper, "His mother threatened me yesterday, but she is high drama when it comes to her son. Auntie O told me my place was with Quig. I ignored both elders. Why can't Quig put one foot in front of the other and keep going like everyone else with heartache does?"

"He can't."

"I don't believe you." Conversations in the busy restaurant ebbed and flowed around us. The smell of so many competing food aromas made me sick to my stomach. That and the whisper-thin chance I might be harming my husband. My hands trembled until I clutched them together. Then both shook.

Herbert studied me before responding. "That's why we are so careful in our mate choice. Why I couldn't bond quickly with Sharm. She won't commit to me, so I won't risk the true bond. Quig risked it all. On you. The only consolation here is that if he dies, he will have reproduced."

Did everyone know of my pregnancy? Wait a minute—if he dies? Why would Herbert say such a thing? "What you're saying is too fantastical. I don't believe you," I repeated, "and that's not why I came over here. You were one of the five people with Willim Rosemont when he died. Did you push him down the steps?"

He visibly bristled. "I did not."

That aura flare seemed in proportion with his response, but still. He'd gone to ground instead of talking to the cops. "Did you see anyone else push him? Or strike his head with a gold-plated object?"

He shrugged carelessly. "Wasn't looking at him. Too busy focusing on Sharmila."

Heeding the crowd around us. I leaned forward to say softly, "Grooming her, you mean."

Herbert looked like he'd swallowed a wad of fish bones. Then he quietly said, "I didn't kill Rosemont. It was a fluke we even met up at the restaurant that evening. Our three couples dined separately at the same place and left at the same time, deciding on the spur of the moment to have a drink together elsewhere. Dr. Rosemont had had a few already."

That was no help at all. I tried another tack. "Is the skeleton in his wall my stepsister?"

His gaze pierced my soul. "It's undetermined. Kimberly's dentist moved to Arizona after his office burned, so comparing the teeth with her dental records is out. Harvesting DNA from the bones is dicey. It's definitely female though because of the hip shape. Rosemont was a womanizer, big time, and he was into rough games. Probably left skeletons all over town."

I shuddered in disgust. "I'm glad he's gone. Why didn't someone stop him years ago?"

"Several women agreed with you, but Rosemont was too powerful. People looked the other way at what he did."

Until they didn't. Someone took the law into their own hands and put the man down.

"Join me for lunch?" Herbert asked.

"No, thanks. I couldn't eat if tried. Nothing stays down."

My thoughts wouldn't settle as I left Southern Tea, so I walked to the other end of the block and watched the fountain flow in Johnson Square. Life went on, no matter what happened. I didn't accept I had life or death power over Quig.

I had enough trouble managing my own life.

Beads of sweat trickled down my spine. No answers to be found out here in the ninety-degree temperatures. I crossed at the light and returned to the shop.

"Everything all right?" Gerard asked.

"What?" I quickly re-ran his words in my head. "Yeah. I'm okay. Just distracted. Going to the stillroom. Call if you need me out here."

The calming robin's egg blue walls and the lush ferns framing the window helped settle me so that at least I felt like myself. But stray thoughts kept charging into my head.

Had I harmed Quig by leaving him for a few nights? Was I being selfish?

And yet, Herbert's comments about Quig's welfare supported Milly Quigsly's. In all the years I'd known Quig, he had never been sick a day in his life. If he truly was ill, it might be the flu or a new virus going around.

It was too unbelievable that he'd die if I didn't go to him.

What about my stake in the matter?

He'd stolen my freedom of choice, used airborne pheromones and biochemical touch-bombs to force my interest. I had every right to be outraged by his actions. Every woman in the world would feel the same way.

I coasted on my outrage for a few more minutes, but the thrum of longing for Quig beat strongly inside my heart. It wasn't fair that I missed him so much. That I wanted to curl into fetal position and shut everything and everyone out.

Been there.

Done that.

Didn't help.

Where did that leave me?

I couldn't stay at work. I couldn't go to Sage's apartment, and I wasn't going home. But I had to move. I paced the stillroom to sort through the chaos.

I'd been out of his clutches for two nights and a day, and my love for him burned brighter than ever. How long did grooming attraction last? Shouldn't I be less in love with him by now?

Gerard looked in on me, then ducked out and returned with a stool to me. "Sit down, Tabby. Your face is deathly pale. Want me to call Quig?"

"No," I said. My staff didn't know I'd slept at Sage's place for two nights. "I'll be okay. I got some bad news today. A friend is sick and possibly very ill."

Sage pinged me on our twin-link. *I'm coming.*

"You shouldn't be around sick people," Gerard said. "Think of your baby."

"I know." The walls pressed in on me. I couldn't be still.

I had to keep moving.

My emotions swooped and soared all over the place, like a kite caught in tree during a hurricane. Gerard wanted to help, but oddly I resented his advice. Everyone wanted to run my life. The only one who understood me was Quig, and I couldn't go to him.

Sage burst into the stillroom. "What's wrong?"

"Everything."

Sage glared at Gerard. "Sister time. Leave."

Gerard must've agreed because I heard the door between the stillroom and the shop close.

"Tell me," Sage said. "Let it all out."

"I can't stop missing Quig. He's the one I need to talk to, but I can't go to him. I don't have answers yet."

"I do. I've never seen you this upset, Tabs. Get hold of yourself."

"I can't. According to three sources, he's in dire straits. Milly said it outright. Auntie O hinted at it.

Herbert said the same thing a few minutes ago. Now I'm beginning to think I'm *killing* the man I love. The weight of it is too much to carry. My wheels keep spinning because doing the right thing for me is the absolute wrong thing for him."

"Do you trust him?"

"What a bizarre thing to ask. The man manipulated my emotions. That wasn't trustworthy." I couldn't stop pacing. I tugged on my ponytail.

"What about before? You said he only started doing this recently. What about before all this happened?"

"Maybe. I thought I didn't, but that was anger talking. Yes, I trusted him. Even when I was a little kid. He always did what he said he would do."

"He's been your friend for more than twenty years. Even if he is not trustworthy about this one thing, given your decades of history, too much is at stake if he's seriously ill. This is the wrong time for you to be ruled by pride. Come with me." Sage grabbed my arm and led me into the alley.

I tried to shake her off but couldn't. "What are you doing?"

"Taking you to see him. It's the only way to find out if he's about to die."

"I can't. I shouldn't. Don't make me do it. I thought you were on my side."

"I am on your side. You are making yourself sick with worry. The best thing for you is to check on him. What happens next is up to the two of you."

We marched up the steps to Quig's apartment. Our home. My eyes misted with tears, my feet plodded woodenly.

Sage kept tugging until we reached the top landing.

She placed my hand on the lock pad until it beeped. Then she opened the door. "Whatever is happening, you need each other right now. Don't risk everything. You could lose the baby if you stay this upset."

My baby.

I cradled my womb with both hands.

Our baby.

I hurried inside my home.

Chapter Eighteen

The apartment felt musty, the air dank. I would open the windows to ventilate the place except the temperature was in the upper 90s outside. Why would anyone choose to be pregnant in August? Perspiration drenched my clothes. I needed to change out of my damp things, and my clothes were in our bedroom.

When I entered the room. I gasped in horror. Quig lay there, pale and stiff, as if he were in rigor mortis. His eyes didn't open when I approached. I was too late to save him!

No.

It couldn't be.

He couldn't be gone.

My heart fluttered. I shed my wet clothes and climbed in with him, matching our lengths and sharing my energy and warmth with him.

Please don't be gone. Please come back to me. I love you. I missed you so much. I don't want to be without you. Wake up, please.

His heart thumped very slow but steady as if he were in a form of stasis. I pulsed energy into him until the rhythm increased. Then I slowed the flow to a trickle because sharing more at that rate might harm the baby.

I stuck to him like glue.

After a bit, his color returned, and his muscles softened. I felt so tired and happy. Relief overwhelmed me. Scant seconds later, I fell into a deep sleep beside him.

~*~

When I awakened at twilight, Quig cradled me in his arms. It felt so natural, so right.

"You came." His voice sounded like gravel rumbling in a cement truck. "You saved me."

"I don't understand this at all, but I don't wish you any harm. Ever. We've always been friends."

"About time you remembered that," he murmured.

"What other surprises are in store for me?" I sat up out of his reach.

He sat up too, alarm etched in his gaunt features at the distance between us. "That's it. You know everything. You are my Achilles heel. Without you, I am literally nothing. I can't exist without you."

"Don't guilt trip me." Skepticism surged through me faster than a rip tide. "Because you gave me your 'everything'?"

"Yes. It happens when a male of my lineage finds his mate and risks the true bond." His voice broke. "I thought you felt the same way. I never dreamed you'd leave me."

"Definitely a guilt trip. You did this to yourself. I didn't do it to you. Why didn't you go to a hospital?"

"Because my illness isn't viral or bacterial. It's bond-related. When you said you didn't want to be with me, it skewed the bond. I didn't have the will to go on. I've served my purpose. In some insect species, the female devours the male after copulation."

"Leave insects out of this." Alarm pulsed through me. "We are talking about us. Human beings. I said I needed a few days to get my head straight after you manipulated my feelings. I had hoped with distance I could detox and learn how I truly felt. As I recall from that exchange, you kept questioning me asking if I wanted to be with you until in the heat of the moment I said I didn't. I never intended to leave forever. I love you, Quig. I always will. But you took unfair advantage. You must see that. Forcing my emotions was wrong."

"All I know, all I've ever known, is you're the one for me. I'm a victim of this as much as you are. More. You hold my life in your hands. I've never been so vulnerable."

I should be rational about this, should weigh the consequences of what I said, but the hurt felt too raw. "Why can't you see things my way?"

He opened his arms to me. "Because I lose you that way. We're bonded, babe. My life depends on you."

I didn't dive into those arms, as much as I wanted to. "Listen. I'm too tired to discuss this, too beat to walk back to Sage's place. I'll stay here through the night, and we'll talk in the morning. No more grooming me. You have to promise."

His expression fell with his arms. "I can't promise that. It's like asking me not to breathe."

"I see." I could sleep on the sofa but it seemed miles away. I quickly thought of a simplistic solution. "Stay on your side of the bed."

He rolled away, but in the morning, I woke on top of him, my arms and legs wrapped around him tighter than a kudzu vine.

"Did you do that?" I asked.

He grinned, once more looking like his old self. "You did that all by yourself."

Chapter Nineteen

Steam heated my face even as I realized how at ease I was, how right I felt with him. This must be his doing. He'd somehow called me in my sleep, and I obeyed like a faithful hound. Here I was holding onto him for all I was worth.

As I started to move away, he kissed me tenderly. And I wanted that, needed that basic reassurance that my husband cared for me. He wanted me. I wanted him, no matter what the cost.

Stop giving in! My thoughts insisted when the kiss ended, and he wrapped his arms around me, lightly keeping me close. *This is that darn bond manipulating you. You aren't acting on your own accord.*

Or was I?

This was so confusing. I couldn't make sense of my feelings. How did one know if abiding love could be coerced? A part of me wanted to forgive his actions. I'd never had feelings that ran this deep for anyone. Not even my twin.

My leaving had physically hurt Quig. I hated that my reaction inadvertently harmed him. And I would never injure him like that again. I wasn't a cruel person.

"Please stay, love," Quig whispered so softly I almost missed it.

"I want to, and that's a problem. I learned nothing by leaving. Instead, I cried and ached for you. Am I addicted to you?"

He chuckled softly. "I certainly hope so, but not because of what I did. I'd rather you felt strongly because you value all the aspects I bring to our union. I'm utterly devoted to you. I care deeply for your health and well-being. Our lovemaking is amazing. And I will be a good provider for you and our family. You will never stress about paying bills again."

My smile fell as he completed the list. "I loved everything you said except for the part about money. I can't be bought."

"Trust me, I know that. Your reservations right now strike ice-cold fear in my heart. I'm a desperate man, and debate isn't my strong suit."

I turned my head so I could see him better. "I want to be here with you but I'm afraid of losing myself. Do you have similar fears?"

"I didn't before. Now, I have them. Even so, I don't blame you for leaving. If someone strongarmed me in any way, I'd protest. I've always wanted to please you. And my parents. But it's hard to do both."

"Give me an example."

He thought about that for a moment. "I went against my family's wishes in moving to Bristol Street. They wanted us to live close to them, to live in a more forested environment instead of an urban cityscape. But your happiness means more to me than pleasing my parents."

"I'm deeply flattered, but I don't want to come between you and your parents. Being married should build family, not tear it apart."

"I know what you really want me to say, what I need to say, but it's hard. I've never shared this part of myself with anyone...I've wanted you to be exclusively mine since I was eighteen. You always made me happy, and I lost myself in your beautiful eyes. It took twelve more years for you to look at me with love. I yearned for you every one of those nights. I reached for you in my dreams, but you weren't there. Over four thousand nights. Dad said it was character building. Mom urged me to move on. But I couldn't. I knew we would fit perfectly in love and life."

Snark curled inside me and lashed out whip fast. "Forcing my emotions took care of that."

"No, it doesn't work that way. If a pair isn't meant to be, the attraction fades. The upside is those incomplete unions don't cause death, but the people drift in and out of relationships for the rest of their lives. You never broke a date with me. You even asked me on a few dates."

"Oh." I digested that information and knew it was true. Good for us. But then I thought of another pair. "Sharmila and Herbert?"

"They will marry. Herbert is very persuasive. Unlike me, he is a skilled debater."

People said actions spoke louder than words, and Quig had always been kind and considerate. He'd listened to me, responded in caring ways. Plus, he was a darn good kisser.

Quig sniffed the air and rolled out of bed. "I need a shower."

Once he left, I lay there for a few moments, wanting to touch him again. Quig didn't know it, but he was a darn good debater. I slid out of bed and joined him.

~*~

After the shower, he directed me to the bathroom mirror and hugged me from behind. I met his eyes in the mirror.

"If I was into tattoos," I said, "I'd get a heart-shaped one with your name on it."

"Whatever makes you happy."

"I'll think about it."

"I couldn't eat or go to work after you said you didn't want to be with me," Quig said. "I may not have a job anymore. None of that mattered because I didn't have you. You are my world, my universe."

"I'm not going anywhere."

"I hoped you'd say that. The effect of the true bond with a female is that I gave my life to you. I literally cannot live without you if you say you don't want to be with me."

No pressure there. I turned to him. "I believe you. And you will never hear those words from me again. I only said it last time because you kept pushing me so hard with that very question. Now that I know why, I will always protect you. Words matter. I get it now." That true bond might be a fairy-tale like condition, but I loved being his person. If he was bad for me, I didn't want to wake up from this fantasy.

He'd always protected me, looked out for me, made me happy. From the very start. According to Quig, the pheromone part wasn't active when we were young. I always looked forward to seeing him in those early days. Still did.

I understood how special abilities could not be denied. All paranormals needed to exercise those talents to feel peace. Quig couldn't be anyone but himself. Same for me. I still didn't appreciate him manipulating my emotions, but he'd caught the raw end of that action by entrusting his life to me without telling me. If I said I didn't want to be with him, he'd die. That was a very serious consequence. And he never mentioned that downside until I returned to him.

He loved me that much.

The thought of living in a world without him made my eyes water, my knees sag. He held me close. "You all right?"

I leaned into him. "I am now."

~*~

A long while later, I stirred. "I need breakfast, and then since it's my day off from the shop and we're okay, I'm going sleuthing."

"We're better than okay. We're great." He stroked my back. "I'm coming with you."

"I wouldn't have it any other way, but what about your work?"

He grinned. "It's Saturday. No work today. Besides, I have a vested interest in your safety, the most important of which is that I don't want to be apart from you today. I nearly lost us both. I can do better. I can and will protect you."

"All right. I'm happy to have company. It's always more fun with someone else along."

We dressed, ate, and were headed to the door when my phone rang.

Chapter Twenty

I answered the phone. "Hello."

"This is Captain Kenzo Haynes of the Historic District Savannah Police Department. Ms. Quigsly, your assistance is needed this morning."

I gazed at Quig, then switched the call to speakerphone. "How may I help you, Captain?"

"I need you here to observe the interviews I'm conducting this morning. Your perspectives are fresh and result in new avenues of investigation. How soon can you get here?"

I hoped this was about the case. "I'm headed out the door now with Quig, so we could be there right away, if we cancel our other plans. I assume it is okay if he accompanies me. May I know who you're interviewing?"

"Bring him only if he's no longer contagious. I've got Peaches McVeigh the singer and her drummer, Grey Roads. This is our first in-depth interview of either of them since Nowry's first interview. I wanted to follow up with them and see how they act in the hot seat."

Contagious? What did that mean? I skipped over the new official finding to ask for a favor. "Interesting. I would love to ask them a few questions."

"Absolutely not. You will be here in a listening-only capacity. This is an active homicide investigation."

Wow. Nothing like being slapped down when I was doing him a favor. But I might learn plenty about these people simply by watching them. Still a win for me. "So, Rosemont's death is no longer considered an accident?"

"Correct. The strike on Rosemont's head led to his death. That was verified two days ago by our interim medical examiner, Dr. Henry Quigsly, who filled in when he let us know of his son's sudden illness."

His words spun through my head in different orbits, out of sync, out of time. Quig's dad had been doing his job? That was good, but nonetheless a surprise. I struggled to say something relevant. "I didn't realize Henry had filled in and reported Quig's 'illness.' But it is nice to have that official confirmation of Rosemont's murder."

"The faster you get here, the better." With that the phone went dead.

"Change of plans. We're headed to the police station." I arched an eyebrow at Quig's inscrutable face. "Did you know your dad reported you were ill and filled in for you at work?"

His shoulders relaxed. "News to me, but my parents were on top of things, as usual. Dad covered for me when I needed it most."

~*~

We sat in a tight airless room the size of the adjacent interview area and viewed the process through a one-way mirror. First in the hot seat was the drummer, Grey Roads.

He looked rangy, as if his limbs were longer than normal, but perhaps the tight jeans and long-sleeved clingy black T-shirt added to that impression. His pasty skin appeared anemic in the brightly lighted room, and his shoulder-length hair tangled around his shoulders. Not tangles, those were dreads.

"State your full name for the record," Haynes said.

"Grey Roads."

"Is that your full name?"

"Yeah."

"No middle name?"

"Don't need it, so I got rid of it."

"Grey Roads is your legal name?" Haynes' voice sounded skeptical.

"Yes, we established that. People think drummers are stupid, but we have to be smart to understand all the rhythms that make up music. We're as creative as other musicians and as smart as scientists."

"Got a musical chip on your shoulder?"

"No. Just stating the truth," Grey said. "If not for drummers, then bands, ensembles, vocalists, you name it, wouldn't sound right."

I heard noises like something being patted. Grey's hands were under the table. Was he making those sounds?

Haynes leaned over the table. "What are you doing?"

Grey's chin rose, challenge sparked in his eyes. "Working out a groove on my thighs. They wouldn't let me bring my kit inside."

"Not if my cops want to keep their jobs. Knock it off."

The verbal exchanges were so rapid-fire I hadn't had time to do much but listen, but that changed now. I doubled-down on my focus to study Grey's aura through the thick glass. It looked twitchy in places and foggy in others. I had no idea what that combination meant. So far, based on my observations of other auras, it appeared he was telling the truth.

"You were with Lilah Acworth the night Dr. Rosemont died?" Haynes asked.

Grey nodded.

"State the answer for the record."

"Yep. Lilah and I left the restaurant with him and Peaches. We ran into Herbert and his girlfriend smooching outside. As a group, we decided to grab a nightcap at a club on River Street. Rosemont smelled boozy, like he'd been drinking heavily."

"Was he inebriated?"

"He held his liquor like a man, if that's what you're asking. Probably could walk a straight line better than me at that point. I wasn't feeling much pain either, but I was also cruising on adrenaline from the wedding we did that afternoon. The rest of the band went to a private party. I needed time to decompress so I asked Lilah to join me for dinner."

"Did you witness any trouble at Dr. Rosemont's table?"

"Didn't know he was in the same joint, not until Peachy stopped at our table after she went to the ladies' room."

"And?"

"And she was on a date with him. Peaches asked us to join them for a nightcap after dinner. Lilah said yes before I could turn the invite down."

"You didn't want to go?"

Grey shook his head. At a piercing glance from Haynes, he continued. "Didn't need more booze. Was in the mood for some very personal attention."

Haynes seemed to ponder that. "What happened next?"

"Nothing, really. The lawyer guy and his cop girlfriend were outside, and they joined our group as we walked together to the steps."

"The historic stone steps that descend to River Street?"

"Yeah."

"Any conversation or observations about the walk?"

"Peaches and Rosemont talked privately a few times, which was annoying. They have some history together."

"What did they say? Be as exact as possible."

"I couldn't make out their murmurs, but she walked close to him, closer than she ever walked with me. We've hooked up a few times but nothing ever came from it. Rosemont, he never had to work at wooing her. He so much as looked at her, and she trotted to his side. Every damn time."

"To recap, you heard nothing of their conversation, and you're basing their intimate vibe and behavior on their alleged history?"

"Sure, but no, that's not right. I did hear him mention 'those were the days.' I remember that line because that's when Peaches fell back to walk with me and Lilah. Seemed like his version of the old days was a good memory for him and not so great for her."

This information fascinated me. Must be lots of water under that bridge, dirty water at that. Did Peaches have a personal motive to kill Rosemont? I really wanted to know more.

Captain Haynes asked, "What happened next?"

"We got to the steps and the lawyer-cop couple decided they'd rather part ways with us. We gathered in a circle for our goodbyes, Rosemont with his back to the steps. All of a sudden, he tipped backward and plunged down the stairs. He fell to the first landing." Grey shifted uneasily in his seat. "Rosemont never moved after that. The spark went right out of him."

"Did he say anything?"

"Maybe. Not entirely sure of this because it makes no sense. I might have heard, 'Not now,' under his breath."

The whole time Grey spoke his aura flared. That likely meant he was lying. Only how much of this conversation was a lie?

"You're certain no one in your group of six was out of your sight or caused him to fall?"

"I didn't see anything. I told you everything I know."

During that statement, Grey's aura returned to its resting state. Truth.

Or he was an excellent liar.

~*~

After Grey was dismissed, an officer led Peaches into the room, seated her in the same chair as Grey. Peaches glared at the observation window as if she knew we were in here. Her aura was difficult to decipher. Had she erected an energy barrier? If so, was she an energetic like me?

Her answers to Haynes' questions about the night tracked the drummer's, except she firmly denied having a personal relationship with Rosemont. Her aura remained static the whole time. Dang, she was good.

Peaches' denial must've irked Haynes. "Savannah is a small town, McVeigh. I can't believe you hadn't crossed paths with the man before."

"I didn't say that," Peaches countered. "I denied having a *romantic* relationship with him."

"Did you collaborate on a project with him?"

Her eyes telegraphed fury, but her aura remained locked down. "No."

"Buy one of his hand-carved ducks?"

"No."

"Attend one of his parties?"

"No and hell no. He's not my style."

"And Grey Roads is?"

Peaches leaned back in her chair, barring her arms across her chest. "Grey is, um, cathartic, at times. He's a way to vent steam with no strings attached. It works for both of us."

"Did Grey have reason to kill Rosemont? Was your drummer jealous of the doctor?"

"Not jealous. He knew I was Rosemont's companion that night. Lots of people talk to me when I'm out. It's part of being an entertainer. Grey knows the score."

"And yet you're older than Grey?"

Peaches sighed. "Not supposed to remind a woman of her age, Captain. But, yeah, I'll bite. Grey liked the fact that I was a cougar, in and out of bed. Satisfied?"

I laughed out loud, then smothered the sound with my hands.

Quig patted my shoulder. "She's a tough nut to crack. I predict Haynes won't get anything else from her."

"That's about what he got from the drummer," I whispered back. "These interviews aren't helpful to him or to me." Even as I spoke, it dawned on me that from Rosemont's position before he fell, only a person with a certain talent could have gotten to him. And that person needed to be physically strong to conk Rosemont hard enough on the back of the head and then tug him down the stairs.

Someone like me.

Someone who could go invisible.

I'd had the thought before because it was a possibility. But now I knew, truly knew, that it was the only way to get at Rosemont. Did I have an alibi for the night he died? Yes, of course. My dinner party in our apartment. I was with Sage, Larry, and Quig that night.

My alibi was also Larry's alibi. And Larry was the only other person I knew who had an invisibility talent. Shoot.

Just how many invisible people were running around Savannah?

~*~

Captain Haynes called us into his office afterward. "What did you learn?"

I paused to collect and sensor my thoughts. It was important that I tell the truth, but I could darn well omit the invisible part. "Besides what was said, the only new information I gleaned is that Grey thinks he's a good liar. He's not. Peaches showed no truth deviations in any of her answers. If she lied, she's darn good at it."

Haynes stared at me. "I figured that out myself, but it's good to also have your confirmation. How did someone get to Rosemont? Too many witnesses present for someone to sneak up on him."

No time for spinning an answer. Had to wing this. "This puzzles me too. Perhaps there was a group pact and one of them did it and swore everyone else to silence, but it doesn't usually work that way."

Haynes leaned toward me, his eyes eagle-sharp. "How do you mean?"

"It's too many people to share a secret. Someone would've blabbed by now."

"I need more, Ms. Quigsly. If it wasn't a group conspiracy, how could it happen? Give me an out-of-the-box solution."

Didn't expect that request. He wanted me to pull something out of the air but make it real evidence? I was no sorcerer. But an idea glimmered in my head. "Maybe someone lay in wait and a conspirator in the group provided a slight distraction at a key moment?"

"Considered that, but it's a longshot. Even with the poor lighting, once everyone heard the fall, the perpetrator would've had to slip away without a sound or sighting. Given the number of people present and no report of anyone else, that is unlikely. There are no good answers. Rosemont was clearly struck on the back of the head. Just as clearly, no one saw it occur."

"I understand your frustration. I feel that way too. Other than walking through Rosemont's house and finding a woman's skeleton in his office wall, I haven't had time to wrap my head around what could have happened. But I'd like to help. If possible, may I visit his office, car and home again?"

"You let me down, Quigsly. Hell, both of you did. The evidence doesn't stack up in the case." He caught Quig in his burning gaze. "Why were you out for medical reasons three days this week, and yet you look hale and hearty today?"

I glanced over at Quig, knowing he couldn't tell the

head cop the truth. I'd nearly killed him by walking away from him. What would Quig say? My grip tightened on the arms of the chair.

"I don't get sick very often," Quig began, "but when I do, I go down fast until my system fights off what ails me. Not up to full speed yet by any means, but I am strong enough to sit through interviews, not that I learned anything new either. Surely, you must've heard similar accounts of Rosemont's last night from Detective Nowry's witness interviews."

Haynes scowled and slumped back in his chair. "It bothers me that everyone's story matches so well. That's why I'm leaning toward a conspiracy theory."

Uh oh. Identical stories triggered his cop intuition. Mine too. I knew of a paranormal explanation that filled in the gaps, but no way would I mention it.

Before I found a way to respond, Quig said, "Rosemont's fall to his death must've seared in everyone's memory. That's why the answers are similar."

"Coincidence," Haynes said. "Never trust it."

An idea surged out of the soup in my head. "What if someone hypnotized the five witnesses?"

"Hypnosis might explain it." Haynes sat up straighter. "Either that or it's one of the bizarre ideas floating around the squad room. Some guess aliens with a ray gun zapped him, causing him to fall. Someone else said the attacker wore a superhero cloak of invisibility, as if this were a fantasy movie. Regardless, Rosemont didn't fall on his own accord. The forensics don't lie. What's the answer? I need this problem to go away, like, yesterday."

I squirmed in my chair, not liking the way his

intensity warmed my cheeks. "I don't have enough information either. I don't know whodunnit. Not yet."

The intensity in the captain's eyes morphed into serious speculation. "You trust that art school gal that dyes her hair weird colors?"

"I've known Fawn Meldrim for a few months. I trust her vibe and what she says. In other words, she seems on the up and up to me."

"She was always an odd kid," Haynes said. "Came to my attention when Metro intervened in her family situation due to her father's public drunkenness. I felt sorry for her even if she did look weird. I know that's not PC to say these days, but it's the truth. Now she's in art school, and her weirdness makes sense. Never met an artist with both feet on the ground."

My brain reeled. First, from the stress of figuring out on the fly that PC was political correctness. Second, from his unexpected sympathy for Fawn. And third, for him classifying all artists as unbalanced. As a candle and soap maker, I qualified as an artisan. That was kissing cousins with being an artist. Which meant he didn't respect my vocation either.

Quig cleared his throat. "Unless hypnosis or magic were used, I don't see a way forward with the information at hand."

"Not good enough." The captain shook his head. "Can't prosecute without tangible evidence."

No way would he consider an invisible murderer. Even if I found the invisible assailant, he or she couldn't be tried in a court of law. Guess that's where the Paranormal Council came in. And their assassins.

"Any identification on the skeleton in Rosemont's wall?" I asked.

"I spoke with Dr. Henry Quigsly yesterday, and he bracketed her age to 12-17 years old."

My eyebrows rose. "How'd he do that?"

"Femur bone is what he said. Followed it by saying there was no wisdom tooth emergence, so the victim was likely under seventeen."

"So, we are looking for a missing young lady, ages 12 to17."

"Right."

~*~

Quig and I dined at the Pirates' House after leaving the station. He must've been tired from our time apart. I surely was. Now, the captain suddenly expected a miracle solution from me, and I couldn't make that happen.

I turned my attention to our server and then the menu. We each chose seafood off the menu. As we waited for our meals, I became conscious of the conversations around us.

Couldn't discuss Rosemont's case in a public place, nor get involved in a relationship conversation that someone might overhear. That limited our options.

Quig must have had the same thought and picked up his phone. "I have some messages to return. Do you mind?"

"Don't mind. I'll do the same thing." I dug out my mobile phone and zipped through emails and social media, landing on my Solitaire app. Except I couldn't focus on the cards.

A lot had happened in the last few days. The murder investigation loomed like a giant thundercloud over my shoulder, but my marriage took center stage. I'd been miserable without Quig. He'd nearly died. I couldn't breathe at the thought of nearly losing him. And yet, I loved a man who used biology and biochemicals to make me his girlfriend, fiancé, and now his wife.

My time away hadn't cleared my head, even without his interfering presence. Worse, every moment I was away, I became more and more miserable.

Violet's warning from the day Herbert had asked us to go over and check on his aunt-turned-cat suddenly made sense. She'd said to forgive Quig. That he couldn't help being who and what he was.

I understood that as I had much about my talents that might need forgiveness, especially if I became the next assassin in my family.

Not helping.

Two facts about me stood out in my mind. I loved him. Deeply, and I was as emotionally connected to him as he was to me. Not just through his actions. Something inside me had recognized him all along. That was why I never felt right around other guys, even in my youth. He'd always been the one for me. Just took me a long time to figure that out.

For better or worse, I loved Quig. According to him, he had no control over his body's reaction to me. He'd even gone for the true bond which meant his life was tied to my loving presence in his life.

He literally couldn't live without me. And I was sure that I didn't want to live without him.

Our food arrived, my crab stew and his seafood gumbo, and we dug into our savory lunch. As we ate, the nearby diners cleared out, and I figured we could risk talking quietly about the case. I asked, "What do you know about Peaches?"

"Well, for one thing, she's one of us," he said.

That was news to me. "One of you or one of me?"

"Something in between is my guess. She had her eye on Herbert early on, but he wasn't interested. She then turned to me, but my heart was already yours."

Peaches better stay away from him. It took me a long moment to tamp down that flare of jealousy. "Interesting. On another topic, did you know that stuff your father reported about the skeletal remains?"

"I did. No one asked for the information. My dad probably saw my notes to that effect. I had planned to share it with the captain, but I got blown severely off course when you left."

My hackles rose. "Don't guilt trip me. I didn't know anything terrible would happen to you. I was reeling in shock. I needed time."

"Our communication skills needed improvement. But we're past that now. Right?"

"I love you. That never wavered." I stopped before saying his mom was a mindless puppet. Whew. Close call. "I agree to talk things out from now on. I didn't plan to leave you permanently and said as much. Once I learned of your trouble, I raced home. I had no idea utter incapacitation was possible, and I feel awful for causing your distress."

"I didn't know it would strike so fast. When you walked out the door after saying you didn't want me, I collapsed. I have always been in love with you, Tabby. You are my world."

"Now I know. I won't leave again, but that doesn't give us a golden ticket to the future. We will disagree sometimes. Especially about your talent."

"Never said we wouldn't. That's okay. I'm glad you understand the whole situation."

It galled me that he'd risked his life to totally bond biochemically to me. And that if I died, he'd die. He'd given up his freedom too, and his penalty was much harsher.

Even so, we were still newlyweds in love. We'd said, "I do." The double meaning of those two words were more binding than our marriage vows.

The server returned with the bill. Quig covered the expense, then snagged me with his heated gaze. "Let's go home."

That spark in his eye got my motor running too. "Sure."

But when we approached our alley steps, a cluster of people blocked our way. "Who are they?" I whispered to my husband. "Other than Herbert and Althea, I've never seen them before."

"I figured this might happen someday," Quig muttered. "Nobody ever wants the entire Paranormal Council to darken their doorstep. Lucky us."

"And it's only mid-day," I mused, thinking how unlucky we were at this moment. "Thought surely they'd be midnight visitors."

Chapter Twenty-One

"What a surprise," I said, at once forming an energy barrier around Quig and me. "Would you like to come upstairs?"

"Thank you, Tabby," Althea said. "We seek a private word with both of you."

I felt pressure in my head, as if someone was testing the protection I'd made. Deliberately, I pushed more current into my barrier, and the pressure eased. Was that from Althea or someone else? Her aura looked calm, truthful. If it wasn't her, who was it?

Sage reached out right away on our twin link. *Tabs, what's going on?*

I'm okay. But the Paranormal Council just paid me a call.

Good grief. Want me to come over?

I got this. Or so I hoped.

I'm here if you need me.

Thanks.

The group followed me up the stairs and oohed and aahed over the special handprint lock. Quig brought up the rear with Herbert, and I wondered why his friend came out of hiding from the police. For that matter, why were these people here?

Unless…they wanted Quig to serve on their board because of his education and public career. I'd fight that tooth and nail. Darned if I'd let either of us commit to something so high octane.

We needed to get back on track as a couple and prepare for our new arrival. Both of those would stress our relationship naturally. There was no room for added tension. Accommodating this group's wishes wasn't on my to-do list.

Now was not the time to get snarky. I'd be the epitome of hospitality and get them to leave as soon as possible. "Please have a seat in the living room, and Quig will bring over our kitchen chairs so that we have enough seating. I've got iced tea and my aunt's homemade cookies. Give me a moment to pull things together."

Herbert and Althea took me up on the refreshments, the others did not. I left the tea pitcher, extra glasses, ice, small plates and the cookies on our island counter in case anyone changed their mind.

Althea cleared her throat, and everyone turned her way. "Thanks for agreeing to see us on short notice. I apologize for not reaching out ahead of time, but Herbert surprised us by coming out of hiding for the Paranormal Council's called meeting today. I've been officially appointed Interim Senior Magistrate. We must know what happened to Rosemont because it may have bearing on our operations. Further, if the entire council is at risk of attack, our community will suffer. Our group never assembles in one place too long for that reason. With that said, let me introduce everyone."

Althea rose and circled the chairs to stand by Quig. "Everyone knows Dr. Quigsly, the Medical Examiner and Coroner for Chatham County." She moved to my side. "Some of you may have met his new bride, Tabby Winslow Quigsly, the candlemaker for her family's Book and Candle Shop on this same block of Bristol Street. She's Oralee Colvin's niece and an energy talent."

Thankful for how she'd couched my ability, I waved my hand as she said my name, my curiosity firing like a 21-gun salute at the steely-eyed stares. Yikes. Unless someone spoke to me directly, I would keep my mouth closed. Safer that way.

Herbert rose and dove into the cookies again. He seemed ravenous.

Althea made her way back to the sofa. "Council members, when I call your name, raise your hand." The group nodded as one, which creeped me out. "Kelsey Flowers, is a Hospice worker and an empath."

My immediate impression of Kelsey was that of a shy, retiring rose with her plain clothing and bobbed hair. I wondered if she was a "yes" person on this board.

With a nod at Herbert sitting at the counter and wolfing down cookies, Althea continued. "Herbert R. Ellis is an attorney currently on the lam from the cops. He's a mirror talent as is Dr. Quigsly. They can deflect emotions or bad energy to their source." Herbert raised his hand but didn't budge from his perch. "Next, we have Reverend Clark Gaudry. He is clairaudient, as in he hears voices that we don't hear. As for me, I'm a white witch who uses practical magic and healing for the greater good. I'm also Larry Rau's aunt. Any questions so far?"

I kept a tight rein on my reactions so my face wouldn't betray me. It was all I could do not to startle uneasily at her wrongheaded name for Quig's talent. Mirror talent was a far cry from parasitic manipulator, which Quig and Herbert said other people called their talent. Regardless, let her be wrong. I'd never betray that secret.

Quig and I exchanged a glance. "None here," he said. "Please continue."

"Tabby, we heard you examined Rosemont in the morgue. Did you learn anything from the body?" Althea demanded, her gaze fixed on me, her aura still calm.

"Nothing of ground-shaking importance." I glanced at my clasped hands to gather my thoughts before meeting her gaze. "I viewed Rosemont's body as asked. His head wound kept drawing my attention, and I mentioned that. After another look, Quig determined that injury happened before he died."

The way Althea's head twitched reminded me of a small bird. "He was bludgeoned?"

Quig cleared his throat. "I reexamined the bones and tissue to distinguish between perimortem and postmortem," he said. "With the police report only indicating a fall, I initially considered his wounds to stem from his plunge. However, with in-depth study, I determined the fatal blow occurred before the fall. My father independently confirmed this finding."

"Impossible. No one else was there to strike him. I was one of the five people with him," Herbert said around a mouthful of cookies.

I held my breath in case anyone mentioned invisibility. Outwardly, I appeared a tower of calm. Would they think it weird that I'd shielded Quig and myself? Too bad. I didn't want any of them sneaking into my head.

"What about his possessions, Tabby? Any hits there?" Althea prompted.

She was full of questions. "Another dead end,

though detecting vibes from possessions isn't something I've tried before. I felt a slight pull toward his knife, er, whitlin' jack."

"For heaven's sake, he wasn't stabbed," Kelsey said crossly. "Everyone knows that."

I cringed at her sharp tone. "My process isn't perfect, nor do I fully understand it. I observed and sensed nothing else."

Althea shot Kelsey a quelling glare, making the young woman flinch, before turning to me and smiling like a shark. "Thanks for accommodating our visit today. We hoped with your clairvoyance ability and possible psychometry talent that you might detect something the cops couldn't."

"I'm an energetic," I added, wondering if they knew about my talents. I wasn't clairvoyant, and I had no idea what psychometry was.

"Semantics." Althea looked down her nose at me. "Marjoram brainwashed you twins into fearing our community. Oralee knew better. Energetics is a term they made up. Rumor has it, you can see and use energy in various ways. That skill often occurs with clairvoyance, the centuries-old name for your talent. I had hoped your skill set included detecting the energy laid down on an object, which is psychometry."

If I argued with her, I'd reveal more of who and what I was. Not happening, so I chose not to reply.

Unfazed by my silence or glare, Althea turned to Quig. "Have you identified the remains from Rosemont's wall?"

He shrugged. "No." Then he rambled on about the difficulty in matching missing persons to old bones, ending with, "Unless we get dental confirmation, it may be impossible to make an exact determination."

"What about DNA?" Althea muttered. "Surely that remained?"

"Though the desiccated marrow scrapings weren't promising, I sent them to the lab anyway. The results aren't back yet. Someone on the council or someone known to them, is more likely to discover the identity by paranormal means."

Althea muttered something I didn't catch and then said, "Does the Acworth girl meet the criteria?"

Quig shrugged. "I can't rule her out."

"Lilah Acworth will declare it is her missing daughter," Herbert tossed into the ring.

"She likely murdered that kid," Kelsey said softly.

My head swam. Althea had assumed Rosemont's leadership role, which might be a motive to kill him. Althea exuded authority and confidence, though I wasn't sure what power white witches had beyond what she'd said. However, Lilah was cunning and vindictive, and if she thought Rosemont snuffed her kid, Lilah would exact retribution. I knew this from personal experience.

I suddenly realized the room had gone quiet while I mused. "Did I miss something?"

Quig touched my shoulder. "Reverend Gaudry asked if he could bless us as a couple."

"But I'm not..." I stopped to glance at Quig before facing the room. "We're not religious."

"It's okay with me," Quig said to me. "It will do no harm."

"Okay-y-y-y."

Gaudry stood over us, both his hands extended toward our heads. The others stood behind him, each one with a hand on his shoulder. "May you hold each other in the highest of light every day," he intoned. "May you navigate joyfully through the storms, rain, and puzzles of your united journey. May your cups overflow with faithfulness, loyalty, compassion, and friendship from this day forward."

Then everyone stepped closer, circling us with hands outstretched like Gaudry's. A waterfall of energy passed over us, and I greedily opened my barrier and soaked it in. I tingled from head to toe with good vibes.

Gaudry added, "Now you will be a shelter for each other and feel no stormy weather. Your combined energy will blot out the cold and foster new life. Companionship will replace loneliness as your lives are now joined forevermore. May your marriage be joyous and fruitful."

When he finished, tears streamed down my face. I dashed them away. "Thank you. That was lovely."

"It was," Althea said, her face glowing with shared energy. "And now we must leave so that Tabby and the baby can rest."

Once they left, I looked at Quig. "How did she know? I was shielded until the blessing."

"White witches see whatever they want to see."

Chapter Twenty-Two

The next day, I worked alone in the shop, while Gerard went to a morning medical appointment. I was polishing my gold-plated candlesticks and suddenly wondered if a candlestick could be the murder weapon. A man wouldn't have had any place to hide something of that size, but if a woman carried a tote bag, she could conceal a candlestick and conk Rosemont on the head when no one was looking.

From what Herbert had said earlier, at the key moment for Rosemont, everyone was standing in a circle with Willim's back to the stone steps. It would've been nearly impossible for one of them to hit him with a candlestick or similar object from behind without others seeing him or her. *Nearly* impossible because there was the chance of invisibility or a hypnotic command for the others present.

Wait a minute. Herbert had golden candlesticks in his home. I thought harder. So did Fawn Meldrim. I'd never been inside the homes of the other suspects, but it seemed a reasonable pursuit, after I visited Rosemont's place again.

The shop door chimed melodically to signal a new arrival, and in walked our statue artist, Norman Googe. He carried a box of his latest mini-sculptures.

"Good morning. What have you brought me today?" I glanced at the box with keen interest. Norman gave off an edgy energy and that shifted my curiosity into high gear.

"This series is a slight departure from my mythological leanings. I really got into making these angels, and I have four to show you."

Angels. Hmm. Would they be cutesy cherubs, Madonna-like figures, or dark angels? What did it matter? All of them would fit the quirky vibe of the shop. "I can't wait to see them."

Norman set the box on the checkout counter and unsealed the cardboard flaps. His brow pebbled with sweat. He was fumbling the process, and his aura flared.

"What's wrong? Everything you make is wonderful," I assured him.

"I'm anxious because I don't know if I made the right kind of angels. See, I got this message one night as I was sleeping. 'Sculpt angels' it said, over and over again. I ignored it the first couple of nights, but then I realized the universe was telling me something." He ran his fingers through his hair. "I'd never thought about making angels before. I love my fantasy line, but the nudge to change my focus wouldn't go away. I started researching angels and realized there was a whole pantheon of styles. I really loved cherubs, for some reason, but they don't blend into my catalogue. Too cutesy. So I hit upon the idea of them looking more like satyrs. Not furry except for the wild hair. Muscular bodies and normal ears. No tail, of course. And then long narrow wings, similar to angel wing seashells. In a nod to cherubs, there's a cloth draped over the manly bits, but the facial expression is more…sensual."

"They sound intriguing."

Harley leapt off his shelf and nosed around the box. Then he rubbed up against it and lay next to it on the counter. Looks like Norman's new stuff made a favorable impression on the cat.

Norman gave a nervous grin. "I was hoping you'd say that."

He pulled out the first one, which was in the same grey-brown finish as his other works. I couldn't look away from the statuette. Though it stood barely a foot high, the entire piece commanded my attention. The musculature was amazing. Compelling. The face riveted me, and those half-lidded eyes were so sexy. The tangled stone hair called to me, and I stroked it. The wings were perfect, not too much to overshadow the piece, but enough to show it was an angel. Best of all, he'd imbued this piece with desire.

"Say something," he begged. "I'm going a little crazy here.'

"Norman, this is so original and wonderful. Pardon the pun, these angels will fly out of the shop."

"You really like the angel?"

"I love it. Everyone who sees this will want it too."

"All four have the same face, but they are in different poses. I hope that's okay."

"I'm sure it will be fine. Let me see the collection."

Without further ado, he pulled the remaining sculptures out. Every one of them charmed me. The sitting one, the one with a lyre, the one with a full-sized bow and arrow, the very first one with his come-hither invitation.

"Oh, Norman. These are amazing. They aren't as much of a departure as you think. Your customers will recognize your style and buy them on the spot. New customers will be enchanted. I'm doubling your prices on these. They are your best work to date."

"Wow. Really?"

"Yes. And don't hate me for asking, how soon can you make more?"

"Depends. I don't force my art. When I follow my muse, the good energy comes. Sounds dopey I know, but you must do the same thing with your candles and soaps. They are all different and yet there's a bedrock sameness to them that brings people back to the store. People wouldn't see my work if not for your shop."

"I don't believe that, but I am happy for you. I hope you will remember The Book and Candle shop when you become rich and famous."

"That's not my goal. A steady income and fewer side jobs would be nice, but art isn't steady. Some days I don't feel like it, and it's best not to work when things are off."

I knew that feeling. "Same here. When I'm not in harmony with my materials and space, the work falls short. That can make for hectic experiences if I have time-sensitive orders. Like you, I don't keep a large inventory of stock. I work at it every chance I get, but on my own time."

"We are kindred spirits."

"Yes. Creatives are that way." We logged his items into the system and barcoded them, and Norman left, looking happier than I'd seen him in a while.

As the day went on, I realized that I felt like myself. I couldn't have felt such joy about Norman's angels if Quig had turned me into an automaton. No question in my mind that I was in control of my thoughts. As to whether my love for Quig was truly mine, it felt real. I couldn't imagine life without him. If that was an illusion, I didn't want to hear otherwise.

I marshalled my arguments in case Sage was against Quig.

I can feel you down there churning your thoughts and thinking of me, Sage purred in my head. *What's up?*

What's up is that I've had time to reflect on what Quig did, and I accept it. My feelings for him are real, even if he accelerated or enhanced them in the beginning.

Tabs. What happened to your outrage and shock?

He nearly died. In bonding with me, his fate is intertwined with mine. If I die, he dies. If I leave him, he dies.

What? How is that possible?

I believe him, Sis. What's more, I love him. Despite his abilities, despite his deliberate omission of key facts about his talent. If I focus on his methods, I am a house divided.

What brought this on?

Angels.

Now I know you've lost it, but I'm happy for you. I've got a plant delivery this morning, and I was just heading out. Good to know you have forgiven him. It may take me longer, but I will come around.

~*~

Later that day, Peaches McVeigh dropped by the shop and introduced herself. "We haven't met before, but I need to talk to you if you can spare the time. I'd like to speak with you privately."

"Please join me in the stillroom so we are less likely to be interrupted."

Peaches nodded and followed me. "I want to state my case. I know you're helping the council and looking for the person who took out Willim. I didn't kill him. Not that I didn't want to at times. But he's helped me throughout my career. I owe him, and I'd never stab him in the back professionally or literally bash in his head. He's always been there for me. It's weird that he's gone."

She'd said a lot in those few words. Her aura looked truthful, but what if her singing ability gave her the power to moderate her outside energy? I reeled under the prospect of Peaches being here for misdirection. Hurriedly, I found something to say. "I've dealt with loss myself, and it's never easy."

Her aura twigged a weird way. Did I trust it, or was she continuing to misdirect me? I was trying to figure that out when she spoke again.

"There's loss and there's loss. Willim and I had a love-hate relationship."

My focus sharpened instantly. "Oh?"

"He was instrumental in my training."

My brain somersaulted over that. Her training? Were they the same kind of talents? Or was it something awful like Jeanine went through? Paranormal bootcamp in the woods with male domination over all aspects of her life and body.

"A mentor? Like Larry Rau's brother?" I asked.

Her cheek twitched, but she nodded. "Since you weren't raised in the community, you probably are unaware of training. The Paranormal Council has hidebound traditions designed to keep each generation in line. It's similar to a military approach in that the mentor breaks you down and then builds you up in the community's way. We learn what's expected of us as paranormals, what we are allowed to do with our talents, and what we cannot do."

Sounded like Peaches had also suffered from the instruction. "Jeanine Acworth told me about Johnny Rau's brutal and aggressive mentorship. She wasn't allowed to deny him anything."

"Like I said. They break each of us down and then remold everyone into a cooperating, rule-following person. Willim didn't skimp on any training, but he never forced himself on me. Later I realized he used his hypnosis talent to make me think I wanted him. Though the hypnosis faded with time, I still had that groupie feeling around him for the rest of his life."

I didn't believe her, so I asked pointblank. "Did you feel coerced? That's what Jeanine hated."

"No, I didn't. I was a willing participant. When the training was over, he dropped me as a steady lover. My heart ached because he didn't care for me that way. I had genuine feelings for him."

Was that a tear in her eye? "Wasn't he married at the time?"

"Yes, but he was the head mentor, and he cherry-picked me for himself. I've thought about it in the intervening years. He got me gigs around town, kept my career on track, so it evened out in the end."

It dawned on me that her situation of being manipulated was akin to mine. "I understand, and it sounds like that training leaves people with a lot to grapple with regarding self-worth and identity."

"Sounds like you're familiar with the process."

"I wasn't trained like you were. Sage and I never had to do that. But I've had people try to take advantage of me over the years."

She looked me over. "We forgot about you girls. Neither Marjoram nor Oralee ever talked about you two, and you didn't take part in any of the community's programs or outreach. And yet somehow, here you are, a fine candlemaker and a woman who's making a name for herself as an amateur sleuth. Plus, you snagged the most eligible bachelor in town. How'd you manage that? Half the women in this town threw themselves at him, me included, and he never blinked."

"Quig and I have been friends since childhood. Our romantic feelings evolved. But that's neither here nor there. What did you want to speak to me about?"

"I needed to tell you in person that I didn't kill Willim. He watched out for me throughout my career."

"At what cost?" I asked.

"None for me, except for the initial disappointment. He considered the favors as repayment for the fringe benefits during training. He was a powerful man. Revered and feared by all. He had dirt on everyone in this city."

Interesting, and I wanted to know more. "Do you two develop a personal relationship later?"

"We both have needs and enjoy each other's company. We were never exclusive. Willim can't settle down with one chick. Never could. Roving eye and all that. We enjoyed our freedoms but often met on Sunday nights."

"Did you ever have a child?"

"No. Why do you ask?"

"Curiosity." Willim wasn't the same kind of talent as Quig. But he had a strong persuasion talent for sure, or he wouldn't have been the Senior Magistrate.

"Be careful," Peaches said. "You know what they say about curiosity."

"Hope that's not true because I love cats." I decided to switch topics. "Speaking of cats, Herbert's cat has been missing for several days."

"Violet?"

"You know Violet?"

Peaches shook with laughter. "Everyone knows Violet. She was quite the siren in her day. Just like Willim. Two peas in a pod."

I didn't understand. "Were they, ah, a couple?"

"Siblings. Rumor has it he poisoned her, and she found a way to survive, but you didn't hear it from me. Look, in all seriousness, I hope you find who murdered Willim. He deserves justice. The community knows you are good at finding answers."

"I don't have answers. Worse, I keep adding suspects to the pool." I eyed Peaches. "Even now I wonder about your motive for coming here. Is this the truth, or are you trying to snow me?"

"Honey, if I wanted to do that, I would've been singing the whole time I was here."

My eyebrows rose. "You're an actual Siren?"

"That talent runs in my family. I coulda gone big time too, but why do that when I enjoyed being close to him? I am set for life, thanks to the windfall I got from Willim."

I did a double take. "You were in his will?"

"Nope. He set up a trust fund for me long ago. The only provision was that I come when he called. I fulfilled my end of the bargain. That honeypot is mine now. I can sing in public or privately without worrying about money ever again."

Peaches kept talking for a while longer, but I wasn't listening. That trust gave her a strong motive. And she was no longer beholden to Willim Rosemont.

Chapter Twenty-Three

Sage showed up at closing time with two pints of ice cream, one for me and one for her. I took the surprise in stride, locked the door, and enjoyed my butter pecan. I tried to eat it slow, but it was so good.

"Thanks for the treat." I scraped the carton wistfully wishing for more even though I was full.

Sage grinned. "I have an ulterior motive."

"You want to hang out with me?"

"That too. Mostly I'm, making sure my niece appreciates the finer things of life. You're probably living on a diet of broccoli, peas, and carrots. She needs to know about the good stuff, like ice cream."

"I am trying to eat reasonably. But if you and Quig have your way, I'll gain fifty pounds with this kid. I want her to be a healthy size, but she has to exit my body through a small opening."

"You're barely two months along. From what I've learned, when it's delivery time you're ready to push her out, no matter the size of the opening. Speaking of my niece-to-be, you made a gyno appointment yet?"

"As I said earlier, I need to coordinate the date with Quig."

"You're doing this backwards. Set up the appointment. He will make time."

"Seems presumptive your way, but I'll figure it out."

She shrugged. "Your body. Your kid."

"Thanks. I appreciate nudges in the right direction,

but I am still enjoying this special news."

"You've told his parents?'

That stopped me cold. "I have no idea."

"That's not good."

"In all fairness, there has been high drama these last few days. I am still getting used to the news. Plus, his mom visited me when he was nearly comatose. It did not go well."

Sage's spoon clattered on the wooden floor. "You have to fix that relationship."

"How?"

"Quig will know how to win her favor."

"Maybe. He says he and his dad humor her when she feels strongly about something. I don't see Quig humoring me on anything. We go toe to toe over some things, like my sleuthing."

"Let's hope being a dad will mellow him out."

"Or maybe it will have that effect on me."

"Get real. You've always leaned toward the tightly wired side of things, like me." Sage cleared her throat. "About the other...did he really almost die?"

"He was comatose. I couldn't rouse him. I shared as much energy as I could spare. Then his breathing sounded better and so did his heartbeat. The whole thing wore me out and I fell asleep. When I woke up, he seemed all there."

"It is risky for him to tie his life to your physical presence. Why would anyone do that?"

I didn't like her judgy tone so I spoke harshly. "Bonding with your mate is a serious matter for his kind."

"Sounds like a heavy responsibility for you. Are you okay with this?"

"It makes me think twice every time I get in a car or cross the street. I must take good care of myself. We have to work out every argument without parting ways." I stared at my hands. "Sometimes I need alone time to figure stuff out. Now, he will always be with me."

"Nah. He's got a full-time job and so do you. Y'all will tag-team raising the young'un. Whoever isn't 'on' will be sleeping, or at least that's my impression from watching young mom podcasters. Quig will be guaranteed backup."

"That sounds better than what I envisioned."

Sage grinned. "That's me, a super problem solver."

Both of us laughed out loud at that.

When we quieted, Sage asked, "If he hasn't clipped your wings, when are we going snooping again?"

"I'm waiting for Captain Haynes or the Paranormal Council to give me access to Rosemont's home, office, and vehicle."

"We're not rule-bound. My lock pick still works."

"No way will Quig agree to a fake sister night right now, and I can't drag him along and endanger his career with unlawful activity."

"What if I ask Larry to distract Quig tonight? Maybe set up a guy's poker night or something. We could go without either of them knowing what we were doing."

"That might work."

"It will work."

But before we started setting that up, Quig called. "Tabby, I'll be late tonight. Bad accident on the interstate with multiple fatalities. A victim is politically connected, and there's pressure to get that autopsy done."

"It's okay," I said, grinning at Sage at this sudden change of plans. "My sister wants to spend quality time with me anyway. I won't be alone."

"Good. Don't wait dinner on me either. I'll eat when I get in."

"If that's what you want."

"It's the best I can do, especially since I've been out on medical leave. What I *want* is to be home with you, to be touching you, romancing you, and celebrating life in every way."

My cheeks heated. "There's always tomorrow."

"I want your todays and tomorrows, but I'll settle for late tonight. Love ya."

The call ended, and I turned to Sage. "That worked out surprisingly well. While I'm sorry there is a bad accident and Quig must work late, now we can go sleuthing without any fussing."

"Great." Sage pumped a fist. "Did you notice a security system at Rosemont's? I didn't pay attention when we were there before."

"Me either, so I hope there wasn't one. We have no cameras outside our shop or apartments. Maybe Rosemont didn't want a video record of comings and goings at his home either."

Sage shrugged. "Let's avoid the police showing up. It's hard to get the right mindset when others intrude."

"I know. We are a good team."

"The best."

"Let's get changed and slip away. Meet you in the parking garage in thirty. You won't have any trouble getting a night out from Larry?"

"Already covered. See you soon."

Sage dashed up the interior stairs to her place. I

locked the shop and ascended the outside stairs to my apartment.

I grimaced at the thought of donning black clothes, our usual sleuthing attire. August wasn't the month to wear black, but the sun would be down, or nearly so. My black pants wouldn't button, so I used a safety pin and made a mental note to buy maternity pants in black.

Sleuthing brightened my spirits, and I was excited Sage could go with me. Just like old times.

I stuffed my work clothes in the hamper. Then I grabbed sodas, a cooler with ice packs, and crackers for emergency rations.

With a quick glance at my watch, I realized I'd frittered the time away. Quickly, I made a last glance around the apartment, leaving a light on by the sofa.

My feet scurried down the stairs at the same time as Sage descended. "How's that for synchronicity?" I asked.

"Perfect." Sage gave me a high five, and we strolled to the garage.

Took you long enough.

Sage grinned at me, so I assumed the cat had included her in the telepathy. I sent my reply to both of them.

Violet? I asked, noting the white cat sitting on my car's hood. *What are you doing here?*

Waiting for you.

Chapter Twenty-Four

We got underway at once. I glanced over at the white pile of fluff on my sister's lap and said, "I've been looking for you."

Violet sniffed. *Wasn't ready to be found. Until now.*

"That makes me curious. What's different?" Sage asked.

It's time.

It was good that Violet was sharing her telepathy with both of us. Still my curiosity meter had pegged to the max. "Time for what? I asked aloud.

Time for my brother Willim to get his comeuppance, that's what.

Sage and I exchanged a look of surprise. I suddenly remembered Peaches telling me that Violet and Willim were siblings. For Sage's benefit, I asked the cat, "Willim is your brother?"

Was. He was my brother. Try and keep up. Now I'm here as a cat, and he's long gone.

"You didn't get along with him?" I asked.

With that tyrant? Hell, no.

"Tell us how you really feel, Violet," Sage said.

Bite your tongue, gal. Not a subject I treat lightly. My brother was a real piece of work. The world revolved around him or else. We're going to his house, right?

"How'd you know?" Sage asked as I parked a few doors down from Rosemont's place. Violet leapt out as soon as Sage opened her door. The cat didn't answer my sister's question.

"Or else what?" I asked as my feet met the sidewalk.

Violet hmphed. *Or else he made sure that person never crossed him again.*

"Why are you coming with us?" I asked.

Revenge. I know his hiding places. Let's enter through the side door. He's gone for good now. Better yet, he didn't have time to conjure up my second-chance trick to turn into a cat or other animal..

All sorts of possibilities entered my mind. "Did you see him die?"

Nope. I would've loved to witness that. I'd pee on his grave, but he's still stuck at the morgue. In a metal drawer, no less. My how the tide has turned.

Sage smothered a laugh as she picked the side door lock. "Got it. No love lost between you two."

The three of us walked inside Willim's home. The air felt still and close. The scent ranged between old folks home and bowling shoes. In the darkness and using my regular vision, I didn't see the energy trails I'd keyed in on before. Did I want to see them again? Shouldn't I look for something else?

Last time I'd been so focused on sleuthing I hadn't noticed the duck decoys. They were everywhere.

Aware that Violet had paused when I'd stopped to let my eyes adjust to the low light, I asked, "Who killed Willim?"

Could be anyone, from the people he manipulated every day to the council, or even his conquests. Man thought he was a regular Casanova.

"I, ah, know he had an arrangement with Peaches McVeigh."

That poor gal never had a shot at independence. Willim treated her like a second wife. Anytime he wanted an itch scratched, he crooked a finger, and she did his bidding.

From her caustic tone, I surmised Violet hated her brother. The depth of her feeling made me wonder who he'd hurt in Violet's life, or if he'd hurt his sister. "She said he gave her a trust fund."

Violet pawed at the air. *Bound to be a catch in the fine print. That man gave nothing away. He wouldn't help me when I needed it, and his wife had to take him to court to get child support to raise his kids.*

My head reared back a smidge at the burst of color. I must've unconsciously switched into my other vision. Violet's aura flared fiercely when she spoke of her brother. I'd learned that "tell" for a human aura indicated a lie. Would a human "tell" translate to the feline world? Or did thoughts of her brother make her emotional?

"What do you want to show us?" Sage asked.

Thought you might enjoy seeing his, uh, used lingerie collection. He sealed each item in a plastic bag so he could savor it later.

"Gross," I said softly as we trailed her through the dark house. "No thanks. I'm interested in finding evidence. I do not need to smell or touch anyone's undies."

You need to see this. Violet nosed a bathroom drawer. *Check the underside for a manila envelope. Undies galore. He bedded the movers and shakers of Savannah and random patients as well. Anyone who caught his eye.*

Sage reached with gloved hands, grabbed the hidden packet, and opened the hasp. She shined her flashlight inside before reaching in. Inside were scads of lacy-barely-there panties. Each individual bag bore a date and two initials. One was child-sized and cotton.

While I dealt with shock and fury, Sage's hand trembled. "If he wasn't dead, I'd kill him." She shoved the packet back in place. "I did not need to see that."

I retreated against the cooler-feeling plaster wall. "Me either. Rosemont was a child molester and who knows what else." I turned to the white cat. "Who was the woman in the wall?"

I have no idea. Didn't know about her until the news came through the barking dog grapevine a few days ago. That's when I began making my way to your place.

The timing of Violet's visit bothered me, but I didn't want to look askance at our good fortune. She clearly had an agenda—to tarnish her brother's memory. He deserved it, but I wished I knew what motivated Violet. "How'd you know where I lived?"

I just did.

That was as clear as mud. Doubts flooded my mind. I realized how much I didn't know about Violet-the-person's life.

"What else do you have to show us?" Sage asked.

There's more but forget it. I'm getting a hinky vibe from both of you. I'm outta here. Look for yourself. Too many bad vibes here. Makes me feel sleazy. Those panties alone will ruin Willim's reputation, so my job here is done. Let me out, Tabby.

"Sure, and, uh, thank you for your help." I padded to the side door and opened it. Violet darted away as soon as the door swung wide.

I closed the door and returned to the bedroom where Sage was now going through a cabinet in his walk-in closet. "Find anything else?"

"Nothing that seems important, mostly I found ducks and more ducks. It's annoying how tidy his drawers are. This man has no clutter, no mess, no disorder anywhere, no unmatched socks. There are no stains or rips on his clothes. How did he live like that?"

"Must've been a perfectionist in everyday life to counter for his messed-up thinking and lecherous behavior."

We aimed our flashlights low and scoured the place from top to bottom, leaving the office where we'd discovered the hidden skeleton until last. I wanted to do another walk-through of that room, but by then my stomach protested with rumbles.

The room started to spin. Oh, dear. I needed to sit down or get the heck out of here. I chose the latter. "Got to go, Sage. Getting hangry."

"Don't want that. Food is our new priority. You must keep your strength up."

"Yes. I definitely need shrimp salad."

"An odd choice. Can you eat that while pregnant?"

"Dang. Don't put the kibosh on my food craving. But to humor you, I'll look it up in the car."

"And where are you going to get that specific dish at this time of night?"

"Carey Hilliard's. We'll get takeout for Quig too. He loves their chicken tenders."

Sage took the wheel. I dove into the ginger ale and crackers that I'd brought with us, which improved my stomach's disposition at once. My phone's search engine found approval for pregnant mothers eating fully cooked shrimp, so I was a happy camper.

We were seated at once in the restaurant, had food before us in very short order, even had the to-go stuff for Quig all neatly packaged. I felt human after I'd eaten. The afternoon ice cream treat had been good at the time, but that didn't stick with me for long. I'd be more conscious of empty calories in the future.

"I noticed something about Rosemont's house," I

said, as my thoughts returned to the case. "Though everything was tidy, his space didn't feel like a home. It felt sterile, as if there was no love between those walls."

"I didn't pick up on that. Now that I think about it, there were no pictures of his kids on display, no artwork or school projects on the refrigerator. Weird."

Her observation triggered one of my own. "There were no family photos in that entire house and no photo albums. I assume he wasn't close to his kids. Maybe he was too busy with his, uh, personal pursuits."

"Don't remind me of those lacy souvenirs." Sage shivered. "Though Violet hinted of more evidence against Willim, we didn't find anything else. Should we be worried we missed something important?"

I hadn't considered that. Once I became ravenously hungry, that was all I could think about. "I'm not worried. Violet's aura flashed as if she were lying while she was there, and given her vindictive nature, she might have teased us about there being more. Then again, I don't know how to interpret cat auras, so I could be totally off-base."

"I hear you. Violet was being Violet. What can we do about that bathroom stash?"

"I've been thinking about that. On the one hand, I don't want anything to do with it. On the other hand, I want this man's 'good' reputation to go up in flames."

"Me too. We need to get word to the cops but in an anonymous way."

"Or, I could mention to Nowry that I dreamed something else needs to be found in that house."

"Yeah. Say it is near water to narrow the search

window for them."

I scowled at her. "It's tempting. But that is an oft-used line of everyone who's ever claimed to be psychic. I'm more thinking along the lines of my intuition is telling me the item is hidden, possibly under something."

"That could work, as long as you leave me out of it," Sage said. "Moving on to another subject, I've been checking out your baby bump all evening, and the baby's aura is less murky now."

"What do you see?" I gripped my napkin tightly. "Can you see hands and feet?"

"Not yet. Just getting a better feel for the overall size. Of your womb. Your babe-on-board may be big for her age, or... my earlier call was right. You could be carrying twins."

"Twins! Like us," I exclaimed, excited by the possibility. Twin sisters who would grow up with each other, like we did. Then reality burst the euphoric bubble. Caring for two infants would be challenging, and I had no idea how to care for one baby. Still, it wasn't definite. Barely even a guess. I needed to schedule an appointment with my obstetrician. The sonogram would sort out if it was one or two kids.

"Auntie O will be thrilled," Sage said.

"Not a word of this twin possibility to anyone, not until I have a sonagram."

Chapter Twenty-Five

The next morning, Quig and I were slow to rise. Neither of us had work today, and for a change, morning sickness wasn't bothering me. Our cuddling sent Harley trotting into the other room. We enjoyed each other's company, and as we drowsed again, a fearful pounding began on our door.

"Go away," I whispered, unready to face the world.

Quig bolted upright. "Uh-oh!"

"What-oh?"

He turned back to me with a sheepish expression. "Forgot to tell you. I spilled the beans last night. My parents know you're expecting. That we're expecting. Mom called as I was driving home last night and they said they would drop by today,. I should've told you as soon as we awakened, but I got distracted. I'm sorry to spring this on you all of a sudden."

"I'm not dressed for visitors." I snagged his gaze. "Your mom will come swooping in and tell me I'm doing everything wrong. Again."

To his credit, his lips twitched. "Here's a tip for getting along with Mom. Nod politely when she gets spun up. Dad quietly beams his happiness when she fusses over either of us. It's her way of showing she cares. But don't worry about our lack of readiness. They are super thrilled about getting their grandson."

As he rose, I reflected on the gender of my child or children, as the case may be. I'd married into a family that only had male children, while my family only had females. If I carried twins, would they be stunned if both were daughters?

Quig pulled on a pair of shorts and a fresh T-shirt. "I'll handle this, but please get dressed and come out as soon as you can."

He whistled his way to the door. I sat up slowly, taking stock of the situation. I'd known this day would come, and I was happy to share the good news with my in-laws, but I'd wasn't ready. Maybe I'd never be ready for Milly's high drama.

Excited voices sounded in the living room, and I snapped out of my fugue. Holy moly! I wasn't wearing anything. What if Quig's mom breezed in here to congratulate me? Yikes. I sprang into high gear, scooping up the dirty clothes from the floor and stuffing them in the bathroom hamper.

Cue the fastest shower on record, then me dressing and tugging wet hair into a low ponytail.

I walked out to a grand feast arranged on my kitchen counter and no sign of my cat. Harley likely scooted over to Sage's when the open door presented itself. Lucky cat.

"We brought brunch!" Milly crowed. "Congratulations on your pregnancy, Tabby. This is such wonderful news. Look at how you're glowing."

While some of my glow was from pregnancy, most came from hustling out here. "Good morning. And thanks. We're delighted with the news." I sidestepped to get plates out, but Quig headed me off and guided me to the table.

In a very light whisper as he nuzzled my neck, he said, "Easy, love. Sit with me and let Mom fuss over us. She's dreamed of this moment for a long time."

Milly nodded approvingly as Quig sat beside me. "Look at you two. Such a beautiful couple, and so perfectly in love."

Heat singed my cheeks. It hadn't been that many days since Quig nearly died from our temporary separation. The same number of days as my last fateful encounter with his mother. Quig tugged on my hand under the table. "It's okay," he murmured in a voice only for me.

Henry helped Milly carry heaping plates to us, served everyone with juice and tall glasses of water. I gazed longingly at the empty coffee pot and gathered that beverage was not on Milly's approved food list for a mom-to-be. *Stop being negative*, I told myself. *Find the positive in this situation.*

"Thanks for this wonderful breakfast. It looks amazing." I beamed at my in-laws with sincere appreciation. "I hope I can do it justice. My appetite has been spotty lately."

"We understand, dear," Milly cooed.

From that point on, the visit became easier. It wasn't until after we'd finished the pecan waffles, veggie omelets, and fresh peaches that Milly pounced.

"We'd love to do a makeover of your extra room for our grandson, with your approval, of course," Milly said. "I have ideas about color schemes and crib styles. With the limited space here, it makes sense to get a crib that can turn into a youth bed, don't you think?"

Fresh panic surged in my veins. Milly, Henry, and Quig would likely be delighted with a forest green room with all manner of bugs painted on the walls. Not what I wanted. "Thank you for your offer, but we have plenty of time. I'm not ready to jump into preparations for something that's happening next year."

Milly opened her mouth to protest, I was sure, when Henry said, "We talked about this on the way over, dear, and the kids will do things in their own time, same as we did. Quig and Tabby know we will help them in any way at any time. Most importantly, they know we are thrilled about the upcoming addition to our family."

Darn if my mother-in-law didn't gulp like a fish out of water for a few seconds, but with everyone's eyes on her, a miraculous change came over Milly. She beamed contentment. "Yes, that's right. Your wonderful news is a blessing to us all."

I gazed over at Quig, noticing for the first time that he'd left his glasses in our room and that his father wasn't wearing his glasses either. My dander rose as I realized both men were doing something to control her. While I was appreciative of not being in the hot seat, this continued mood modification of Milly wasn't okay with me. I sent her pulses of good energy. Mom energy. And she turned my way, beaming at me.

"Oh, I feel so invigorated all of a sudden, as if I've awakened from a good night's sleep. Would anyone else like to walk down to the fountain with me?"

"I would," Quig said, arching an eyebrow at me.

I thought about joining them for a nanosecond. It was already roasting hot outside and getting overheated could likely trigger a round of morning sickness. "I pass. Still getting my sea legs under me, as it were."

Everyone nodded, so I'd made the right choice. Milly tossed a comment over her shoulder, "Make sure she sits while you do the dishes, Henry."

"Yes, love."

Once they left, Henry invited me to help. Together we cleared the table and put away the food. He turned on the dishwasher, and then he ushered me over to the sofa and sat with me. "Quig explained that you *know* and that you also know my wife doesn't know."

Oh, snap. Where was he going with this? "Yes, that's true."

"It's our nature and sincere pleasure to promote happiness in the family."

There was so much I wanted to say, so much I wanted to rail against the manipulation they used on his wife. Poor Milly. Would she ever have a thought of her own? I couldn't hold it in. "I understand it's an automatic part of who you are, something you can't turn off. I won't interfere, though I don't agree it's necessary."

Henry nodded. "Good. Good."

Let it go and focus on the positive. I'll be hanging out with Quig's family for the rest of my life. "I am very grateful you stepped in for Quig at work. He was worried he wouldn't have a job after missing work. I had no idea what would happen to him if I wasn't with him. Your family talent has a serious downside."

"Yes. As does your own." His gaze narrowed. "I understand Marjoram died trying to ease a friend's discomfort, right?"

I found it hard to breathe. "Yes."

"One might have thought she'd take you girls into her confidence, or that she'd love you two more than her friend. That she'd want to see her grandchildren grow up."

My gut clenched. If she'd lived, Mom would have

been thrilled about my pregnancy. Would she have been a Grandmother, Gram, Nana, or the like? Tears misted my eyes. "I believe Mom thought she had everything under control, that her sudden death surprised her. She had no reason to believe that her last night was any different recharge-wise than the others."

"And you are as talented and kind and generous as she was."

Oh. He thought I would repeat Mom's mistake. "Actually, I'm not that generous. Self-preservation runs strong in my veins."

"Mine too." He grinned. "We're not so different, you see. And now that you're a Quigsly, you understand we deal with Milly's mood swings and bossing us around by smoothing out her distress when she gets emotional. While my son and I chafe at redirecting her, we need the family to stay strong, to be there for each other. My Milly has the organizational strengths to run corporations or even the country, but she is my heart. Always has been. Since I am nearly twice Quig's age, I would not have lasted as long as Quig did if she left me now, for any reason."

His reference to my leaving Quig made me feel as if I were in a tank with piranhas. Henry didn't forgive me for hurting Quig. That wasn't in his DNA. But if I messed with Milly, and thus with him, I would bring down this house of cards. Quig would be deadlocked in the middle.

That would be an epic disaster.

But two could play at the guilting game. "You are an excellent poker player. Here I was thinking you and Quig were exploiting Milly. And yet, you humor her natural tendencies to foster her sense of self-worth, despite the fact that you're constantly encouraging her to remain at your side."

Henry got a vacant look before settling on a determined gaze at me. Instinctively, I shielded myself from his attempt to bring me in line. "That won't work on me. Put your glasses on, bud."

He glanced away as if to gather himself. "So I see. Well, nothing ventured, nothing gained. I needed to see if my boy was so addled with love that he hadn't tried to take you in hand."

"He doesn't need to rewire my brain every minute of the day to make me stay. I want to stay. To always be with him, despite what he did to me. And I will grudgingly tolerate what you do to your wife because of the consequences to all involved. But I don't agree with it. I never will."

"You know, for a *candlemaker*, you're surprisingly tough."

His faint praise settled over me like a scratchy blanket. I was tough. Mom's strategy of isolating us and then throwing us in the deep end of life had forged my character with steely strength and determination. It'd taught us twins the "Us vs Them" mentality from the get-go, taught us that there's no place like home.

"Yeah, I am."

Henry beamed. "My son chose well."

~*~

Sage called later that afternoon. Quig had gone to the gym, and I'd been to the grocery store and was now folding laundry on our bed.

"All four Norman Googe angels sold today," Sage began. "That's a record, isn't it? We only had them in stock for less than a week."

"I knew they were good. Maybe I should have tripled the price."

"You could double it again, and they'd still fly out of here. Norman's passion shines through his craftsmanship."

I sank down on the mattress. "I'm delighted. I hope we don't lose him."

"Norman knows what's good for him. He hangs on every word you say."

"Did you tell him yet?"

"I will. Just wanted to let you know first. How hard can I pressure him for more?"

"Don't. I'll call him. Jack up the prices on his other stock on hand." It was on the tip of my tongue to tell her about brunch this morning, but I dismissed the urge.

As a Quigsly, I had divided loyalties. I could not confide anything else to my twin sister that could destroy Quig or his parents if it got out. The baby and I would be buffeted by the winds of change and heartbreak. Not a future I wanted. Sage already knew Quig's secret. She did not need to know more along that line.

"We're doing this," Sage said. "After our first cluelessness and struggle with the shop, we are making a profit. We have repeat local customers. We tap into the tourist trade. Our vendors are loyal."

The wonder in her voice had me shucking the remorse of keeping Quigsly knowledge from her. "Got a feeling it only works if we both stay involved. That will get tricky as life pulls us in different directions."

"Ha! I'm not going anywhere," Sage said, a smile in her voice.

"Me either."

"Did you call the detective about you know what?"

Her hedging around the subject made me smile. "Not yet, but I will."

"Okay. There's something else I learned today. Are you sitting down?"

There was an odd squeak to her voice that ramped up my curiosity. "Just so happens I am. What's the news?"

"Larry says two candidates are under consideration for *leadership* roles. You're never going to believe who they are."

She was talking about the Paranormal Council. Dread rushed in. "It's not us, is it?"

"No. Not that. But close."

"You're killing me."

"Our guys. Quig has the added bonus of his career's high visibility, like Rosemont. Larry's family has a long history of service."

I knew my guy. He would refuse. "Quig won't like this."

"Larry is over the moon about it."

Again, that weird crack in her voice, like static. My breath stilled. "And?"

"And, I'm not."

~*~

What with one thing and another, I didn't make those calls until the next day. I phoned sculptor Norman Googe first. "Great news! Your angels sold."

"Already? I can't believe it. I was worried about the higher price."

"You shouldn't be," I soothed. "We've raised the prices on your remaining merchandise. You are on your way, Norman. I couldn't be happier for you."

"Wow. I can barely take it in." He paused. "Or the paycheck I'll get this month."

"Yes, it will be substantial. Which brings me to a burning question. How soon until you have more angels?"

"Ooh. I don't know. I haven't started anything yet because despite how much you loved the angels, I wasn't sure if others would feel the same way."

Some artists needed handholding. Norman fell into that group. "Trust in it. The angels should be your focus now. That is, until you get fired up about what you want to make next."

"I'm happy to make more angels, but I worry about getting stuck in one lane. I want the freedom to make what I want."

"You'll have it, soon. Right now I highly recommend that you focus on your angels because they have something extra that the other perfectly fine sculptures don't. An intangible quality that resonates deep inside art lovers. It's the purity of your work. Get in that good head space and have at it."

"I'll make more, but I can't promise a certain number. Those other ones poured out of me so fast. Don't know if that will happen again."

"You can do it. Then bring your finished angels to me. I will sell them."

"Thanks."

Call concluded, I felt very good about showcasing more Norman Googe angels. I was glad for Norman's success and that he'd accessed a deeper level of his creativity. It felt great to help him and to help the shop.

I felt less excited about the needed call to Detective

Nowry about Rosemont's undie stash. Would Nowry sense I wasn't telling all of the truth? I could come right out and tell him of our excursion and what we found, but that would complicate matters. Best to tell him a slice of the truth and have his people find the hidden packet.

So resolved, I made the call.

"Nowry."

"I woke up thinking about Willim Rosemont's house," I said. "My intuition insists there is something secret that needs to be found. Something hidden."

"What is it?" he asked flatly.

"I believe the item is in an out-of-the-way place." Ha! That was the truth.

"Tabby, we can't go in there and tear down all the walls."

"I'm not suggesting that. Please, take a hard look inside the house again. I keep sensing the word 'under,' and I believe it's important."

"I'm not ripping up floors either," Nowry groused. "At this point in my career, every day extra that I work means my pension is growing."

"Look. If you don't want my insight, ignore it. I'm letting you know I strongly believe something important is hidden there."

"Will you help us search?"

"Not today. It's my day in the shop."

"Can't you take off? It would speed things up if you came and found whatever is hidden."

"You might as well know, I am pregnant. I've missed several workdays already this week with morning sickness, and I can't keep asking my staff to cover for me."

"You're puking?"

I chuckled inwardly at the revulsion in his words. "Yes."

"Never mind. My team will comb through the place from top to bottom."

~*~

Captain Haynes called me that evening before Quig came home. "How'd you know?"

"I had a nagging feeling about that place," I said with an air of calm confidence. "Did you find anything?"

"We did. The found item had 'under' in its name, and it was taped under a drawer."

"Now you've got me curious. What did you find?"

"You really don't know?"

I crossed my fingers. "My mind is a blank slate."

"It will stay that way for a while as we investigate this new evidence."

He hung up on me.

Not that I minded. I disliked skirting the truth to the police, but it was the best way to get this evidence out there and for me to stay in the shadows. That evidence was their problem now.

Chapter Twenty-Six

Several days later, Quig received two complimentary tickets to the Dinner Club via a courier service. The mystery tickets listed Peaches McVeigh as the entertainment. Quig waved the tickets at me. "Free dinner and a show tomorrow night. Sounds like fun. You interested?"

My cynical side raised its head. Nothing in life was completely free, and I didn't want to owe someone a favor if strings were attached. "Who sent them?"

"Doesn't say. The return address is the club. I'm not a member of the Dinner Club, though I have been a guest there on occasion."

"Seems suspicious that the sender is anonymous."

"Not really. I get freebies in the mail from time to time. Often from charities seeking donations or wanting me to speak at an upcoming event."

Aha! I knew it. "So you'll owe someone a favor later?"

"I don't keep score that way, but I also don't accept all the invites. Look, it's no big deal to me either way. If you want to go, we'll attend. If not, we pass."

That was more than fair. Perhaps I was unjustly suspicious. How could I turn this around so I wasn't a killjoy? "Peaches is a suspect in the Rosemont case," I began slowly. "It could be an opportunity to speak privately with her. I've never been to any dinner club before, and it does sound like something we'd enjoy. If we're under no obligation for the gifted tickets, I'd like to go. Is that okay with you?"

"As long as it's safe for you and the baby."

"I agree. If the music is too loud, I won't last long. And I'm pleased for the opportunity to perhaps develop a new lead on the case. I'm frustrated over not having a clear direction yet."

"The case isn't even on my mind. The tickets say coat and tie dress code, and it's a tech-free place. Everyone has to leave their phones at the door or in their vehicles. It's on Bull Street, a few blocks from here. We could probably walk."

Hmm. I'd be wearing fancy heels. "I'd rather we drive. It's still hot in the evening, and the humidity is off the charts. I'd rather look nice when I arrive at a fancy place."

"Of course. There's a designated lot so parking nearby isn't an issue."

"Good. It's all settled then."

~*~

The next evening, we entered the restaurant's softly glowing lobby, and I was charmed and impressed. This place had a definite sense of "you have arrived." Chamber music played softly through a speaker. I marveled at a stunning life-sized carved wooden dolphin under a corner spotlight.

Dark wood paneling lined the walls. Two leather-covered club chairs faced a fireplace with an impressive rouge and white marble arched façade and an artfully curved white marble mantle. Inside the fireplace were large baskets of artfully displayed magnolia leaves. Original art hung around the room, and a stately Oriental carpet covered most of the hardwood floor.

Quig handed our tickets to the elegantly dressed host.

"One moment, Dr. Quigsly. And welcome back to the Dinner Club."

My throat tightened. I felt like a fraud. This place wasn't in my social strata.

Quig noticed my tension and nuzzled my ear. "What's wrong?"

"This place." I whispered to him. "Everything looks and smells expensive. What if I mess up the etiquette stuff?"

"You'll do fine, I promise." He patted my shoulder and then held my hand. "You look lovely tonight, Mrs. Quigsly."

My jitters eased. "You cleaned up pretty nice yourself."

The host returned with menus. "Right this way. Since it's your wife's first time here, I'll take the long way around so she can see how we've restored this historic building."

Our feet made no sound in the plushily carpeted halls. We passed areas that looked like living rooms and libraries of the rich and famous. Lots of dark wood everywhere, accentuated with classical marble busts on column-shaped pedestals. Oil paintings in a classic old-world style adorned the walls. Vases of freshly cut flowers perfumed every room and hallway.

Wide-eyed by the splendor I saw, I gasped when I stumbled into weird energy. A shift to my other vision revealed the host's aura looked fine, as did Quig's. My gaze drifted to the walls and carpet. There. Those dark energy trails on the floor. Much like the ones at Rosemont's place.

My hackles rose.

"You're tense again," Quig noted when we reached our destination, a well-appointed room with intimate dining areas and a raised stage loaded with musical instruments.

I lowered my voice to a confidential level. "The energy here is troubled. My intuition is on high alert. I feel on edge, as if I shouldn't relax. As if I'm unwelcome."

"You are very much welcome here. We're invited guests. However, I trust your intuition. You sense anything stronger than unease, we'll walk. Personally, I'm hoping for a relaxing evening."

"You and me both."

We were seated at a table for four, stage-front but slightly offset. "Wow. Prime seating," I said. "How'd we get so lucky?"

"Must be living right," he quipped as he settled in beside me.

A server approached in black pants and a pleated white shirt. He memorized our drink orders and left. We took our time scanning the menu.

Unlike a restaurant with many selections, the club offered three dinner options. The entrees included filet mignon, broiled grouper, or saffron risotto with mushrooms. I had no interest in the red meat, and I dithered between the fish or the rice dish.

"Tabby!"

I glanced up at my sister's voice. Quig and I rose to greet them. We sisters hugged, and the guys shook hands.

"Surprise!" Sage said as she sat across from me.

"It *is* a surprise to see you here," I said.

"Larry received two tickets yesterday afternoon, and we decided to come. I'm looking forward to the food and the music. Can't remember the last time I did something like this."

"Me either." I said conversationally, though I knew precisely the last time I did something like this. Never. Coming to a private club for dinner and a show wasn't in my budget. I hoped the luxury didn't go to my head.

Once Sage and Larry gave their drink orders, I took another surreptitious glance around the room and noted a few familiar faces. Althea Morgan sat with Reverend Clark Gaudy and Kelsey Flowers — what were they doing here? I gave them a polite nod of acknowledgement and realized after another scan of the room that, except for Herbert R Ellis, the entire Paranormal Council was present.

That accounted for the edgy vibe. Council members were powerful talents. Get enough people like us in a room, and the paranormal energy revved up. Perhaps that also accounted for my initial misgivings.

I glanced at the rest of the tables. Detective Nowry and an unknown to me woman were seated across the room. And, of all people, Lilah Acworth and her dapper date were two tables away. Could this night get any stranger?

The murmur of conversation in the room increased until dinner arrived on a cart, plated in the three offerings. Sage and I selected grouper, our guys went with filet mignon. Everything was mouthwateringly delicious.

Liquor flowed freely throughout the room, except for me and my husband. No booze of any kind for me while pregnant. And Quig was always on call for his job so he stuck with coffee.

Band members dressed in black sauntered out to check the electronics and lighting. Then they picked up their instruments. An air of excitement swirled through the room. Everyone seemed eager for the entertainment to begin.

The room dimmed, and a sweeping spotlight illuminated every table, even ours. The murmur of conversation halted when the circle of light settled on a doorway.

Peaches strolled onto the stage in a translucent ball gown, her beautiful hair styled in a frothy updo. She launched into a sultry number. Sitting so close to the stage, I could literally feel the music vibrating inside me. Her silky voice soothed my tension. I tapped my feet to the beat and settled back into my chair.

"Is the sound too loud?" Quig asked.

"It's just right. Peaches is an amazing vocalist. I feel so content and relaxed."

"Me too."

During the next song, I noticed Peaches singing to Larry and to Quig. Jealousy jolted through me, and out of caution I shielded Quig, then bumped the barrier out to include our entire table. I wasn't sure why the singer directed her attention our way, but I wasn't taking any chances with my guy, my sister, or her boyfriend.

And especially not with my baby.

The next song frazzled my nerves. Something felt off-kilter, and the music no longer sounded so perfect. It jangled my nerves. Peaches intensified her singing.

You picking up on this? I asked Sage telepathically.

Yeah. This woman is downright weird. Her eyes are

hypnotic and so is her voice. Or so I thought. Now she sounds pitchy.

I don't trust her or anyone here. This was too bizarre. Then I remembered something. *Crap. I'd forgotten Peaches told me what she was. A Siren talent.*

Sage paused a long moment. *Historically, sirens lure men to their death. She can't have Larry. He's mine.*

She's not getting Quig either. And, her music is affecting men and women alike. I shielded all four of us once I felt the energy shift.

That explains the marked difference in her singing. You're blocking her talent. Bet that is messing with her head.

I don't care. I no longer feel good about being here. Should we leave?

No way. Let's see where this is heading.

Peaches gave up singing to anyone else and blatantly stood near our table. She put more and more effort into singing, screaming the lyrics while the drums pounded and the guitars wailed.

What fresh hell was this?

I increased my energy shield every time she amped up her power.

The barrier held, but I didn't know how long I could keep burning this much energy. Wouldn't be long before I needed to start draining people in the room to protect us.

Points in my brain related to the case suddenly connected.

Peaches' mesmerizing ability might have helped or caused Rosemont's death. Did she enthrall someone the night he was murdered? Or maybe not a single person, maybe she spelled everyone at the Stone Steps of Death that night. Her vocal power definitely filled this room and thus caused concern.

One thing became crystal clear. Except for those at our shielded table, everyone else appeared out of it, even Detective Nowry looked dazed.

Low vibrational notes threaded through the angry music. A repeated blast of three discordant notes sounded during an instrumental riff. It lulled me into false complacency until I realized that this tactic was a new sound wave barrage on my barrier. I shook off the sudden lethargy and strengthened our protection.

Lights strobed, adding an unworldly sense to the wild scene. Reverend Clark stood with arms upraised and shouted alleluias. Detective Nowry swept the woman he was with into his arms and began kissing her clothes off. Althea Morgan gyrated wildly in the aisle between the tables. Kelsey Flowers leapt onto the stage to join the band, grabbing a spare guitar and rubbing her body suggestively against the bass guitarist as she played. The beat intensified.

Like jungle drums.

The way my pulse heated in response to the frequency and soundwaves worried me. This was turning into a den of questionable behavior. It felt ritualistic. I felt violated. This wasn't fun or enjoyable, and I was done with playing nice.

I turned to Quig. "I want to go home."

"What?" he asked. "Can't hear you over the music."

Larry seemed similarly afflicted.

The bad vibes were seeping through my energy shield, a little at a time. The vibrations were off-putting on so many levels that I couldn't shield each person individually. I could barely shield us as a group.

I sent Sage another twin-link message. *This is messed up. I'm worried about the baby. I'm leaving. Now.*

Right behind you. This vibe is awful. I've got a splitting headache.

Never thought I'd hear my free-spirited sister complain about music. Stay close to me when we leave so that my barrier covers us.

Tabby, this isn't music, Sage insisted. *They are using sound to compel people to act out.*

That made sense and was an even better reason to get the heck out of here. I rose and tugged on Quig's hand. He got the message and stood. Sage did the same with Larry. We hurried over to the entry doors, only they wouldn't budge.

It appeared they were secured from the outside.

My spirits sank.

We were locked in here with senses-drugging music, and people acting out of character. This wasn't the calm and relaxing evening I'd hoped for. This was hellish and dangerous.

Why were the doors bolted?

What was going on?

Now what? I sent to Sage.

You're the genius. Figure it out before we succumb.

Did you bring your lock picks? I asked my twin telepathically.

No pockets in this gown, and I didn't bring a purse. Sage frowned. *I thought there'd be slow dancing.*

I expected a romantic evening too. But this is wrong on every level. The other guests seem under the music's spell. Will they turn on us en masse? Are we safe?

Detective Nowry shambled our way, and I drew him under my protection.

"This has all the hallmarks of an orgy," Nowry groused. "If the Captain hadn't asked me to keep an eye on you tonight, I'd be over there kissing that stranger again and taking her dress off. When you folks moved to the door, I remembered my assignment and followed you. Glad I did."

"How'd you break free of the music?" I asked.

He shook his head. "You won't believe me."

"Try me."

"My wife spoke in my head. She said to stop being foolish and walk over here to the people I trust. So that's what I did."

"Good man." I leaned close to his ear. "It's as if everyone but us drank the same doped-up fruit punch, like a bizarre initiation ritual."

The music transitioned to another melody. The demonic feeling wasn't as intense, but the crowd inched toward us. Peaches switched from her lower range and gradually the room throbbed with the power of her top register. People halted at my energy shield with their arms spread wide. I felt a huge power drain as they tried to destroy my barrier.

With my reserves bottoming out, I grabbed energy without mercy from anyone who touched the circle. No way was I letting these spelled minions harm people I cared about.

Time stretched and folded on itself.

The music pulsed into something off-key, and the lights strobed faster. How long could I hold out against this multi-tiered threat?

As long as needed. After all, there was a huge energy reservoir in this room.

I showed no mercy about draining my attackers.

They started this fight.

They locked us in here.

Any consequences incurred were on them.

When I cried out in frustration, Sage, Quig, and Larry placed their hands on my shoulders willing their energy into me. I was approaching the point where I might actually kill council members because of the power I'd drained from them.

Not good for my longevity.

Because I couldn't spare my energy for the next idea, I silently mouthed to Larry, "Make us invisible."

"On it," he replied.

At first his efforts made no difference, but then the attackers stopped, as if they had powered down.

Spooky.

This whole darn evening freaked me out.

Did I dare believe it was over?

Then in the next moment, those outside my protective circle renewed their attack, and a jungle beat song hammered at us.

"Save your energy, Larry," I said.

Sweat slicked my entire body as I fielded their attack. Either our side or theirs would win, and it darn well wouldn't be them. I was mightily invested in saving us, so they would lose.

Our backs were against a wall, literally, and there was no escaping this situation. Though I feared for our lives, I couldn't do anything but try to protect us.

Until the door suddenly opened, and we spilled out into the hallway.

Quig cradled my body so my landing was soft.

I blinked in confusion, struggling to make sense of what happened as I scrambled to my feet.

My hand went to my belly, and the baby felt fine. Thank goodness.

Auntie O and Frankie, both wearing ear protection,

shoved us behind them into the carpeted corridor and then slammed and bolted the door. "Sorry we're late, dear ones," Auntie O said. "I didn't hear about this until a few minutes ago. Everyone all right?"

"We are now," Sage said.

Chapter Twenty-Seven

"Auntie O! You saved us!" I said.

"Thanks," Quig said. "Let's talk later. The sooner we leave here, the better."

He took my hand, and we made a mad dash through deserted halls with everyone fast on our heels. Then we stumbled outside into the humid evening air. Though no one followed us, I needed to get far away from this awful place at once.

As soon as I stopped trembling.

My entire body shook so much my teeth chattered. I inhaled several deep breaths to center myself.

"They attacked us. Why?" I asked Auntie O.

"Not here," she says. "Let's get the detective home first. We will reconvene at Sage's place where we can talk privately."

"Okay."

Frankie took the detective's car keys and drove Nowry home with Auntie O following them in their Lexus.

The rest of us piled into Quig's Hummer for the short ride to Bristol Street.

"That was intense," Sage said once we were moving toward home.

Larry fumed silently.

Quig focused on driving.

Were the men weirded out or purposefully not speaking? Their silence bothered me. Between the shivers, the sweaty clothes, and my flagging energy, I was out of sorts, and I wanted answers.

"I don't know about the rest of you," I said slowly, "but that's my first and last time going to dinner and a show. The food was not as good as Auntie O's cooking, and the entertainment nearly killed us."

"You're right," Sage said. "I'm never doing that again."

Quig gave a slight head nod.

Larry glowered at me.

What's going on with the guys? I asked my sister on our twin-link. *Did Auntie spell the men so they couldn't talk?*

Not sure, Sage replied *but their silence is very odd. Let me try something.*

"Larry, do I have spinach in my teeth?" Sage asked.

I pulled down the sun visor and watched Larry in the mirror. He glanced away from Sage.

Holy Cow. She must've spelled them, Sage said in my head. *What the hell happened in there?*

Peaches attacked us, I said wearily. *That much is obvious. We've never done anything to her. I don't get it. And I'm so tired. I could fall asleep right this second.*

Stay awake. You know what you must do, Sage replied. *Gather energy while you can. No telling what else this creepy night has in store for us. I'll keep watch over you since I didn't burn as much energy.*

Good idea. Since we weren't far from home, I plunged into the task, sipping a little energy here and a little there from people on the sidewalk. Though it bothered me to steal energy from people anytime, I didn't take enough that anyone would notice.

Consequently, I was nowhere near fully recharged when we reached the parking area for our place. But I felt alert and that was an improvement.

We hurried inside Sage's apartment without incident. When we locked the door behind us, I felt a wave of relief and, oddly, hunger. "You won't believe this, but I'm craving food."

"Of course you are," Sage said. "Eating for two is an ongoing challenge. I'll make hot tea. Will you set out the fresh cookies?"

"Okay." I nearly tripped over Harley, who'd stayed in the shop when I left and then made his way through the interior cat door of Sage's place. He wove around my legs. "Just a minute, kitty."

The cat sat in the middle of the floor, glaring intently at me. It wasn't the same feeling as conversing with Violet, Herbert's cat, but I sensed he didn't like that I'd put him off, even for a few seconds.

Sage helped herself to a handful of cookies straight from the tin container I held. "Yes. Cookies are exactly what we need," my sister said.

"We got lucky tonight," I told her. "No telling what might have happened if Auntie O hadn't saved the day. I couldn't hold them off much longer. What foul nest of evil was that?"

"It was a trap. That's for sure. We should have passed on those 'free' tickets."

"Sit down and rest, love," Quig said. "I can deal with the cookies."

He could talk now?

About time.

"I'm okay, thanks to leaving the Dinner Club," I said, taking a seat anyway. "But that attack was a near thing."

I caught Larry staring at me several times and then he would shake his head before glancing away. How strange.

A few minutes later, Auntie O arrived. "Where's Frankie?" I asked while Sage poured our aunt a cup of Earl Grey.

"He's fine, but he needed rest after all the excitement. His heart, you know? He went home."

"What was that?" Sage asked. "We were enjoying an evening out and then it turned freaky. I wasn't sure we'd make it out alive. It felt like we were caged with zombies."

"Why did the council attack us?" I asked around a mouthful of cookie.

Auntie O pointed at Larry standing by the window. "He knows."

Larry blushed crimson red. "They conducted a power test," he said. "It's a time-honored method to judge paranormal ability. Testing ensures that the strongest candidates are elected to leadership roles. But Quig and I were unable to take it. Tabby blocked us from the test."

"Why didn't you tell me?" I asked, not trusting him because he should've shared that information earlier, when it would have been helpful.

Quig joined me on the sofa, his arm circling my shoulder. "There was no point in putting us through that kind of stress, especially not my pregnant wife. I don't want a seat and neither does Tabby nor Sage. If you set this up, Larry, you're no friend of ours."

"The council set it up. I didn't know for sure until it happened." Larry sighed and faced us. "I didn't have the chance to show my strength." He turned to me. "I did not ask for your protection. I do not hide behind a woman's skirts or her wall of energy."

My dander rose with every word he spoke. "Whining doesn't become you, Larry. If you wanted out of my barrier and had the power to do so, you would have gone through it. Don't blame me for what you couldn't do."

Larry grabbed his heart in mock agony. "Ouch."

You're being mean to my guy, Sage said in my mind even though she went to stand by Larry.

I spoke the truth.

"Now, now, settle everyone," Auntie O said. "This needs to be a constructive conversation. Give me a minute to recharge with one of Sage's gingersnap cookies."

Sage glanced at Larry, then elbowed him in the side. "Say something. Right now."

Larry groaned at the jolt. "I'm sorry for lashing out at you, Tabby. I tried to go through your shield and couldn't. That bothered me. I thought I'd ace the test, you see. Because my brother did." He gazed at my twin and she nodded in approval.

Then they both looked expectantly at me.

Ugh. I needed to say something. "I accept your apology, and I believe this evening took all of us by surprise."

Larry nodded. "In more ways that I expected. I wanted to prove myself, but I wasn't strong enough. I am genuinely sorry for blaming you. A council member should lead, and I couldn't do that."

He stopped and hung his head. Sage patted his shoulder. "It's all right, Larry. You did nothing wrong."

"Looks like we are all trapped in the lanes our families mapped out for us. My mom and aunt instilled in us the need to hide from the council. When the councilors attacked us tonight, I shifted into defensive mode automatically. It seemed they meant to kill us. It didn't matter to me that they were council or not. They were my enemies."

"We don't know what would've happened," Sage said. "Because Auntie O rescued us. Our family sticks together. And I'm thrilled that none of us are angling for the council after that debacle."

"Speak for yourself. I still want a council seat," Larry said.

"Let's agree to disagree for now," Sage said.

Auntie O and I munched. Sage sighed dramatically and flounced onto the sofa. Larry settled beside her. Quig kept me anchored to his side, though Harley claimed my lap.

"Thanks for waiting for me to begin this discussion," Auntie O said. "I will speak frankly because it is past time for that. Tonight was indeed a power test, for the four of you, and Tabby passed with flying colors. She defended the ones she loves. In fact, it would be unnatural if she didn't."

Sage perked up. "What about me?"

"You have a big heart too, dear, but your affinity for plants and nature keeps you from striking out with your powers most of the time. However, your strong sense of justice can override your innate reserve at times. When you see a wrong, you react."

"I do?" Sage asked. "That isn't what I've done in the past. I've walked away from confrontations unless I was at risk."

"Larry is your true mate, Sage," Auntie O continued. "The wholeness you now feel coursing through your body is your blended energy. He literally completes you in a way you've never been complete before. Your energy is complete now. That's why you've felt so much better lately. He's returned to your life. If you are smart, you'll keep him."

Sage's eyes opened very wide, then she shuttered them for a long moment.

"What about the council members?" I asked. "Where they affected or faking it?"

"A bit of both. They released their inhibitions to enhance the power of Peaches' music. Though I was forbidden from interfering, I don't take orders well. In any event, I didn't take kindly to them sealing you in and pushing a pregnant woman to her limits. Now the council is upset with all of us for different reasons."

"Why wasn't Herbert there if this was a governing board matter?" I ask.

"Herbert is already at risk of losing his seat for not reproducing. Last month they told him that unless he procreated at once, he would be replaced. That would mean three openings on the Paranormal Council. Which is the reason the four of you were tested tonight."

I put two and two together. Sharmila allegedly had a stomach virus. Or did she? Morning sickness could manifest as a vomiting bug. "Sharmila's pregnant?"

Auntie O beamed. "Yes, though it is not widely known. Your children will grow up together, same as Herbert and Quig did. It's best for our community."

"What about me?" Sage asked. "Am I off the hook reproductively now that Tabby is carrying?"

"No. Each of you needs to have at least two children."

Acid churned in my stomach at the crossness of Auntie O's voice. All these years, we'd wanted to know about the paranormal community. Now that we had experienced it, I was underwhelmed. The leadership group was a bunch of powerful talents lording it over everyone else with the excuse of doing it for the "greater good."

Worse, I ached for my twin. I would've gone to Sage and hugged her, but Quig's arm tightened around my shoulder as if he knew my intention. I gazed at my sister. Her tomato-red face told the whole story.

But she wasn't protesting.

Was it possible she'd matured overnight? Tonight's revelations should have shocked her to her core—they certainly shocked me—and yet she appeared composed, as if she took bad news in stride every day. It felt too good to be true.

Auntie O sighed. "For better or worse, the council needs you both to bear children, and, sadly, if you don't manage the feat on your own, they will ensure it happens. Or, I should say, that was the way of past councils. It is absolutely necessary for the survival of our community, and especially of strong talents, like you two."

My aunt let that sink in before she leveled a sharp glance at Larry. "His chance at a seat is partially dependent on you carrying his child. He should've taken action last year, but he wouldn't move in on you while you were dating someone else. This is your chance, Larry. Don't mess it up."

"Yes, ma'am."

"I won't be talked about as if I weren't here!" Sage's aura flared with indignation. "Get out! All of you. Out of my house. Everyone but Tabby."

Ah. There was the volatile sister I knew and loved. Somehow, I knew she hadn't turned into a pushover, just because her energy was complete.

Auntie O made a Pied Piper wave to the guys. "Follow me gentlemen."

Larry went with her out the door to the stairs.

Quig didn't move. "Are you sure?"

I knew he wasn't asking Sage. "I am. My sister needs me."

The door closed softly, and we twins huddled together with our cats. Luna took a while to settle. Harley nestled in my arms contentedly and revved up his purr machine. The soothing vibrations traveled through all of us.

"I can't believe this," Sage said. "The council told Larry to impregnate me? Not happening. I need to be available in case you and Quig die together. I don't have the time or inclination to carry a baby, much less any idea how to parent a kid."

"Easy. We have just as much experience as Mom had, and she did all right. We're living proof. Besides, you and I are not the last Winslows standing. We are now the Winslow-Quigsly combined family. In addition to Auntie O and Frankie, we have Milly and Henry as backup parents. If Quig and I died, our kid, or our twins, will be parented by you and your guy, same as we'd do for you. What's the big deal, anyway, with hearing you must have kids? We know about the low paranormal birth rate and understand that unless the group keeps our numbers up, paranormals will go extinct in Savannah. Larry is crazy about you, and I'm certain you love him."

"I do, but we've never said the words to each other. What if his attraction is pretend, for the sake of getting that council seat?"

"Then I predict he will have exceedingly bad karma. But that's not the case. Larry has genuine feelings for you. He doesn't respond well to being pressured and, from what I've seen, he's deliberate in his choices. If he wanted that seat so bad, I'm sure there were other paranormal women he could've, um, procreated with over the last year or so."

Sage's eyes targeted mine like incoming missiles. "Over my dead body."

"You can't have it both ways, Sis. Which is it?" Though her attitude irked me, my role was to settle her. This was her being her, and me being me. "You want Larry and his council baggage? He certainly wants you and all that it entails. And before you protest, I mean that both of us twins are peculiar in our own ways."

"It's not that. I'd like us to take our time. To figure out cohabitation first. I loved Brindle, but it didn't work. He didn't reciprocate my feelings. His love came with contingency clauses. I couldn't bear it if Larry is faking his feelings."

I groaned inwardly. How did she not see the truth right in front of her? "You'd know, just as you knew when Brindle began making excuses."

"What I *know* is that I'd like to poke holes in all the people who dropped the reproductive ball in earlier generations. With my unpredictable mood swings and energy recharging issues, carrying a baby will be difficult. What if *my* choice is to never become pregnant? Will Larry leave me?"

Sage wanted self-determination, and who could blame her in this situation? I understood her and would always help her. Was something else causing her to hesitate? "Wait. Is this about Lilah Acworth's claim that Auntie O stayed away because one of us inherited her assassin abilities?"

Eyes glistening with tears, Sage nodded. "You're a good person, Tabby. Therefore, I've always known it was me. Even though I've never fired a gun, never thought about doing anyone in, other than generically flinging those words around when somebody crossed me. I mean, how could I go out and whack people and then come home to nurse a baby? Those activities aren't compatible, and I don't need religion to know that."

"I have the same issue. Not the energy recharge part, but what if I'm the assassin? Quig's family is so 'back to nature' that I'm sure they'd consider me a rogue if I became a council assassin. Not that they could or would get rid of me now. But still. They'd be so disappointed. However, let me be clear. I would kill anyone who harmed our family."

We exchanged a nod.

"So would I." Sage giggled, then slapped her hand over her mouth until she pulled herself together. "We're probably both assassins. I vote we don't tell anyone."

"Agreed. The council doesn't need to know anything else about us. Mom had the right of it by isolating us. And I'll be forever thankful that she saved us from having to go through 'training' at thirteen." I thought about that a while more. "Maybe she knew we'd kill anyone that tried to break us down, bootcamp-style. That would've been a terrible outcome too. Especially if a council member was our trainer."

"Maybe, but that doesn't explain everything." Sage tapped a hand on her leg. "I've got a problem with paranormal bootcamp training at any age. I don't want to be a part of a group that does that."

"I agree with you, but I don't see a way around it, except to get that training changed. Maybe without Rosemont, reason will reign and the new council will protect our young people. My kid or kids aren't doing the current training no matter what pressure I get about it."

"I'll back you up all the way. You're right to mention Rosemont. That package of undies in his bathroom really bothered me. I've got a feeling Willim Rosemont is the rotten egg in the middle of this reproductive disaster."

I believed her. "Peaches told me that he was her trainer. He must've trained others through time. Maybe he trained Mom and Auntie O."

"I would've drained that sucker dry in a heartbeat," Sage said. "My training would have been the shortest ever on record."

"He should have been too afraid to train either of us, given our lineage. Our energy talent honed into a weapon would make it easy for a coroner to conclude an untimely death was a legitimate heart attack."

"Roger that. No matter what, I'm in charge of my actions. Everyone else better take a powder and leave me the heck alone."

"Fat chance. The council has designs on every paranormal womb. Here's what I think. Assuming

Willim was still alive and running things, if there was a suspicious death like a heart attack among the Paranormal Council, he might have taken both of us out for good measure."

Sage smirked. "Lucky for us someone else got to him first."

Chapter Twenty-Eight

"You're good now?" I asked my sister.

"I am. Let's face our guys and see what happens. If Larry lost faith in me, it's best to know now."

Harley leapt from my arms as I stood. When I opened the door, Larry and Quig were sitting on the stoop. Auntie O must've gone home.

I gestured to them. "You can come in now."

"Let's go home," Quig said, catching my hand in his and kissing it. "After that, your wish is my command."

"Okay. Sounds good."

We weren't all the way down the steps when I heard Sage shouting at Larry. They'd figure it out, but in case they needed help, I sent them peace and light.

"You want to talk about it?" I asked Quig.

"Nope. Too much talking already tonight, and we're both worn out. If you want to have a conversation in the morning, that's fine with me."

With so much high drama this evening, I doubted I'd sleep a wink, but I did. We awakened when Quig's alarm sounded. He rose as if it was any other workday.

I reached for him. "No, you don't, buddy. You're staying here until I know your thoughts on the council, our baby, and last night."

"You know as much as I do," Quig said. "They didn't pressure me to reproduce, but my parents did. Our talent is the rarest, and with only one male child produced each lifetime, and not every male fertile through the generations, we've become an endangered

243

species. I didn't know about the test last night, and I don't aspire to a leadership role. I thought it was another innocent freebie. You and our family are my focus now. I will be fully present for my son, not running off every night doing things for the 'good' of the paranormal community. Larry can have the job."

"But he must become a father first, according to Auntie O." I made fists in the bed covers. "That's going to be tough. Sage doesn't want to be a mom."

"The Rau family always has council seats. Larry will find a way. We had a heart-to-heart on the steps last night. He would never subject Sage to the group's foul schemes. However, he made no bones about it. She is the one for him. The harsh reality is if he doesn't do what's expected, council will take him out."

They'd kill Larry?

My blood boiled. "That's ridiculous. It sounds like medieval times with this plotting about which bloodlines survive. I am content to be a mom. Sage is a free spirit. Even if she somehow pops out a kid, she isn't maternal. For her kid to survive, we will have to raise it."

"Or it could be fostered by another family with abilities."

"That's not acceptable to Sage. Or to me."

"The decline of reproduction has cost our community dearly. Now, to lose a respected leader like Rosemont is a huge hit. We must ensure the new leaders will be strong in power, authority, intellect, and fertility."

Rosemont was slimy and egocentric as far as I was concerned. "Was Rosemont's murder a power play by another faction?"

Quig paused a moment. "I believe his passing brought everything into a clear focus."

"Don't be putting any halos on that guy. Sage and I believe Rosemont was a rotten apple, which explains why there was a skeleton in his wall. He hurt those he trained. Someone he hurt badly had a perfect motive for killing him."

My husband rubbed the back of his neck. "You have evidence to support that?"

"Yes and no. Sage and I went through Rosemont's place and found a hidden stash of used women's underwear. Not his size. It must be a collection from his conquests. Souvenirs, if you will."

"This is the first I've heard of that."

"Since Sage and I made a secret trip into his place, I notified the police of the materials by saying the information came to me in a dream. Cops found the envelope taped beneath a bathroom drawer, same as we did, and they will investigate."

His eyes widened. "Did you touch anything?"

"Yes, but only while wearing gloves."

"Why tell me after the fact? Puts me in a bad spot."

My emotions flared. "I did it because you have Rosemont on a pedestal. Women hated him. He wasn't the guy you think he was. He molested women and teens. He got what was coming to him."

Quig crossed his arms. "The legal system works on evidence."

"Those undies are evidence. DNA will identify the women and identify their assailant."

"Might help with some cold cases, but Rosemont is dead. He can't be charged now."

"His reputation will suffer. What if he's more than a

serial rapist? Maybe a serial killer. We don't know."

"No we don't."

He looked pensive and thankfully was no longer praising Rosemont. "Look, it's true the legal system runs on evidence, but the paranormal world works on power. Thanks to this conversation, I've revised my suspect list. Fawn Meldrim and Detective Sharmila Belfor aren't strong paras, so I'm taking them off the list." I waited for that to sink in. "But every council member is powerful."

Quig's expression darkened. "I'm undecided about the integrity of those who were with Rosemont that night, but you have the council members as your suspects."

"Yes."

"Good luck with that. Now may I rise, get dressed, and be the Medical Examiner?"

I grinned. "Absolutely."

I dressed, sat with him, and sipped herbal tea in my new "uniform" for summer, a lightweight dress in shades of turquoise and my favorite sneakers.

"What's happening today?" Quig asked. "Will you and Sage seek out council members to interview?"

"Good question. I was wondering where Althea lived."

"Check the online resource of Chatham tax dot org. Properties are listed there by property owner."

"Thanks. I didn't know that." I picked up my phone and clicked to the internet site. "How would I know if the council owned property?"

"That might be harder to trace. If they do, my guess is it would be listed under a partnership or a shell corporation."

"Hmm. Not finding anything at that site for Althea though online I see her Springfield home in Effingham County is listed on that county's tax site." What about Willim Rosemont, I wondered silently. Did he have more properties?

"Stay safe," Quig said, drawing me into his arms for a goodbye kiss before he left. "You are my world."

After Quig left, I turned all my focus to sleuth mode. While it was possible that the Council had acted together to take out Rosemont, my intuition believed this was a crime of passion. That one person was behind Rosemont's death.

Further, I had shown how much power I had last night. If I was right, and there was a rogue element on the board, then I was vulnerable now. No way I would let them come after me or my family. I must be proactive on solving this murder.

And I needed Auntie O and Sage to help me unmask this hidden killer. Going to work at the candle shop and sticking my head in the sand didn't pass muster. Gerard was on the schedule for today with me, so I called Eve to see if she could fill in. She had a conflict, so Frankie agreed to help out again.

Luckily, Auntie O and Sage cleared their schedules and came to my place for a strategy session.

I waved to the kettle of tea and the soda bottles on the counter. "Help yourself. I'm going with ginger ale and crackers."

Sage and Auntie O went with hot tea. Given I'd brewed the Earl Grey they both preferred, I was certain of that outcome. Maybe I'd get lucky with our analysis of the council members.

"I asked you here today to help me narrow

Rosemont's suspect pool. It's past time that I made
progress with this investigation. After last night, I had
an epiphany. Rosemont was the strongest council
member. It is unlikely he was taken out by someone
with less power. Since the most powerful people of the
community serve in leadership roles, they are my top
suspects. Council members are Herbert R. Ellis,
Reverend Clark Gaudry, Kelsey Flowers, and Althea
Morgan. Since Herbert is on the outs with the council
and in danger of losing his seat, I'm removing him
from the suspect list. Althea is a mother who got
promoted into a crappy job. Even though she's a witch,
she's dealt fairly with me. I don't think she did it. Do
you agree with removing Herbert and Althea?"

"Yes. Makes sense to me," Sage said.

Auntie O cleared her throat. "Herbert is a fine man
from a good family. I don't think he did it either.
Althea has taken on a lot of responsibility that she
didn't want. She's always seemed levelheaded and
calm in my presence. But I'm undecided on her."

I nodded then turned to my twin. "Sage?"

"Of these people, I only know Herbert. I don't trust
anyone but him."

"Okay, Herbert's out, Althea stays on the list. " That
leaves Clark and Kelsey, and Althea as suspects. I'll
give a brief run through of where I am. Afterward,
chime in if you have information. The Reverend Clark
Gaudry is about forty years old, an authentic faith
healer and a clairaudient, and that combination helps
him heal those who come to him."

Auntie O added, "I know more of his history. He
burst onto the Savannah scene with his 'act,' drawing
huge crowds. The Paranormal Council became

alarmed, tested him, found his power to be genuine, and added him to our ruling body. He serves as advisor and spiritual leader for the group. They keep him too busy to make headlines, and now he heals people without the publicity."

"They controlled him by getting him under their thumbs?" I asked.

Auntie O's lips quirked. "Something like that."

"Sage, you got anything to add?"

She took a moment before speaking. "I've never believed in faith healing and view that man much as I would a con artist. Clark looks sleazy to me. I don't like him, and I wouldn't trust him to carry a bag of groceries across the street."

I nodded, expecting nothing less from my twin. "That brings us to Kelsey Flowers. She's a year younger than Sage and I are. Kelsey is a Hospice worker and an empath. I got a good vibe from her when we spoke not long after Rosemont passed. Anyone know more about her?"

"Darling Kelsey came on board after her uncle, a former member, died in his sleep," Auntie O added. "Rumors flew once she became a council member, specifically that she'd killed her uncle. But those must have been sour grapes because she's helped many people since then. She's topped me off with energy after tough jobs. Could she have killed Rosemont? Sure. Would she? That's where I keep getting stuck."

"Kelsey sounds too good to be true, but I've been hanging out with my suspicious twin lately." I turned to my sister. "Sage?"

"Same response as I had for the reverend with one addition. Who's to say she doesn't have a dark side?

Kelsey took part in the test and thus is on my Naughty list."

"Aren't you a vault of insight today?" I asked.

"You asked my opinion."

"I did." I cleared my throat. "That brings us to Althea Morgan. She's Larry's aunt and a white witch. She's about five years younger than Rosemont. For her to be on the council and become the Interim Senior Magistrate, I assume she rose within the ranks of the community. With motherhood approaching for me, I trust she's a good person."

Auntie O's face clouded. "Althea was one of Rosemont's first trainees. Which accounts for her rise to power. He 'made' her so he trusted her to follow his lead implicitly. He kept her close, the same way he kept Peaches close to him." She paused for a moment, then her face flushed. "He would've kept me close if I'd agreed. I didn't."

"He wasn't afraid of you?" I asked.

"Not for a second. He always thought he was the most powerful person in the room. Thought he'd live forever, too."

"You could've taken him, right?" Sage asked.

"If it suited me. But I stayed away from him after training. He hurt me in ways I'm still realizing. So, yeah, while I could have killed him, I didn't. He used brutal tactics and psychological warfare to wear me down. In short, he was power hungry and an ass." She paused for a moment. "I have no proof, but I always believed he killed my husband."

My forehead wrinkled as my brows rose. "That son of a gun."

Sage growled. "Bastard."

"Further," Auntie O continued, "I also believe he killed your father. Adam Winslow disappeared without a trace. Marjoram was so upset by Adam's vanishing act, I searched everywhere for years. He was there one moment and gone the next."

"Why would Rosemont harm Dad?" I asked.

"Rosemont always had a thing for Marjoram. She never wanted anything to do with him. It didn't matter to him that she was happily married. He wanted her and when he didn't get her, he retaliated. He was big on retribution. I always thought he took out both men."

Sage's hands clenched into fists. "Did he train Mom?"

"No. Larry's uncle did."

"Ugh. Small world." My hand splayed across my belly. "All this talk of reproduction and killing is surreal. No wonder Mom hid us from the council and community. She protected us from Rosemont. He was a monster."

"If he wasn't dead already," Sage gritted, "I'd kill him right now."

"Me too," I added. "He hurt our family. And Auntie O suffered too much." I reached for her hand. "Nobody should hurt you, ever."

Auntie O gave it a squeeze. "Thanks, dear ones. You don't know what that means to me."

I glanced over at my twin. "Sage, anything to add about Althea?"

"I hate her too. Because she's council. She must be as rotten on the inside as her mentor was."

"Okay, so recapping, we have a faith healer, an empath, and a white witch on the suspect list. It goes against the grain that any of them would kill their boss, but I don't know much about white witches. Auntie O, would you share your impressions of them?"

"It won't help you decide who killed Rosemont. A white witch uses her talent for benevolent reasons. They have a special connection with nature and a policy of doing no harm. Also, white witches are clairsentient, which means they can read a person through body language or emotional cues."

I blinked. "So, Althea was Rosemont's profiler? She told him which people were trouble?"

My aunt's cheek twitched. "Yes."

"And now she's in line to be the top dog of the whole she-bang." I mulled this over. "Any chance he 'broke' her during that training? As in twisted her mind to something dark?"

"I don't know, but the point of training thirteen-year-olds is to shape their talent and force their obedience." Auntie O's shoulders slumped. "It is possible, but if Althea has an evil side, she hides it well. I've never heard anything bad about her."

"She must be the killer," Sage said, putting heat in her words. "She has the strongest motive, she was his trusted subordinate who had full access to him, and she waited for the perfect opportunity."

"Her aura never spiked or twitched oddly when she spoke to me. But I trust our opinions. If you think we should start with Althea, Sage, we will. She wasn't part of the group that night. Can she go invisible, Auntie O?"

"Again, I don't know. But multi-talents are rare among paranormals. It is unlikely that she can hide in plain sight."

"Does she have an invisibility cloak?" I asked.

"How do you know about those, Tabby?" Auntie O asked. "Not many exist, and they're closely guarded."

"Not as close as you think. A suspect in an earlier case used an invisibility cloak his girlfriend loaned him to sneak in and talk with me."

"Really?" Auntie O continued. "As far as I know the maker created three. Everyone believes that two of them were destroyed by the council. What are the odds she used the last cloak?"

"My air math is bad. But if it wasn't Althea who used it the night of Rosemont's death, someone did."

Sage beamed. "Let's confront her at her home."

"Her place is spelled and warded," Auntie O said. "You won't get in there. Speaking of which, great job on warding the shop and your apartments. You gals are really coming along."

"Not like we had a lot of choice," I said. "People were coming after us."

"Don't sell yourself short. You two learned critical problem-solving after Marjoram passed. You learned how to identify a problem and fix it. I'm very proud of both of you."

"Thanks," I said, "but it was a lesson hard-won. Why didn't y'all tell us this place was warded?"

"It was a very strong ward your mother made to keep the council unaware of your presence, fueled by her intentions. Sadly, it faded when Marjoram passed. I'd forgotten about it, until we had a parade of council members traipsing through here. Anyway, you will never forget to ward your homes now."

She was right, but I didn't like feeling that my mom and aunt had paid a higher price. Even so, that was a conversation for another day. "If we can't get into Althea's home, can we check out Clark and Kelsey's homes this morning? It would be good to drop them from the list for good."

"Yes," Sage said.

"I've been wondering if the council has a list of everyone's paranormal talents. Do you know, Auntie O?"

"My parents talked about them creating a list like that. Council had such a list when I was a teen, but it was 'destroyed' not long after. It became a double-edged sword, because it was a threat to every paranormal in Savannah."

"I don't see how," I said.

"Some unscrupulous paranormals decided to come after the Rau family. They got names and specific talents from that list. A list that only existed for a few years in the council's hands."

"Oh no! Which feeds into what my intuition had telling me all along. The council is dirty."

"I believe they masterminded taking out Larry's brother," Auntie O said.

"I see." And I did.

Though it seemed logical to have a list of powers, it was downright scary that it could be used as a hitman shopping list. Though Clark, Kelsey, and Althea all had the power to heal, only one of them was also a witch. Althea. We'd start with surveillance of her home.

~*~

Sage and I parked near Althea's two-story white farmhouse with a faded blue metal roof near Savannah. The front porch brimmed with pots upon pots of ferns, flowers, and herbs. Trees towered over the house and the shrubs on the sides of the house were nearly as tall as the porch roof.

As soon as the coast cleared, as in no one was coming or going on the adjacent road, we tried to slip onto her property, but we couldn't get more than a step without being shocked. "Dang. Auntie O was right. Her wards are strong. I truly thought we'd find a way in," I said.

Sage arched an eyebrow. "Really? The top dog on the Paranormal Council probably has a houseful of secrets. Too bad we're not on her A-list and allowed inside."

Though we watched her place with the intent of staying all day, after two hours we gave up in favor of the sandwich shop down the road. Would she know we'd been there?

That question wouldn't go away.

Chapter Twenty-Nine

Before Quig left for work the next day, he asked, "Will you and Sage keep staking out Althea's place?"

"Not much point. That property is heavily warded."

"Be safe."

"Will do," I managed after our goodbye kiss. Then I leaned against the kitchen counter and returned to that property tax assessor site with a new direction in mind. There were six Chatham County properties listed for Dr. Willim Rosemont. Wow. What was he doing with six places?

Something stirred my senses.

Oh. The door didn't close immediately behind Quig, though it was shut now.

That was odd. Even more odd was Harley suddenly streaking off through the bedroom door. Something was afoot.

I stilled, seeking answers to soothe my unease.

My senses told me I wasn't alone, that I was in danger. *Sage, I'm in trouble,* I sent her through our twin-link.

Where are you? I'm at my nursery property a few miles out of town, not at home, Sage replied by return thought.

Home. Darn it, she wasn't close enough to help. What could I do?

Suddenly, Althea Morgan loomed in front of me, and I couldn't look away from her odd eyes. Her pupils were dilated so much that her irises looked black. She tossed an invisibility cloak on my sofa. "Tabby Quigsly, you are causing me endless grief, and I can't tolerate that. I've worked too hard to reach the top."

Ohmigod. Althea *was* Rosemont's killer. I knew it in my bones.

And now she'd come for me.

Suddenly, my joints froze.

My brain too.

I tried sending a SOS to my aunt, who lived next door, but my telepathic message stalled. If I could yell, she'd hear me, but no sound emerged from my mouth. What? Why was this happening?

Was I having a stroke?

If so, my body would've collapsed. Instead, I stood frozen like a powered-down robot, unable to access my paranormal abilities, speak, or move. That left one conclusion.

Althea controlled me.

Fighting panic, I took stock. I could still breathe and think. Autonomic nervous system worked. But nothing else was available. I was trapped!

She'd locked my brain inside a frozen body. She must have superpowers to do that. Even if I managed to regain full function, how could I defeat such a powerful talent?

Despair threatened to dash away the flickers of hope.

Only, I couldn't give up.

Except for looking up or down or blinking, I couldn't move anything else. I was aware of what was happening and where I was, but I couldn't react.

Fear welled up in my body like a waterspout, churning my gut, disrupting my thoughts.

Got to do better.

Must rein in the panic.

Althea's aura flared dark and violent as she ripped the phone from my tight grip and threw it on the floor. "I left you alone for years, Tabby, but you are hunting me now, and I can't have that. You are a powerful wild card, nearly as strong as me, and I am within my right as our community leader to have you put down, like the rabid mongrel you are."

She jittered around the room. Sometimes she passed through my field of vision. Was she doing a bizarre victory dance? Boobytrapping my home? What would happen next? Would she kill me here in the apartment or elsewhere?

Not ready to die.

I had a whole life to live, a child to bear. Worse, if I died, Quig died. No way would I be responsible for orphaning my kid or kids. I'd beat Althea somehow.

My emotions shouted to strike at her now, barrage her with energy spears, and suck every drop of energy from her body. If only I could access my power, I would fight her with everything I had. But I had to bide my time. Tears welled in my eyes, hazing my vision.

Damn it.

Not now.

I needed to see. It was all I had. Again, I tried to send a telepathic message. *Sage, I am in trouble. Help!* But the message stalled like a blinking computer cursor on my mental screen, same as my earlier SOS to Auntie O. I broke into a cold sweat, my breathing and heart quickening. My hands tingled painfully like frostbite. I couldn't feel my feet at all.

How could I break free?

Should I bend light and go invisible?

No. Althea didn't know I had that talent. Besides, if she touched where she'd locked me in place, she'd know I hadn't gone anywhere.

Think, Tabby! If she lost her focus, my functionality might return. I had to watch for my chance. Then hit her with everything I had.

"You and I are taking a trip, girlie. Sadly, you will disappear." She snapped her fingers in front of my nose. "Follow me. We're leaving now."

My body obeyed her command. I tried to stick my feet to the floor, but no luck with that either. A protest welled in my throat, and there it lodged.

But I was alive.

As long as I was lived, I had a chance to escape.

Althea had captured me by stealth, neutralized my paranormal and physical attack, silenced my verbal protests, and now she controlled my movements.

It felt like I was marching to my death.

No, no, no, no.

Cloaked in invisibility, she walked ahead of me and mentally ordered me into her vehicle beside the dumpster. I sat there, mute and furious, while she placed a scratchy burlap sack over my head, and then the car began moving.

I counted three rights and four lefts before I lost track of the turns. Heck, she could be driving in circles around Savannah's historic squares for all I knew.

I'd been kidnapped.

Althea might be super powerful, but she wasn't working with a full deck. Her dilated pupils, flaring dark aura, and signs of anxiety meant she was wired to the max.

Would Quig go catatonic if I wasn't there when he came home tonight? I hoped not. After all, I hadn't left of my own accord or said the words to break the bond. I would never say them.

I needed Quig and Sage to rescue me.

How would Althea kill me?

Would she cosh my head or shoot me? Perhaps kill me with her talent? How many minutes of "me" did I have left?

My thoughts churned.

She patted my left knee. "Relax. You won't die today, Tabby. As a pregnant paranormal, you have high value. The rest of your life will be lived out in captivity. Once we get Quig's kid out of you, my son will impregnate you. After I have my biological grandchild, I'll auction off your womb. Several infertile couples in our community will pay a king's ransom for a child of your power."

Her words infuriated me.

The fate she described would be hell on earth. My womb wasn't for sale. I'd find a way out of this. I had to. Otherwise, I'd lose everything and everyone I loved.

She didn't allow me to protest.

Silently I fumed.

Finally, we turned onto a long gravel lane and then stopped. Althea's car door opened and then she removed my hood. "Walk through that door."

I stumbled into glaring sunshine, my clothes soaked with sweat. Quickly, I tried to find a landmark, but I'd never seen these worn-out industrial buildings before.

"Move." She gave me a paranormal shove.

My traitorous legs sped up to her forced pace.

"Good. Now go down the steps."

Inside the building, the sunlight faded quickly. The further I descended, the darker it became. This place smelled dank, as if it had been sealed for years.

Althea floated an orb of light in front of her, barely enough illumination for me to see the steps. After the landing, I went down a second flight of steps. The air increasingly smelled moist and moldy.

No way was breathing stagnant air good for me or my baby. Or babies. I quickly squelched that thought, fearing this woman could read my mind. If she knew I carried twins, she'd sell them, likely to different people to maximize her profits. I would fight that like a wildcat. At some point, she had to power down. My only choice was to wait for a chance to strike at her.

Before I even made out features in the dark area, Althea shoved me into a small cell with metal walls and jail bars facing the empty corridor. She ordered me to sit on the metal bunk. Then I heard the damning clang of the cell door, the clatter of metal keys. "This is your new home."

As soon as the white witch left with the orb of light hovering over her hand, darkness swallowed me. I tried to move. Not happening. I yelled for help. Only my lips didn't move. No sound emerged. Darn it. I tried sending my twin a message, *Can you hear me?* I asked.

Nothing.

Time passed slow as molasses, and still I couldn't move, speak, or use telepathy. I was imprisoned underground and literally under Althea's tight control.

Much as I wanted it to be otherwise, I had only bad options.

Chapter Thirty

When I'd counted candles in my head for several eternities, an actual light flared in the distance. From the simple pattern of the approaching steps, it sounded like one person headed this way. My neck and back were so stiff from sitting up. My bladder was so full I had pee chills. If I was stuck here for months or years, this jailer better be bringing me lunch.

The light stopped outside my bars. I couldn't rotate my head to see him or her. My visitor shook a paper bag. "Hey, wench, dinner is served," a man said.

At his voice, the command to sit on the bunk lifted. That likely meant I could talk. "Dinner? What happened to lunch?" I blinked at the raspiness of my voice. I turned my head to see a guy. Not just any guy. Peaches' drummer.

"Stay seated on the bunk while I'm here if you want food or water," Grey Roads commanded. Then he placed a small brown sack and a mini bottle of water on the floor inside the cell. "I'm keeping you on two meals a day, so you won't get too heavy to deliver that baby naturally."

"Get me out of here, Grey. I'm claustrophobic and need to use a bathroom."

"No bathroom here. Just that five-gallon bucket in the corner," he cackled. "If you want permission to use it now, I get to watch."

I mentally reeled at his Peeping Tom personality. "That's private."

"Girl, you don't get it. You have no privacy. You're mine. Mom said I could do anything I wanted with you, once we get a shock collar and senses-numbing chain fitted on you."

A collar?

They planned to treat me like an animal.

I shuddered. "No. I don't want any of this. Please let me go. Keeping me here is crazy."

"You're the one who will go crazy." He snickered. "No one is stronger than my mom. She's legendary in how she messes with people's heads. And bodies. You'll be begging me to take you in a few days, just for the privilege of having physical contact. And I'll touch every part of you, in every way. Forget about daylight and freedom, you're never seeing either again."

"My family will find me."

"Fat chance. Ain't nobody but me and Mom knows where you are. That cell has special metal in the walls. Good old Rosemont built it to hold council prisoners. He always thought he was the smartest one in the room, but my mom put the idea for the cell in his head. He used this hellhole in recent years for his training. Nobody but him and mom knew the location of this place then. Now, he's dead, and she ain't coming to take care of you. That's my sole job now. You better treat me nice if you want to eat."

I hung my head. "I want to go home. Please, I need sunlight and good nutrition for the baby to thrive. We'll die in here without that."

"You'll die in here anyway. The only way you're leaving this hole is in a body bag." He and the light moved away, once again leaving me in total darkness.

My spirits sank. Suddenly, I felt a freedom I hadn't

had before. Thank goodness. In the dark, I found the pee bucket and squatted over it.

Chills racked my body as I let loose.

Oh. Oh! Nothing had ever felt so good.

When I finished I shook a bit because there was no tissue. How could I survive these primitive conditions?

My knees trembled, and I wanted to curl into a fetal position on the concrete floor. But I didn't. They hadn't won yet. With one hand on the wall, I paced around the cell to the bars, then walked very slowly along the bars until I found the paper sack with my shoes. I snagged the bag and water bottle, then followed the wall back to the metal bunk.

I ate half the peanut butter and grape jelly sandwich before I wondered if it was drugged. Even though I was ravenous, I stopped eating. What about the water? Was it tainted with a drug? Maybe. But I would get too dehydrated if I didn't drink.

Damn it.

This wasn't right.

But according to Grey, this place was isolated. No one would hear me if I screamed. Thus, I decided there was no reason to drug me. Maybe I was rationalizing, but at this point I didn't care. I downed the rest of the food and drank all the water. And wished I had more of both.

How could I get word to my family and escape?

I tried sending a telepathic message to my twin. Like before, it sat there in my head. I used every curse word I could think of. This couldn't be happening to me. Darn Rosemont for creating this underground prisoner stash.

Wait.

Was this one of the six places I'd found for him in the property records listings?

No way I could check from here. Maybe Quig or Sage would check Rosemont's listings and find me. Or maybe they'd find my phone and see what I'd been researching. I clung to that faint hope. I couldn't give in to despair. Not if I wanted to thrive and deliver a healthy baby or babies.

Tears spilled down my cheeks.

How could I manage labor and delivery alone? Though that seemed less awful than Althea and her psychopathic son assisting.

I had to escape before then.

~*~

I dozed a bit, walked some cell laps, and used the bucket again. Wished I had more water. Wished I had clean clothes. Wished I was free to do as I pleased. Finally, my energy burst subsided, and I lay on the hard bunk.

Reality sucked.

I didn't know where I was.

Nobody that cared knew my location. I couldn't contact them. Couldn't summon anyone.

The walls blocked paranormal energy, or so Grey had said. Now that I could move around, what if I stuck an arm through the bars? Then it wouldn't be in the metal cell. Could I send a message through my fingertips?

Nothing to lose.

I tried it.

Couldn't tell if it worked.

Eventually, I lay down by the bars, one arm extending through the narrow opening and used that hand as a focal point to send a SOS signal. I kept refreshing the message, keeping it going for all I was worth. Somebody would notice the beacon and come. I had to believe in that. I couldn't, no I wouldn't, live the rest of my life as a prisoner.

Time passed.

I tried singing, but my heart wasn't in it, and the effort made me thirstier.

What did I have on me that could double as a weapon? My hair tie. Laces from my sneakers. Not much help there. Despair settled around me like a blanket of sandspurs.

I had to think positive.

Had to believe I'd be rescued.

The cold floor put a chill in my bones. I didn't care. Sending this signal was the only offense I could mount. I fought sleep as long as I could.

My eyes drifted shut.

Sometime later, a door above creaked open. A hint of light appeared on the stairs. Mild cussing and foot stomping ensued. "Get out of my way," Grey yelled. "Scat."

I listened even as I silently retreated to the bunk. I must be ready to take advantage of any opportunity. Hope flickered, a wisp of possibility in my realm of darkness. Whatever this development was, it might be my salvation.

"You stupid cat. Go on!"

A cat? How'd a cat find me? Could it be Harley or Violet? The faint light of hope in my heart flared brightly.

I heard the step pattern change as the man rounded the landing and transitioned to the lower set of steps.

Then the cat yowled, and I heard a thud, thud.

Did he kick the cat? What happened? The absolute silence gave me chills.

"Hello? Is anybody there?" I asked, rising to stand by the jail bars. My eyes adjusted to the deep twilight, but I didn't see a flashlight or a lantern. I didn't see or hear Grey either.

What did that mean?

Was something worse coming for me?

I shook all over in that crystalline moment. I'd never felt more alone, more afraid. The stench of the cell, of my unwashed fear slapped at my normal senses and nearly swamped me. I was going to die today.

This was bad.

Very bad.

I closed my eyes and sent Quig all my love, sent Sage my eternal regrets, told Mom I'd be with her soon.

A ghostly apparition appeared on the floor. In the palest twilight, the cat stalked my way. I blinked with recognition, tears flowing unchecked down my cheeks. I knelt and extended my hands. "Violet?"

Of course it's me. You see anyone else in here? It's only me, myself, and I to the rescue. The feline moved steadily forward, her upright tail twitching at the top end.

I petted Herbert's cat. Her fur felt delightfully soft. I felt a bulky object near her mouth. "Oh my gosh. You have something in your mouth? Is this what I think it is? Keys? You are amazing. Thanks for finding me."

Got your message loud and clear. Good thing I was already on the way to you. That hunk of dog poop over there planned to mount you tonight. He broadcasted his thoughts throughout the area. I ran the last two miles, then I tripped him on the steps and pawed the keys from his pocket. Rescuing is exhausting work.

Violet dropped a set of keys next to the bars of my cell. "Thanks." I scooped them up and tried several before I found the right one. The cell door swung open. "Let's get out of here."

Not so fast, Missy. I didn't spring you only to be caught again. We must drag that sorry sapsucker into your cell and lock him up. We can't have him setting off an alarm right away.

"Understood."

We tugged, pulled, and rolled the unconscious man into the cell. By we, I mean I did all the hard work while Violet supervised. Once Grey was inside the cell, I took everything out of his pockets and carried it with me along with his shoes. Even if he somehow managed to escape this stronghold, I hoped this might slow him down.

We locked the cell door and went up the stairs. "Did he bring a meal?" I asked, looking around where he'd fallen.

No food here. Told you, he came for a bootie call, Violet said in my head.

When we got outside, the moon was still rising in the eastern sky. Not so late after all.

Violet arrowed for the nearest woods. I followed her, and our passage stirred up a swirl of mosquitoes. I tossed Grey's items in the bushes and plunged after Violet, smacking bugs and trusting the cat had a plan. Still, as the darkness closed around me, I needed the reassurance we weren't running blind.

"Where are we going?" I asked.

Herbert's house. It's closer than your place. No one would think you'd go there. They won't know I rescued you either.

And when we get there, I can call my family.

No need to wait. Use your telepathy. Nothing is jamming

you now.

Oh. Right. *Sage?* I pinged her on a pinpoint wavelength through our twin-link.

She answered in my head at once. *Tabby! Where are you? Are you okay? I've been going out of my mind trying to find you.*

Althea kidnapped me and stuck me in a council jail cell underground where my senses didn't work. Help came from an unexpected quarter, and I now I'm running for my life on an empty stomach. We're headed to the swamp. Don't tell anyone Violet rescued me. Our destination is Herbert's house. Can you and Quig meet me there with clean clothing and shoes? I never want to see this dress again. Oh, and tell no one where you're going.

On it....Is it okay if Larry comes?

I guess. I mean, sure. Don't forget Quig. Tell him right away that me and the baby are safe, and I love him.

Gotcha. Just so I don't run into the wrong person, who else is on her team of bad guys?

*Grey Roads, Peaches' drummer, is helping Althea. He's her son. She plans to use my womb as her paranormal cash cow. He planned to...*my thoughts scattered. I willed them to be strong. *To take advantage of me tonight.*

I'll kill them both. She doesn't get to say who gets pregnant or when. He will be tortured before I kill him.

Thanks for the support, but I'm not sure the two of us combined could stop Althea. Escaping from her and this foul site is my priority. See you soon.

I tried pinging Quig with the words "I'm safe." I knew his aura inside and out, and it should have gone through if he had any receptors. But the communication felt dead, broken. Next, I sent an image of an open cell door. Hopefully, he'd get it, or Sage would tell him.

Violet urged me to hurry, but my body didn't slink through ankle-high hidey holes in the brush like a cat's did. I had to smash my way Godzilla-style through branches and vines, and it slowed me down.

We hadn't gone far when I ran out of energy.

Just a few more steps, I kept telling myself every time I stopped. I could do that much.

Breaths came heavy and fast. I tried to calm my breathing, but it was pointless. I needed air. I leaned against a stout pine, hoping and praying I wasn't hyperventilating. No rescue squad would ever find me in here. A helicopter couldn't land in this bramble to collect me. Hell, I didn't even know where here was.

Don't stop, Violet said. *Trouble follows us.*

I realized I'd somehow tapped into the tree and it had shared energy with me. Didn't know I could do that. I kept the draw going. "What? How's that possible?"

Then, I heard a baying sound. Hounds. Crap. Someone was tracking us! It had to be Althea. How did she discover I'd escaped so soon?

Where did she get the dogs?

Chapter Thirty-One

I'd never felt so hot, miserable, or scared. The worst trifecta ever. All I could do was keep the white cat in my sight and keep going. Everything ached, and I couldn't draw a full breath no matter how hard I tried. I tripped on a briar vine and splatted on the ground, banging my knee and chin on something hard. Ow! I got back up and started trotting again.

The fresh blood drew mosquitoes the size of quarters. If I ever got out of here, I was never ever entering the swamp again.

Hurry up. The dogs are gaining ground.

"How can we outrun them? I'm spent, Violet. If I stop for a bit I can recharge in the woods."

No stopping! You can and will keep going unless you want to be pregnant in a hole in the ground for the rest of your life.

"No, thanks."

Keep moving. There's a boat ahead. You will paddle us away from the dogs. They won't follow us through the swamp water.

"Uh, sure." I'd never paddled a boat in my life. How hard could it be?

I tried to focus, but my mind kept skittering around. Had I escaped one dangerous predator for another? Still, I managed to cobble my thoughts together. Paddling the boat would make it harder for the hounds to track my scent. It should give us a reprieve. I hadn't seen any security cameras in the facility or outside of it. Hopefully, Herbert's place would be a safe haven.

One hundred and twelve more steps and the way opened. An abandoned dark green kayak rested on the closest bank. Bald Cypress trees grew in the black water, surrounded by their knobby roots poking straight out of the water. The air felt thick and smelled like a compost pile. I had no idea how I was seeing anything in the dark of night, but I was thankful I no longer had to run through thick brush.

Violet leapt into the kayak. I waded into the water, carefully pushed off, climbed in, and lifted the small paddle. "Which way?" I asked.

Away from here.

So, I paddled and paddled some more. My arms weren't as tired as my legs, thank goodness, but paddling was hard work. In a boat this tiny, you couldn't do more than two strokes at a time before you had to paddle on the other side. There wasn't a current to work against us, but the reverse was also true. There wasn't a current to help us.

I used my talent to draw energy from anything I encountered. The trees, the fish in the water, the frogs croaking nearby. If it was alive, it was fair game. I needed to be ready for what came next. It was slow going, as if I were using a trickle charger, but I wasn't getting weaker. That meant something.

Violet kept sniffing the air and adjusting our course. The baying of the hounds abruptly ceased. I assumed they'd reached the bank where we'd embarked.

"Are we safe now?" I asked Violet.

Not yet. You won't be safe as long as Althea is alive. She will keep coming after you until she gains her objective, her own grandchildren. And not just any grandchildren.

Powerful grandchildren. Your kids will be the strongest in several generations.

I pondered that for a few moments. My kids would be awesome. Did that mean I carried more than one child, as Sage suspected?

My paddle struck the bottom, so I switched to the other side. Same issue. "Uh Violet, it's very shallow here. We can't go any farther in the kayak."

The watery route kept the hounds off our scent and bought us time. We're near Herbert's place now. We can walk from here.

I glanced around the dark cathedral-like swamp. "What about alligators and snakes?"

What about 'em? This is their home. We're the trespassers here. As long as we make noise, and you have that paddle to whack anything that approaches, we'll be fine.

In short order, Violet's white fur darkened with mud. She looked as bedraggled and miserable as I felt. I couldn't complain though. It beat the alternative.

I was free.

No longer imprisoned in that blasted cell. Suffering a little tonight was better than rotting in that cell for the rest of my life.

The swamp transitioned to squishy wetlands and gradually firmed to become solid ground. I yawned and kept moving, using the wooden paddle like a walking stick.

The side of Herbert's house came into view. I matched Violet's quick pace across the manicured lawn. We raced to the front door. Locked.

What? Herbert's car was parked in the yard.

Where was he?

I shot my twin a quick message. *Sage, we're at Herbert's house. Something feels wrong here. I've surely found trouble again, and I'm not up to full strength. Hurry!*

Before I could retrieve Herbert's hidden key, the door wrenched open, and Grey Roads grabbed my arm, wrestled me to the floor, and hogtied my limbs in front with duct tape.

No! That wasn't possible. I'd left him locked in my cell. All that effort to get away, gone in a second.

This wasn't the escape of my dreams.

It was a nightmare.

Chapter Thirty-Two

Grey slapped my face, then he pinched my nostrils tight. "Thought you could run away from me? No way. You're mine, woman. From now on, you will do whatever I say, whenever I say."

I didn't respond. Couldn't, not with duct tape sealed over my mouth and around my limbs. Panic welled as I needed air. I struggled against him.

"Yeah, bitch. Like that. You can't breathe unless I say so."

He got off on seeing me struggle. I headbutted him, and his grip loosened. I drew a quick breath then he pounced on me again. He bit my shoulder, hard. The hope and vitality I'd felt in the last hour fled. I hurt all over, but all things considered, I was alive. And I began siphoning streams of energy from him. He didn't even notice.

When I quit fighting, he let go and rolled to his feet.

I drew in ragged breaths of fresh air and more of his energy.

"Where'd that damn cat go?" Grey asked. He kicked my thigh with his bare foot, then howled in pain. "You better be nice to me, or you're sleeping with the fishes tonight, wench, despite Mom's plan to make you our pet. I've killed before, and I'll kill you in a heartbeat."

I felt a small victory that he'd hurt his foot. I should've blasted him with an energy spear right away, but he'd been so quick to tape me that I'd missed that opportunity. Now I was totally at his mercy. Or

275

was I? I continued stealing energy from him. Help was on the way. I needed this power boost to survive until it arrived.

I hoped Violet got away.

Althea appeared as a shadow figure in Herbert's living room. "Do you have the package?" she asked.

Despite my poor circumstance, I marveled that Althea's essence manifested here, and it could speak. How could a living person do that? More to the point, was it a vulnerability? Could I attack her shadow and hurt the woman? Perhaps if I got to her first and then took out Grey, I'd have a better chance of escaping.

"Got her. She's not going anywhere," Grey said. "The cat ran off, but I'll wager it's nearby. Release your neighbor's hounds again, and we'll be done with Violet for good."

"I give the orders around here," Althea snapped. "Lucky for you that I came out to check on the package or you'd still be in a cell. Tabby wouldn't have escaped if you'd kept your pants zipped."

"My zipper had nothing to do with it. The cat attacked me and stole my keys."

Remember what you are, Tabby, Violet announced in my head. *Draw energy from the ground and stop them. The earth here has special powers, same as Bristol Street.*

You're safe? I'd been pulling energy from trees and wildlife, but I'd never pulled energy straight from the ground. These were desperate times. I'd do whatever it took to survive.

Save yourself. Althea released those hounds, and they're coming here. I'm sneaking around the house and entering quietly through my cat door. I'll stay hidden unless Grey gets rough with you.

Will do. I closed my eyes and focused on the energy reservoir beneath Herbert's home. I called upon the souls there to give me strength and courage to stop the people who'd captured me. Then I fired an energy spear into Althea's shadow figure, hoping it could damage her.

"The *package* needs to be demoralized and subdued." Grey pounded his fist on the dining room table. "The way we're broken in training. She's way overdue for that humbling experience."

"Perhaps but take her and go to ground elsewhere. I have my own trouble to deal with. Cars are coming down the lane over here."

"Oh, I plan to take her."

Althea's figure wavered. "You hurt that baby, and I'll turn you into a eunuch."

I punched more juice into the spear lodged in her shadow, needing to stop her.

"Not planning to hurt the kid. Just rough up the woman. Put more marks on her."

"Is the nullifier on her?"

"Forgot it. I barely beat them here."

"You idiot. She's a strong telepath. Her family is likely on the way."

I poured more energy into my spear in Althea. She cried out and wavered until she wasn't there. I thrilled at the victory. One tormentor down, one to go.

"Mom?" Grey yelled.

My family *was* on the way. Meanwhile, I fired off energy spears at his heart.

Though my strength faded quickly, I kept pulsing energy into his heart until the door opened.

~*~

Quig ripped the duct tape off my mouth, turned, and dove onto Grey. I stopped pulsing supercharged energy into Grey's heart and struggled to sit up.

Quig got in several good punches, then Grey fell hard, banging his head on the floor. He didn't move again.

Then Quig's arms encircled me.

"Am I dreaming?" I asked.

He softened his voice so that only I could hear him. "Not a dream, love. You're safe now. Neither Althea nor her son will hurt you ever again."

"What happened to her?"

"Sage asked the cops to check here every few hours, so they were already in the area when you said you were coming to Herbert's place. They rushed here and the place next door to neutralize any threats. Both the woman and her son must have had bad hearts."

I could feel my eyes rounding. My energy spear had killed Althea? I didn't know what to make of that.

"How do you know that without doing an autopsy?"

"I just do." Quig kissed my brow.

~*~

Ten minutes later, Detective Nowry arrived. "Lucky for you I was in the area. My timing couldn't be better, and I need Tabby's statement while it's fresh in her mind."

After Nowry turned on his recorder and made a note of my name, the time, and the day, he nodded at me. "Begin."

I cleared my throat. "Althea Morgan kidnapped me yesterday. She expected me to bear her grandchildren once I gave birth to my baby. She and her son are crazy as sprayed roaches. They locked me in a cell in an abandoned industrial complex nearby. When Grey came this evening, I escaped through the swamp. Intuition guided me here. I thought I was fleeing to safety. But he anticipated my route and grabbed me. Then he bound me with tape and threatened me. He pinched my nose shut saying he controlled everything about me, even when I breathed. I thought he'd kill me."

Shivers raced down my spine, despite the August heat. "Grey bragged that he owned me. He bit my shoulder and kicked my thigh. Then he clutched his chest and collapsed. I hope he's dead."

Nowry cleared his throat. "He is. Not a mark on him either. You know anything about that?"

"I didn't touch him. If I could've walloped him, I would've. What about Althea?" I continued, moving the conversation along. "She kidnapped me and killed Rosemont. She snuck into our apartment and took me captive. She's bad news for sure."

"She's dead. Our team found a gold candlestick in a cabin nearby where she was hiding. Forensics will swab it for DNA. If genetic material from Rosemont and Althea is present, we will list her as Rosemont's killer as well as your kidnapper. Anything else?"

"No. That's it. I want to sleep for three days."

"Once the forensic team processes you, and they take your clothes into evidence, you're free to go."

Ugh. Much as I hated the delay, I knew it was standard procedure. The police needed solid proof of crimes. "Be sure to swab where Grey bit my shoulder."

"We will."

When they finished with me, I took my second-ever

shower at Herbert's house. I dressed quickly in the clean clothes Sage and Quig brought. I looked at Quig. "Let's go home."

Chapter Thirty-Three

The next day before work, Auntie O and Frankie, along with Sage, Larry, Gerard, and Eve gathered in our apartment.

"Catch us up," Eve said. "Tabby was missing for a day and now she's home. What happened in between?"

With Quig at my side, I felt strong enough to tell the horror story again.

"A cat rescued you?" Gerard said, once I finished. "Cool."

"Violet was awesome. She tripped Grey on the steps and brought me his keys."

"Cats rule!" Sage pumped a fist in the air.

"I don't get it. Althea had the head spot on the council," Larry said. "Why'd she kidnap you?"

"She claimed I was causing her grief," I said. "While I did nothing to her, she was a suspect in Rosemont's murder. Sage and I staked out her home two days ago. Althea found out and became incensed. She entered this apartment wearing an invisibility cloak, then took total control of my body."

"I've never been so scared in my life," Quig said. "I can't believe I inadvertently let her in. All that money I spent on security, and she beat it."

"We kept trying to find you," Sage said. "It wasn't going well. Then, we saw your phone on the floor, reviewed your search results, and saw those properties Rosemont owned. We had decided to check the locations one-by one-when you messaged me."

"Was that industrial site on the list?"

"Yeah, but we would have checked it last. I'm glad you escaped when you did."

"Me too. Althea said she'd keep me pregnant the rest of my life. Said she'd auction off my womb."

"She had some nerve to even consider such a thing," Auntie O fumed. "Frankie and I found her collapsed in that abandoned cabin. They say she suffered a fatal heart attack. She apparently had a congenital heart condition that her son, Grey, also inherited, so stress killed both of them."

I translated between the lines. I'd killed Althea and Grey with energy spears. It was either kill them or live the rest of my life in captivity. I'd done what was needed to survive.

"Was the skeleton in Rosemont's wall Kimmy?" I asked, hoping no one dwelt on the so-called inherited heart condition coincidence.

"Yes."

My head turned toward Quig. "You're certain?"

"Absolutely, and I wouldn't be surprised if Althea was jealous of her, flew at her in a rage, shot her, and dumped Kimmy's body on Rosemont's doorstep."

I blinked for a few moments, unsure of what I could say. Did he have inside information? "That solution seems a stretch, but it ties everything together nicely."

"The important thing," Sage said, "is that those suckers will never bother us again."

"Will the Paranormal Council come after me?" I asked.

"No." This from Larry. "They are moving forward with a clean slate for everyone."

I heaved in a sigh of relief.

Quig kept a firm grip on my hand. "With Rosemont and Althea gone, the average age of council members is lower. Newer, more contemporary policies will be enacted. The long-overdue updating of the ruling body's charter will finally occur."

"Thanks so much for the rescue," I added with a nod toward the people who'd saved me. "Anyone seen Violet?"

"Nobody has seen her today that I know of," Larry said. "But, she'll turn up."

"Shouldn't we be concerned about her wellbeing?" Sage asked. "She's quite a clever cat. She's welcome to live with us if she doesn't want to stay with Herbert."

Eve's eyes twinkled with delight. "Herbert and Sharmila may have something to say about that."

"Let's return to the council," I said. "Who's on it? Is it too soon to know?"

"Not too soon. I accepted a seat," Larry said.

Sage's eyebrows rose to her hairline. "You did? First I've heard of it."

"You knew I wanted it before they ran the power test at the club. When they called me last night to join without testing, I couldn't refuse. Council service runs in my family."

Sage narrowed her eyes. "You're not training any young girls, are you? Because I draw the line at that. We're a couple now. A *committed* couple."

"No. Training is already suspended and pending review. Which brings me to a question I've long wanted to ask you. We are a committed couple, Sage." Larry knelt in front of my sister. "I've loved you for years, Sage Winslow. You are the woman I want to spend my life with. Will you marry me?"

Sage blinked but remained silent.

Answer him, Sage! I shouted through the twin-link.

Where's the champagne and fancy dinner? she groused. *Where's my engagement ring?*

Give him a chance. He's smart, and he's crazy about you.

"Sage?" Larry asked. "You're killing me. Will you marry me?"

"Yes," Sage said softly. "I will."

Larry drew a ring from his pocket. "This was my mother's. It's a moonstone with diamonds on each side. I'd be honored if you'd wear it. But if you don't like it, I will buy any ring of your choice."

Sage reached for it eagerly. "I love it."

They kissed, and we congratulated them.

"Our family has a lot to celebrate today." I glanced up at Quig. "Want to do the honors?"

Quig nodded, his somber expression revealing nothing. "Last night when Tabby was being cleared by medical personnel, they ran a sonogram to check on the baby."

"Don't stop there," Sage shrieked. "Tell us what they found."

Quig drew me into his lap and hugged me. "We're having twins. Too soon to know the gender."

"I knew it," Sage whooped. "They'll grow up here on Bristol Street, same as we did."

Happiness bathed me all over. "That's the plan."

"When I spoke to Herbert earlier, " Quig said, "he announced he is staying on the council. He also shared his good news. Sharmila agreed to marry him. They will have a private ceremony because she's expecting a child."

"Goody for her," Sage said. "That means they still need one more person for our ruling body. They better not be thinking of the Winslow twins."

"I've heard the news about this," Auntie O said with a sly grin following. "Our Eve was tapped for a leadership role, and she agreed. The council will be strong and powerful with these young talents."

Eve blushed. "It's true. The best way to effect change is from the inside."

A knock sounded on the door. Auntie O answered it and waved Detective Nowry inside.

"Looks like a party in here," Nowry said, crossing the room and handing me an envelope.

"What's this?" I asked.

"Your payment from the captain. You solved the case and more. Althea killed Rosemont. She kept a journal in her house that revealed everything."

I tried to return the packet to no avail. "I don't want this money."

"If you have an issue with the amount, take it up with Haynes."

"I'm not his employee."

"He knows you're freelance, and he won't tap you for every case. Only the ones we can't get a handle on. You have the special knack for getting to the bottom of things, Tabby."

"Yes, she does," Auntie O said proudly.

"Can't stay. I'm in the midst of reopening at least a dozen missing persons cases."

"What?" I thought hard for a moment. "Is this related to the package you found in Rosemont's house?"

"Yes, it is. Thanks to your intuition, some families

might be getting answers soon. You didn't hear it from me, but Rosemont might have been a serial rapist and possibly a serial killer." With that, Nowry grabbed a handful of cookies and departed.

"Wow." I glanced at Sage. "We had a hand in that."

Sage crowed. "Rosemont's life won't be remembered as picture perfect anymore."

Everyone started talking at once. I heard them, though their voices faded against all the thoughts running in circles in my head. First off, I was very glad they'd found proof linking Althea to the murder. And Rosemont got his comeuppance too.

I glanced at my happy family, thinking back to the beginning of this case. Back to when the winged lion winked at me. The universe had sent me a message that whatever came my way, I could handle it. Working together, my family had done that and more.

Auntie O and Frankie had settled matters with his family, Sage and Larry were engaged, and Quig and I were expecting twins, much to our delight. His parents would be super pumped by the news. Gerard and Eve were now our family by choice.

When Mom died, I wasn't sure where I belonged. Now I knew the answer.

I belonged with my blended family.

~*~

Clouds filled the sky over Bonaventure Cemetery. Sage and I, along with our guys, had brought a picnic lunch to our grandparents' plot. They were unique in that they were both felled by the same assassin's bullet.

I loved the feel of this historic cemetery. Centuries old oaks flanked the shady lanes, and their branches full of Spanish moss gave the place an ethereal feel.

This graveyard was the resting place of many of the city's movers and shakers through time.

The Ghost Dog ran up to my side and mugged me as usual. His chilling presence didn't give me goosebumps. Instead I felt right at home.

As usual, we began with the ritual blessing for Dwayne and Rosemary, as well as Mom's cremains, which we'd brought with us.

After lighting a tea candle and placing it on the headstone, I knelt beside my twin as she spoke the honorary words in a reverent voice. "In the name of the heavens and earth and all the directions, we share our love for Rosemary, Dwayne, and Marjoram. May their ways of spreading peace and joy be reflected in us as we make our spiritual journeys. Grant them a sacred rest, peace, and radiance until the new day dawns. So be it."

"I don't know about the rest of you," Larry said, "But I'm starved. Let's dive into those sandwiches."

"Oh yeah," Quig said. "Bring on those shrimp po'boys and chips."

Three days had passed since the showdown at Herbert's home by the river. Quig and I had spent most of the time together and tried to find a routine, but it was hard to accomplish because so much had happened.

My energy spears had taken out Althea and most likely Grey as well. I hadn't come to terms with killing those two people, although their official death certificates said they'd died of heart attacks.

"You haven't eaten a bite, Tabs," Sage said. You okay?"

"Yeah. Still trying to process what happened. I

should have listened to you when you said Althea was the killer. I naively thought any mom couldn't kill. But I was wrong. So wrong." I dropped my voice. "I killed two people. I'm the next family assassin."

"Oh no you don't," Sage whispered back. "You don't get to have all the fun and notoriety. I would've done the exact same thing in your place. You are not a bad person."

My lips pressed together. "My head accepts that, but not my heart."

"Get over it. You did what you had to do."

"It will be different now. We've tried to go back to normal but it isn't working."

"Our old normal is gone because we no longer fear the council or the paranormal community."

"Good point. Mom would be proud of us. We're making money with the shop, we're in stable relationships, and babies will be born next year."

"Pretty much the trifecta every parent hopes for."

"I'm glad our kids will grow up together on Bristol Street. We did all right, so they should too."

Feeling much better, I showered each person present with love and good energy. Our future glittered bright with promise.

We'd taken everything the schemers on the council had thrown at us and beat them at their games. Plus, the word had spread far and wide that Mom and Auntie O had raised strong, stable talents without the benefit of training. Hope and new life was spreading like wildfire through our paranormal community.

Best of all, nobody with a grain of sense would ever mess with the Winslow twins again.

About the Author

Valona Jones is a pen name for Southern author Maggie Toussaint. She writes mystery, suspense, and dystopian fiction. Her work won three Silver Falchion Awards, the Readers' Choice Award, and the EPIC Award. She's published thirty novels as well as several short stories and novellas. Maggie is a member of Mystery Writers of America—Southeast Chapter, and the Sisters in Crime Guppy Chapter. Maggie and her husband live in coastal Georgia where live oaks and heritage cast long shadows. Her website is https://maggietoussaint.com

Author's Note

Thank you for coming along on this wonderful journey with me. I hope you've enjoyed this fictional visit to Savannah, GA. In writing A Magic Candle Shop Mysteries, it has been my honor to show you the area through the eyes and senses of my paranormal amateur sleuth, Tabby Winslow Quigsly. Speaking of Tabby and her twin sister Sage, I have long been fascinated with twins. We have a set of twins in my father's line: his grandfather was a twin. As far as I know, twins didn't follow down through "our" twin's descendants.

Remember, you can always help authors out by leaving online reviews about our books. No need for anything lengthy or in-depth. Honest reviews are needed, and they make a difference to the author and to other readers.

More Books by Maggie Toussaint

Thanks for reading *Flamed Out*. A list of my works of fiction follows.

A Magic Candle Shop Mystery Series, paranormal cozy mysteries
Snuffed Out (writing as Valona Jones)
In the Wick of Time (writing as Valona Jones)
Tallowed Ground (writing as Valona Jones)
Candle With Care (writing as Valona Jones)
Flamed Out (writing as Valona Jones)

Seafood Caper Mystery series, culinary cozies
Seas the Day
Spawning Suspicion
Shrimply Dead

Dreamwalker Mystery series, paranormal mysteries
Gone and Done It
Bubba Done It
Doggone It
Dadgummit
Confound It
Dreamed It
All Done with It

Lindsey & Ike Romantic Mystery Novella series book (novellas 1-3 included), cozy mysteries.
"Really, Truly Dead"
"Turtle Tribbles"
"Dead Men Tell No Tales"

Cleopatra Jones Mystery series
In for a Penny
On the Nickel
Dime If I Know
"No Quarter" (novella)

Single Title Mysteries
Death, Island Style
Murder in the Buff

Mossy Bog Romantic Suspense series
Muddy Waters
Hot Water
Rough Waters

Single Title Romantic Suspense
House of Lies
Second Chance
Seeing Red

The Guardian of Earth Futuristic Mystery series
G-1 (writing as Rigel Carson)
G-2 (writing as Rigel Carson)
G-3 (writing as Rigel Carson)

Short Stories
"High Noon at Dollar Central" (A Dreamwalker story)
"Sand Dollar Secrets" (A Cleopatra Jones story)
"The Trouble with Horses" (A Seafood Caper story)